BY ADRIENNE YOUNG

A Sea of Unspoken Things

The Unmaking of June Farrow

Spells for Forgetting

Sky in the Deep

The Girl the Sea Gave Back

Fable

Namesake

The Last Legacy

Saint

A
SEA
of
UNSPOKEN THINGS

A SEA *of* UNSPOKEN THINGS

A NOVEL

ADRIENNE YOUNG

DELACORTE PRESS

NEW YORK

Published in the United States by Delacorte Press, an imprint of Random
House, a division of Penguin Random House LLC, New York.

DELACORTE PRESS is a registered trademark and the DP colophon
is a trademark of Penguin Random House LLC.

ISBN 9780593598702

Printed in the United States of America

Book design by Caroline Cunningham

For Adam,

my first friend, and the only one I get to keep for life—

first heartbeats to last

A
SEA
of
UNSPOKEN THINGS

ONE

We were made in the dark. I used to hate it when Johnny said that, but now I know it's true.

Sunlight flickered on the windshield as I turned the wheel and the road curved, tightening. Trees pressed in like a wall on both sides of the cracked asphalt, making the old highway that snaked through the Six Rivers National Forest look impossibly narrower. I could feel that cinching in my lungs, too, the air squeezing from them just a little more the deeper into the forest I drove. I'd expected that.

From above, the little blue car would look like an insect between the giant, towering redwoods, and even just imagining it made me uneasy. I'd never liked the feeling that I couldn't see into the distance, like the whole world might have ended on the other side of those trees and I wouldn't know it. I guess, really, it had.

There was no world without Johnny.

The thought made the ache rising in my throat travel down my arms, into the fingers that curled around the smooth leather of the steering wheel. It had been three and a half months since I got the call that my brother was gone, but I'd known at least a day before that.

The part of me that wasn't constructed of bone and blood had just . . . *known*. Maybe even down to the minute.

I glanced at the duffel bag on the passenger seat, the only luggage I'd brought for the two weeks I'd be in Six Rivers. I couldn't remember now what I'd even packed. In fact, I hadn't even been able to think of what I might need. In the twenty years since I'd seen the tiny, claustrophobic logging town, I'd done my best to forget it. I'd avoided these winding mountain roads, using every excuse I could think of to keep from coming back to this place. But there was no denying that leaving Six Rivers and never looking back had come at a cost.

Only days after I turned eighteen, I left and never returned. I'd spent my youth hidden in the labyrinth-like forest before I'd all but clawed my way out into the light. Now, my life in San Francisco was exactly what I'd made it, as if I'd painted it onto a canvas and conjured it to life. The days that made up that version of me were filled with gallery openings, poetry readings, and cocktail hours—things that made me forget the sun-starved, evergreen-scented life I'd left behind.

But that cost—the unexpected conditions for that disentanglement—wasn't just the home I knew or the memories I'd made there. In the end, the price I'd paid had been giving up Johnny. There was a time when I thought we could never truly be separated, because we weren't just siblings. We were twins. For half of my life, there was nowhere I existed without him, and it didn't feel like we were knit together by only blood and genetics. We were connected in places that no one could see, in ways that I still didn't understand.

There had always been a kind of blur that existed between us. The anecdotal stories about twins portrayed on viral social media posts and afternoon talk shows weren't just entertaining tales that skirted the line of the supernatural. For me, they'd always been real. Sometimes, terrifyingly so.

It wasn't until I left that I felt some semblance of separation from Johnny. In a way, it felt like he had slowly been scraped from the cracks of my life, just like Six Rivers. In the beginning, he would make the trip down to the city on visits that were hardly ever planned. I would come home to find him cooking in my kitchen or standing fully clothed in the shower with a wrench to tighten the dripping faucet. He would just appear out of nowhere before vanishing like a ghost, and he never stayed long. He was a creature of quiet, unnerved by the buzz of the city and the twinkling lights it cast on the bay. The visits became less and less frequent, and he hadn't shown up like that in years now.

Johnny wasn't one for phone calls or emails. Half the time, he didn't even respond to text messages. So, my only window into his quiet life in Northern California was the Instagram account he kept updated. From 349 miles away, the bits I got to see of my brother's existence in the redwoods were through the lens of the old analog camera we'd found sitting on top of a neighbor's garbage can when we were sixteen years old. Twenty years later, he had still refused to switch to digital, and after he started the Instagram account, it soon became filled with those little bits of the world that only Johnny seemed to notice. Sunlight gleaming on dewdrops. A swath of lace-like frost clinging to a pane of glass. The owls.

Always, the owls.

Even when we were kids, I knew that Johnny was different. He'd always found comfort in places that most deemed lonely, disappearing for hours without a word, and I would *feel* him go quiet. That stillness would settle right between my ribs, and when I couldn't stand it anymore, I'd go and find him lying on the hot roof of our cabin or tangled high in the branches of a sixty-foot tree. He'd been pulling away from the world for as long as I could remember, but when the photographs of the owls started popping up on his feed, I remember the cold sensation that filled me. He was drawn to them—the secretive creatures that only came out in the darkness. And deep down I knew that it was because he was one of them.

If you'd have told me when we were kids that Johnny would end up a photographer, I probably would have thought it was both surprising and not at all. Growing up, I was the artist. My hands itched for pencils and paintbrushes the way Johnny's mind itched for the quiet. In the end, both Johnny and I wound up trying to capture moments and people and places. Me with my canvas, him with his camera. But eventually, the drawings that filled my notebooks felt like the blueprints of a prison—a way for me to plan my escape. And eventually, I did.

Johnny had spent the last two years working remotely for a conservation project documenting five different owls in and around Six Rivers National Forest. The opportunity had seemed so serendipitous that I should have known there was something wrong with it. Johnny had never been lucky. Stars didn't align for him and opportunities didn't just drop into his lap. So, when I heard that Quinn Fraser, director of biology at California Academy of Sciences, was looking for someone to cover the Six Rivers area, it should have felt off. But only two weeks after I'd sent Johnny's work to Quinn, Johnny was hired.

I hadn't been able to shake the feeling that in a way, that made all of this my fault. The project was the first job Johnny ever had that wasn't logging, and at the time I'd thought that maybe, finally, it would be the thing that got him out of Six Rivers. But only weeks away from the study's end, Johnny was out on a shoot in Trentham Gorge when a rogue bullet from a hunter's gun slammed into his chest.

My fingers slipped from the steering wheel, instinctively finding the place two and a half inches below my collarbone, where I could still feel it. I rubbed at the phantom ache, pressing the heel of my hand there until the throb began to recede.

The image unfurled, replacing the view of the forest outside the windshield. In my mind's eye, tree limbs bent and swayed, creating blurred shapes of light that punched through the forest canopy high above—a flashing glimpse of the last thing Johnny had seen as he lay there on the forest floor. The rendering had been cast across my mind on a loop, making the connection between me and my brother more than just a sense or a feeling. Now, it was something that felt tangible and tactile. Now, it was *too* real.

Accidental firearm deaths weren't unheard of in the wilderness that surrounded Six Rivers, especially during the elk season that brought hunters from all over the country to town. I could remember more than one that happened when me and Johnny were kids. But I also knew that *accidents* didn't happen in that forest. Not really. There was almost nothing that was random or by chance because the place was alive—intentional.

It was that *feeling* that had compelled me to pack my bag and drive to Six Rivers. It had rooted down into my gut, twisting so tightly that it made it almost impossible to breathe. Because the link between me and Johnny wasn't just intuition or some cosmic connection. I'd felt the white-hot heat of that bullet pierce between my ribs. I'd seen the forest canopy swaying in the wind. I'd also felt that bone-deep sense that had been coursing through Johnny's veins. That despite what the investigation had uncovered about what Johnny was doing out in the gorge that day, he wasn't alone. More than that, he was afraid.

I returned my hand to the steering wheel, watching the blur of emerald green fly past the window. I'd grown up feeling like the trees had eyes, each tangle of roots like a brain that held memories. I could feel, even now, that they remembered me.

I read once, years after I left, that they could actually speak to one another. That they had the ability to communicate through the network of fungi in the ground over miles and miles of forest. And I believed it. They knew what happened the day my brother died. They'd watched as he grew cold, his blood soaking the earth. And that wasn't all they knew.

I forced my gaze back to the road and let my foot come down on the brake as the sign appeared in the distance.

SIX RIVERS, CALIFORNIA

4.5 MILES

A reflective white arrow pointed in the direction of the hidden turnoff on the only sign I'd seen in the last half hour. The blinker clicked on, and I let the car drift onto the gravel track that disappeared into the trees. Almost immediately, the silence grew thick in that way I remembered, making my ears feel like they needed to pop. It was an eerie absence of sound that resonated around the car, broken only by the crack of rocks under the tires.

The light had changed, too, adding to the stillness. The canopy far above diffused the sun into nothing more than glowing, golden air that hovered, suspended between the trees. The whole scene gave the innate feeling that you were leaving the world behind, entering into some imaginary place that didn't really exist. I wished that were true.

The blue dot blinking on the dash's GPS crept along the hairpin-turn road, deeper and deeper into the sea of green that covered the screen. The national forest was almost completely uninhabited by people except for the town that lay at its center. The map took me around turn after turn until the trees began to spread out just enough to reveal a house here and there. They were almost camouflaged against the colors of the landscape, with moss-covered roofs and wood-plank siding that was dotted with pine knots. The little red pin on the map crept closer until the cabin finally came into view.

The car rolled to a stop and I went stiff in my seat, eyes pinned to the old blue 4Runner parked out front. A nauseous, liquid feeling pooled in my belly as I shifted the gear into park. The cabin we'd grown up in was tiny, with two square windows that looked out at the road and a screen door that had once been painted a rust red. Pine needles that looked at least a foot deep were piled up around the porch like drifts of snow. As soon as I opened the car door, I could smell them.

My stomach turned a little as I let my eyes drift to the next house up the road. Set back in the trees, at the end of a long blacktop drive, was the Walkers' place. The windows were dark, the drive empty, but it still looked lived in. Looking at it almost made me feel like I was right back there again—eighteen years old and no idea that everything was about to change.

I forced my gaze back to our cabin, but it took a few seconds for my foot to lift and touch down on the ground. It took much longer for me to actually get out. Almost immediately, I could feel my brother spilling from inside the walls of the house we grew up in, thickening in the air around me.

"I'm here, Johnny," I breathed.

My hand clenched painfully around my keys as I rounded the car and got my bag, slinging it over my shoulder. My reflection moved over the windows of the 4Runner, and flashes of my younger self were there, behind the glass. Riding in the passenger seat with Johnny driving and Micah in the back. Flying down the highway sipping a lukewarm soda with music blaring from the only speaker that wasn't busted. I could see my bare feet propped up on the dash and catch the scent of burning oil leaking through the air vents.

I stepped up onto the porch, eyeing a fluttering square of white behind the screen door where something was taped to the window. I pulled the handle, and the springs creaked and popped as the door opened. It was a folded piece of paper with my name written on the front.

I opened it, reading the handwritten script.

James, welcome home. Please come by the office when you get a chance.

—Amelia Travis

My spine straightened when I saw the name. Amelia Travis was one of the rangers stationed in the national forest, a replacement for the decades-long tenure of Timothy Branson, who'd had the position in our town when I was growing up. The purview of the ranger who occupied the U.S. National Forest office mostly entailed things like permits and protections and land management. But they were also the closest thing we'd had to law enforcement, which meant that Johnny's death ultimately had fallen into Amelia Travis's jurisdiction.

She'd been the one to call me that day. I could still clearly remember the nothingness that had seized my body as the woman's words buzzed against my ear. Like every inch of empty space in the universe had hollowed me out. It was still there, a chasm that had no end, no edges.

I refolded the paper and lifted the mat, finding the rusted key that had been kept there for decades. It took a few tries to turn it in the lock, and I had to shove my shoulder into the door to get it open. But when it did, that chasm within me stretched so wide the whole earth could fall into it.

The presence that had hovered around the cabin was so heavy on the other side of the door that it knocked the wind from my lungs. My brother was like a gathering smoke in the air, choking out the oxygen. Like at any second, I'd hear him call my name from the other room.

James?

His voice echoed inside of me and I pinched my eyes closed, trying to push the overwhelming feeling down. I'd waited for that tether between me and Johnny to dim after I got the news that he was gone. I was sure that at some point, it would grow thin as he pulled away from this world. But the hope I'd held on to that I would walk through that door and finally begin to sense his absence was a point of fading light now. He was still here. He was still everywhere.

Growing up, my connection with Johnny was something that had always just existed, like the color of the sunlight when it came through the kitchen window or the familiar sounds of the forest at night. When I left home for the city, I finally experienced what it was like for that connection between us to stretch. He was still there—always there—and I didn't realize how grafted into me it was until there were miles between us. But long before that, I'd begun to recognize when that feeling settled into my gut, telling me that something was wrong. I'd learned the hard way to listen when that happened.

For months before he died, I'd had the nagging sense that something was going on with Johnny. He was harder to get ahold of than usual. Less responsive to my texts. When I tried to press, tugging at the thread of that unsettled instinct, he'd pulled away even farther.

Maybe farther than he'd ever been from me. But then he was gone, and now I was convinced that all of it had been some kind of premonition of what was coming.

When I opened my eyes again, the saturated colors of the space came into focus, painting a scene that made my heart come up into my throat. The navy checkered sofa and corduroy armchair were still set neatly on a fraying Turkish rug that half covered the scratched wooden floor. The fireplace was stacked with large, misshapen stones, and a shelf on one wall was filled with dozens of books. One corner of the rectangular room was carved out as a small kitchen with an old green stove and a window that looked out into the forest. Even the mismatched pottery dishes on the shelves had a humble charm to them, glazed in shades of brown and cream.

I let my hand slide over the tops of the books, reading their spines. With just Johnny, me, and Dad living here, the place had always been distinctly masculine in a way that hadn't changed at all. Every detail was the same, as if it hadn't been years since I'd left. As if I'd walked out that door only days ago.

We were seventeen when Dad took a temporary logging job up in Oregon that turned out to be mostly permanent, and our mother had left long before that, extricating herself from the hungry forest after years of being trapped here. Pregnant only three months after high school graduation, she'd married our father for no other reason than the fact that that's what you did. He got a job with the logging company, and she gave birth to not one but two babies. She named us James and Johnny, and I couldn't help but wonder if that's because she wished we'd both been boys. Like maybe she could somehow spare me her own fate if I wasn't a girl.

Only a few years later, she was gone. If I had any memories of the woman, they were folded so deep in my mind that they couldn't be summoned, and the ones I did have of my father were like faded pictures that blurred at the edges. It was this place I remembered most. The cabin, and Johnny. But my mother's story had been a kind of cautionary tale for me as a kid. One that haunted me through adolescence, all the way up to the day I left. I'd spent all those years trying not to become her, but when I got on that bus to San Francisco, it wasn't just to dig myself out of the hole my mother had trapped herself in. I was running from more than that.

An engine rumbled outside, growing loud before it was interrupted by the screech of brakes. Through the window, I could see the red truck pulling into the dirt drive, and even from this distance, with only the shape of his shadowed profile visible, I recognized him.

Micah Rhodes.

I let the duffel slide from my shoulder and hit the ground by my feet as I took a step closer to the window. Instantly, I started counting the years since the last time I'd laid eyes on him, but I already knew the answer: twenty. It had been twenty years, and somehow, I could still feel that rush of blood beneath my skin.

Smoke, the wolflike dog that had shown up on our doorstep when Johnny and I were teenagers, was in the cab beside him, and at first glance, a shiver snaked up between my shoulder blades. The dog should have died years ago, but he looked exactly the same. Just like the cabin. As if he was part of the immortal landscape that was this life.

The engine cut off, and for nearly a minute Micah just sat there. I could already see his nerves, and something about that made me feel just a little less crazy. I wasn't the only one dreading this moment. I'd hoped there was a way to avoid it altogether, but for all its miles of trees and trails and ravines, Six Rivers was much too small for that.

He raked a hand through his hair before he got out, and when I could finally see his face properly, my stomach dropped just a little more. His denim-blue button-up was opened over an old T-shirt, his jeans faded. This was a version of him that was achingly familiar, always a bit thrown together, everything about him worn in and frayed.

His not quite blond, not quite brown hair had been the same shade since we were kids, but it was much longer now. It waved at the ends where he had it tucked behind his ears, and the scruff along his jaw was the same color. His face was different, less youthful than it had been all those years ago, of course. But the light in his eyes had changed, too. There was less light in them now.

Smoke was whining the moment he jumped out of the truck, pacing the drive with his sharp, tawny eyes on the cabin. His ears were back, his head ducked low, like he could feel it, too—Johnny. He was tall enough that the tips of his ears reached my waist, with huge paws at the end of his long, lanky legs. Wide, uneven paint strokes of varying shades of gray covered him from head to toe.

Micah's gaze dropped from the top of the roof to the front door, and I was suddenly overcome with the hope that he wouldn't knock. That he would just turn around and leave, sparing us both the tidal wave of heartache that was seconds from running ashore.

Johnny and Micah had been friends since we were kids, and he was the only person I could think of that might know even a fraction of what it felt like to lose Johnny. They'd been inseparable for most of our lives. All three of us were.

He started toward the porch, and I forced myself to reach for the door. As soon as it swung open, Smoke scrambled up the steps, his whimper stuttering into a cry when he saw me. He nearly knocked me over, meeting my height when he jumped up, and I couldn't help the smile that broke on my lips or the rush of emotion that followed it. He pushed his nose into my shirt as my hands stroked down the length of his face and scratched behind his ears. When he slipped from my grasp, he leaned into me so heavily that I had to counterbalance his weight with my own.

Behind him, Micah was staring at me. There was no hiding that stiff, rigid shape that straightened the line of him, and the same tension that drew his shoulders up was now snaking around me, too.

"Hey, James."

My name spoken in his deep voice made the less familiar parts of him snap into focus. Just like that, we were sixteen years old again, staring at each other like we were waiting to see who would be first to cross the line between us.

"Thought I'd beat you here," he said, catching the edge of the screen door and holding it open.

When he just stood there, I realized he was waiting to be invited in, and that was unfamiliar, too. After our dad moved to Oregon, Micah had spent so much time here that he practically lived in this house with us.

I swallowed. "Do you want to come in?"

He hesitated for just a moment before he finally crossed the threshold, and the door closed behind him. As soon as it did, the room felt even smaller, like everything left unresolved when I went to San Francisco was taking up what little space there was.

"Was the drive okay?" he asked.

"Yeah." My voice came out a bit misshapen.

His hands slid into his pockets, and he watched as Smoke's nose went to the ground. Anxiously, the dog explored each room of the small cabin, as if checking to see if Johnny was here. I'd had the same urge when I walked through the door.

"I dropped off a few things earlier." Micah's eyes moved to the kitchen. "There's milk and eggs in the fridge. Bread. The market will be closed already, but you can go by tomorrow and get anything else you need."

He was talking fast, and I didn't know if that was the nerves or if he was just trying to get this over with as quickly as possible. When I didn't respond, he searched for something else to say.

"I left a bag of dog food, too, if you're sure you're okay with Smoke being here. I don't mind looking after him," he said.

"It's fine."

Despite my best efforts, I still didn't sound like myself, and Micah seemed to notice. His eyes ran over me a little more slowly, as if he was tracing the bloom of red that I could feel creeping up my throat, into my cheeks.

He glanced toward the window. "There's still not much in town, but the diner is open. Sadie Cross owns it now, actually."

Sadie. The mention of the name made me blink. She'd been Johnny's

on-again, off-again girlfriend for years, the epitome of the kind of girl
who ended up like our mother. And if she was still here in Six Rivers,
running the diner, I guessed she had.

"It's really the only place to eat or get coffee around here, but there's
Wi-Fi there now. Pretty decent cell service, too," he added.

"I'm not here that long, Micah." I said it for myself as much as for
him because it felt like a necessary reassurance for both of us.

"I know." He met my eyes again, making that bloom of red feel like
a tangle of flames. Then he stepped around me, disappearing into the
hall.

I closed my eyes, letting out an uneven breath before I followed,
and the click of a lamp being turned on sounded just before I rounded
the corner. Yellow light washed over the wood paneling of a shadowed alcove just outside the closed bedroom door, where there had
once been a twin bed pushed against the wall. Now, it had been replaced by an old wooden desk, and I felt some sense of relief that not
everything in this place had remained unchanged.

Dozens of papers, handwritten notes, photographs, and envelopes
were pinned to a corkboard that was hung on the wall, and a laptop
was sitting closed in the middle of the mess. When I spotted Johnny's
camera bag beside the chair on the floor, I had to look away.

"This is everything." Micah gestured to the desk. "Not the most
organized, but you should be able to find what you need."

I crossed my arms, eyes running over the remnants of Johnny's
work. It was haphazardly sorted, arranged in teetering piles, and when
I caught a glimpse of his handwriting on a notepad, I couldn't let my
gaze linger too long.

"I would have been happy to pack all this up for you, James. You
didn't need to come all the way up here," Micah said.

He'd said the same thing a couple of weeks ago when I called to let
him know I was coming. He'd insisted, really, even offering to drive
everything down to San Francisco himself. It didn't make sense for
me to be here. Compiling and submitting Johnny's work for the conservation project had been my excuse for coming back, but the look

Micah gave me now was a suspicious one. Like he knew it didn't quite add up. And it didn't.

Eventually, we'd have to have that conversation. I just hadn't figured out how to do that yet. I didn't know how to tell Micah why I'd come, because I could hardly make sense of it myself. I'd just been certain that I'd *had* to. Between the feeling of that bullet in my chest and the guilt that I carried for leaving Johnny behind, I couldn't let go of the feeling that there was something *more* to all of this. Like the forest had finally balanced the scales. Like she'd waited all this time to punish us for what we'd done.

Finally, I let my eyes meet Micah's, and I could see there was some part of him that was thinking the same thing. That we'd gotten what we deserved, just twenty years late.

He cleared his throat, dropping his gaze. "I told Olivia you'd be coming by."

"Olivia?"

"Olivia Shaw."

I wished I could pretend I hadn't thought about Olivia in years, but that wasn't true. Proximity in a town like this meant that your friends were chosen for you, and Olivia Shaw had been in our same year at school. By the time we were teenagers, a natural distinction had formed around us. There was me and Olivia, and Johnny and Micah. Then there was Johnny's girlfriend Sadie, and Griffin Walker.

As soon as that last name flitted through my mind, I felt instantly colder.

"I can give you her number," Micah continued. "She's the art teacher over at the high school now. Johnny was using their darkroom for the project, and some of his stuff is still there. You should be able to set up a time with her to go by."

I nodded slowly, trying to recall the details of Olivia's face so that I could reconstruct them into how I imagined she would look now. We hadn't kept in touch after I left, and I'd always wanted to believe that had been a mutual decision. But the truth was, it wasn't.

After a few long seconds, Micah exhaled. "Are you okay, James?"

I blinked, unsure if I'd heard him right. Was I *okay?*

"We don't need to do this, Micah." My voice was a tightrope.

That stiffness in his shoulders resurfaced, his lips pressing into a line like he was biting back what he wanted to say. We were both good at that. At least, we had been. I hadn't answered his call after I got the news about Johnny for this very reason. I didn't want to fall apart with Micah, because I couldn't.

"Fine. Just call me if you need anything," he said.

He went back to the door, and I didn't let myself breathe until it was closed behind him. I stared at the floor as the truck's engine roared back to life and listened as it backed down the drive. By the time he was gone, my knuckles ached, fingernails like knives against my palms.

I leaned into the wall and sank down, back sliding along the wood panels until I was sitting on the floor. That's when it really hit me— the enormity of Johnny's presence that lived between these walls. The bits of him that clung to the objects around me hadn't dimmed. There was no indication of them fading away or flickering out.

Down the hall, Smoke was watching me. His focused golden eyes bored directly into mine with an intensity that seemed much too human to be real, like he could feel it, too. Like he could sense Johnny in the still air between us.

We watched each other for a long time before he inched his way across the rug. When he reached me, his nose found my hair and he whimpered again. That was the thing that finally undid it—all those bound-up tears that I hadn't been able to let fall. The tightly spooled grief pulled taut behind my ribs, unclenching just enough for me to feel the ocean of pain inside me.

I pressed my forehead to Smoke's, breathing through the emptiness that filled the cabin around us. A place where Johnny shouldn't be anymore. But somehow, he was.

He was there the first time my heart beat, the first time air entered my lungs, the first time the sun touched my face. But now, he'd gone back to the dark without me.

TWO

❧ ———— ❦

I could have walked the distance to town in about as much time as
it had taken me to get in the car and drive. After several miles of
nothing but wilderness on the old highway that cut through the national forest, the town of Six Rivers appeared, flanking each side of
the road with a string of buildings.

Main Street was nestled in an area that had been hollowed out
back when the gold rush brought people west, but in every direction,
the trees thickened like a protective membrane, concealing it from
the rest of the world. As a kid, it had felt to me like a shifting maze
you were never meant to escape from.

I stood on the curb with Amelia Travis's note clutched in my hand,
staring at the green decal of the U.S. Forest Service crest pressed onto
the glass door of the office. The last time I'd walked through that door,
I'd been an eighteen-year-old girl with rehearsed words on my lips,
only minutes from telling a lie that would change my entire life.

I pulled the door open and the warmth inside the office instantly
sent chills over my skin. A single desk sat at the back of the small
room, and the cramped space was made narrower by the filing cabinets
and a Formica counter at the back that housed a coffeepot. National

Forest Service posters with curling edges and faded, vintage-style art-work depicting fire safety slogans and office policies were pinned to the walls. They were the same ones that had been there years ago. But all evidence of Timothy Branson, the ranger who used to be stationed here, was gone.

Within seconds of the door closing behind me, the patter of foot-steps knocked overhead. I looked up, eyes following the sound across the water-stained ceiling tiles until it was coming down a staircase on the other side of the wall.

A woman in a uniform appeared with what looked like a ream of unopened printer paper beneath one arm. She stopped short, a look of surprise widening her eyes when she spotted me. Her dark hair was streaked with gray at the temples, and it was pulled back into a lazy ponytail that revealed the soft wrinkles framing her oval, sun-worn face. The arm of the tan button-up she wore displayed the same crest that was on the door.

"Hi there." She came around the desk, setting down the paper. There was a polite smile on her lips, but the question in her eyes was assertive. Direct. "How can I help?"

I stared at the engraved letters on the badge pinned to her chest. The name read TRAVIS. When my eyes traveled back up to meet hers, I tried to place the sound of her voice as the one that had called me that day. The one that had told me Johnny was gone.

I glanced down at the note still clutched in my hand before lifting it into the air. "I'm James. James Golden?"

Understanding slowly settled into her expression, her dark brows lifting just slightly. "Oh, yes. I'm sorry." She rubbed at her temple. "I must have gotten my days mixed up. I thought you were getting in tomorrow." She took a step forward, extending a hand. "It's nice to meet you, James."

I shook it as her eyes ran over me. She was probably thinking that I looked like Johnny, which I did, if you were looking in the right places. There was always a beat of silence when people learned that we were twins, as if they were trying to connect those dots between us.

Johnny had a brawny, tall frame that towered over mine, but our coloring was an exact match from eyes, to hair, to skin tone.

"I tell you, out here time is a slippery thing. But I hope your journey was all right?" She attempted a more genuine smile. "Can I get you anything? Tea, perhaps?"

"I'm okay, thank you."

Amelia gestured for me to sit, and I took the chair in front of the desk, where stacks of files were piled in rows.

"Still getting settled, if you can believe it. I've been in this posting for almost two years and still can't seem to get a handle on this paperwork. But it's good to finally meet face-to-face." She lowered herself into the seat opposite mine, and my gaze dropped to the gun holster and gleaming pair of silver handcuffs that rested at each of her hips. "I know we already spoke about this on the phone, but I want to offer my condolences again. I'm very sorry for your loss."

"Thank you." I cleared my throat.

"I want to assure you again that this case is being handled with the utmost care. Johnny was a friend, and as you can imagine, the entire town has been just devastated by what happened."

"There haven't been any more developments?" My voice was thick, and I hoped it didn't read as emotion. The last thing I wanted was for this woman to pull out a tissue and comfort me. There were more important things to get to.

A frown changed the shape of her face. "I'm afraid not. I know this is hard to make sense of, but the working theory right now is that whoever fired the gun likely had no idea they'd even struck someone. Johnny wasn't wearing his safety gear, and honestly, we see these accidents happen every year. It's almost impossible to track down who's involved, especially with a bullet like that."

"A bullet like that?"

"Yeah." Her head tilted just a little, a note of confusion in her tone. "I thought I mentioned that the last time we spoke on the phone. . . ."

It was possible she had. I could hardly recall the details of our conversation now.

"We were lucky in that we were able to recover the bullet from Johnny's"—Amelia paused—"*body*." She cleared her throat before she continued. "We sent it to Sacramento to be analyzed, but it belongs to a very old gun, most likely a hunting rifle that was made before production required serial numbers. Most guns like that aren't registered, either, and unfortunately, hunters from all over the country turn up in Six Rivers during that part of the season—for the elk." She stopped herself. "Of course, you know all of that."

I did. Hunting season in Six Rivers was rivaled only by the town's obsession with the high school's soccer team, which had won the state championship many times over the years. In a town like this one, both resembled religious holidays.

"The point is, there's no real way to even know who exactly was in the forest that day, let alone that week. In fact, it's most likely that whoever took that shot was a visitor to the area."

"So, that's it?" The words felt flat in my mouth.

Amelia was silent for another beat. "Not exactly. I've been doing weapon checks on my rounds to verify permits, and I will continue to do so, but the season is over now. And it's important to keep in mind that the odds of finding the gun are almost . . ." She didn't finish. She didn't have to. "I just want to be sure there isn't anything else you can tell me about Johnny that might be relevant."

"Relevant?"

She shrugged. "Anything you know about the days leading up to your brother's death. Anything you think might be helpful."

I swallowed. "Johnny and I hadn't talked for a while."

"I gathered that."

My focus on her sharpened, studying the tilt of her mouth. She was looking right at me now with an acute attention that made me feel uneasy.

"I just got the impression that you two weren't keeping in touch, per se. I mean, when's the last time you visited?" Her eyes didn't leave mine, and I suddenly had the distinct feeling that she knew the answer to that question.

"It's been a long time."

"Yes, well." She folded her hands on the desk. "Family can be complicated."

Her tone was still light, but there was a weight to the words themselves that made me uncomfortable. I didn't know if it was my own paranoia or just the fact that I didn't know or trust Amelia Travis. But that look in her eye wasn't simple or naïve. And I was willing to bet she didn't trust me, either.

"Look, in my experience, it's only a matter of time before the details begin to surface. It might take weeks, months, even decades," Amelia said. "But I give you my word that I'll continue to exhaust what resources are available to me. As long as I'm stationed at this post, I can promise you that."

The pain below my collarbone woke again, and I discreetly pressed my knuckles to it, trying to breathe through the searing ache. I'd just stepped out of a coffee shop when it first exploded in my chest, followed by the feeling of hot blood soaking my shirt. I could still feel the cold in my fingertips. The gravity-spinning rush that had made me feel like I was falling. But I'd known right away that this wasn't like the other times. I knew, as the cup slipped from my fingers, that Johnny was gone. In a blink, that image had cast over my mind like a veil. Treetops swaying, the flicker of light. I could still see it, even now.

"Now, there are a couple of other items we need to cover. I wasn't able to track down anyone else for notification of Johnny's death. Are you his only family?"

"Yes," I answered.

"No one else back in San Francisco?"

My fingers dropped from the phantom hole in my chest, landing in my lap. "It's just the two of us. Our dad passed away years ago."

"And your mother?"

I shook my head. "Left a long time before that. We've never had any contact."

Amelia nodded, making a note on the pad in front of her. "You two grew up here?"

My eyes settled on hers, trying to read the look of them again. She had to know the answer to that question. So why was she asking it?

"That's right," I answered.

"When about did you leave Six Rivers?"

"About twenty years ago? When I left for school."

She tapped the end of her pen against the paper. "Twenty years ago. That would have been right around the time that kid died, right? Griffin Walker?"

I kept my hands clasped in my lap, fingers strangling one another. "What?"

She smiled, letting out a breath. "Sorry, my head's been in all this paperwork, like I said. Reviewing old files and cases, trying to get a handle on the history of this place. That must have been a difficult time."

"It was," I managed, looking for any possible exit from where the conversation was headed. I'd gone to great lengths to erase that time from my life. And I didn't like to think about what anyone following that trail would find. "Was there anything else?"

"No, I just want to be sure I have all the contact information for any other next of kin, in case more details or questions come up."

"It's just me," I said, trying to look more relaxed.

She set down the pen, squaring it with the edge of the notepad. "Look, I know I'm an outsider here," she said. "It's not exactly easy coming into a tight-knit community like this, especially when you're here to enforce rules and regulations. But if you need anything while you're here, or if you come across anything that might be helpful in regard to Johnny, I hope you'll reach out."

She was right that Six Rivers didn't exactly welcome strangers. Timothy Branson had learned that almost as soon as he'd taken the position. He'd been under the impression that the posting would be a simple one. But between the hunters, the semi-transient loggers, and the overly protective town residents, he'd gotten more than he'd bargained for. It didn't matter how long he was here or how entrenched in the town he became, he'd never been one of us, and that had made it difficult for him to do his job when Griffin Walker died.

"Anyway," Amelia said, "the real reason I asked you to come in is because I wanted to be sure you got these."

She pushed back from the desk and stood, going to one of the cabinets. A hand lifted the keys from her belt, and I watched as she unlocked the one closest to the wall and pulled a bag from the shelf inside. Through the clear plastic, I could see the dark blue checkered fabric of Johnny's jacket, and immediately, that seasick feeling returned to the center of my gut. Within seconds, he was there, filling the space of the small office like slowly rising water. I was already getting to my feet, as if preparing to try and keep my head above the surface.

Amelia handled the bag with care, holding it out to me slowly. "These are his things we recovered from the scene."

The scene.

There wasn't a single moment of each day that I wasn't thinking about the fact that Johnny was gone, but hearing those words forced me to actually imagine it. Johnny, laying in the forest, that blue jacket just barely visible in the thick green ferns.

My hands felt numb as I took the bag from her, fingers curling around the soft shape of the jacket inside. Amelia was still speaking, but I couldn't hear her anymore. The sound of her voice bled into a kind of white noise as I stared at that blue-and-black pattern. The jacket had belonged to Dad and was one of the things he'd left behind when he went to Oregon. After that, it became Johnny's.

I nodded in an attempted answer to whatever Amelia was saying, tucking the plastic bag beneath my arm and turning for the door.

"James?"

My name was too loud in my ears, my face flashing hot with the tears I was desperately trying to swallow down. I looked back, one hand clutched tightly to the metal knob on the door.

"One more thing." Amelia paused. "Johnny's ashes. They're still being held at the morgue in Sacramento. Should I have them sent now?"

The tightness in my chest twisted. Ashes. There was no way I could begin to conceive of that. How was it possible that Johnny, everything he was, every memory he had, every thought and feeling, was now just . . . dust? How could that be when he was still *here*, alive in the air around me?

"I'm not sure how long I'll be here exactly," I said, voice strained as I searched for some kind of excuse. I didn't want them. I couldn't bear to think they even existed.

Amelia gave me a sympathetic nod. "Of course. Maybe I could have them sent to Micah then?"

I stared at her, caught off guard by the mention of Micah's name.

"I just mean, I know you all are practically family, and he's been the one dealing with things up to now," she added, by way of explanation.

Dealing with things. Was that an implication that I *hadn't* been? But when I searched Amelia's eyes for any sign of an accusation, I couldn't find it.

"Sure." I nodded.

Better Micah than me, I thought.

"Okay, then I'll take care of it. And please remember, if there's anything I can do to help while you're here, you have my number."

"Thanks."

I was out the door before the word had even left my mouth, gulping the cold air down into my hot lungs. My hands shook as I pulled the car key from my pocket, my breath fogging in spurts as I tried to fit it in the lock. As soon as I was inside, the door slammed behind me and I set the bag on my lap, tearing the plastic open until I could touch the jacket inside. My fingers moved over the softened flannel, the image of Johnny flashing in my mind. The color was faded from its original rich blue and the snap buttons had lost most of their shine.

Johnny's phone, a small ring of keys, and a money clip with his ID were secured inside a smaller sealed bag, and I set them on the passenger seat before I held the jacket up to me, lining up the shoulders with mine. There, inches below the collar, was the bullet hole torn through the fabric. In the exact spot where the pain had been throbbing for months. It was surrounded by a dark bloodstain that looked black in the dim light.

I let the jacket fall onto my lap and brushed my thumb over the stiff flannel, thinking that the sight was reassuring, in a twisted kind of way. An anchor to the reality that Johnny was really, truly gone. But I went still when I felt something take shape beneath the heap of fabric. Something round. No, it had a cylinder shape.

I sniffed, unfolding the jacket until I found the inside pocket. The object inside made a weak laugh escape my lips. It was a roll of film.

My head tilted back, finding the headrest. I used to find rolls of film around the house all the time, collecting them in the fruit basket where they would live for months, until Johnny got around to developing them. If he did at all. He left them everywhere. In the cupholder of the 4Runner, tossed inside a boot, poised on the bathroom sink beside his toothbrush.

I slipped the canister back into the pocket and bundled the jacket onto the passenger seat. When I started the car, the headlights washed over the pavement, illuminating the fine mist that drifted through the air. The diner across the street was the only thing lit up downtown, aglow with the warm light inside. SIX RIVERS DINER was painted in an ochre yellow on the glass in an old style that was rubbed off at the edges. The window was slightly fogged with condensation, making the people inside look like moving smudges.

What Amelia had said about this town was still wedged beneath my skin. It was a skipping rock on the surface of my mind, taking me from one thought to the next.

I'd all but erased my life here after what happened—after what we *did*—moving to San Francisco so I could disappear into the city's eight hundred thousand people who didn't know anything about me or this place. But it wasn't just my secret, or my story. It was Johnny's, too. That had always been true about everything.

THREE

Micah Rhodes had always been an expert in the unspoken, and there was a time when I was one of only a few people who knew that language.

The bacon sizzled in the skillet as the coffee dripped, and I eyed the bowl of apples on the counter. He had gone to more trouble than he'd let on, filling the fridge with several days' worth of groceries.

We'd never been good at talking about things. *This* was the way he had always communicated with me. And as much as I used to hate it, as much as it stirred to life a hundred memories I wished I could forget, I couldn't deny the fact that in some ways, it was just so much easier.

I tapped my phone screen for the tenth time, checking for a notification that he had texted. I wasn't sure if I was hoping he would or wouldn't. Through the years, there were times I was sure I never wanted to see him again and others when I'd had to force myself not to get in the car and drive back to Six Rivers. I was eternally pulled between two warring beliefs. I'd lived years alternating between both of them—the idea that leaving things with Micah the way I did was the biggest mistake I'd ever made, and the certainty that it was the only thing I'd done right. For both of us.

I leaned into the counter, watching out the kitchen window, where the lush forest stretched in every direction. The little stone fire pit out back was encircled by two weathered Adirondack chairs that sat in the small clearing of trees. The red-painted shed out back was just beyond it, its roof piled with golden pine needles and a series of rusted yard tools leaning against its side. The whole scene was almost too perfect to look at. Like something that would be sketched onto the pages of a book. But it had never felt that way to me.

My gaze focused beyond the tree line, to where the Walkers' place sat back in the forest. The drive was still empty, the windows dark, and I let myself hope for a moment that Rhett Walker no longer lived there.

Amelia's mention of his son Griffin hadn't exactly been out of nowhere. His death was the biggest thing to happen in this town in the last twenty years, a tragedy that shook Six Rivers to its core. Griffin Walker had been the boy next door long before he was the promising young athlete with a scholarship to Stanford. He and I were the only two kids from our high school who had a way out of this town. But he never made it.

I forced my attention back to the stove, fishing the bacon from the skillet with a fork and setting it onto the plate beside two fried eggs and a piece of buttered toast. Smoke hadn't moved from his spot at my feet, sniffing the air with a whine buried in his chest. The animal was even bigger than I remembered, his eyes so clear and focused that it was a little unnerving to look at him straight on.

"No, Smoke." I pointed the fork at his untouched food bowl in the corner. "Your breakfast is right there."

I tore the toast in half, using it to break open one of the eggs and soak up the yolk.

His front paws shifted just a fraction, his gaze still locked on my plate. When he whined again, I sank down, scratching down his back with both hands. He was an enormous dog, but somehow still lean and slender.

"I think Johnny has been spoiling you." Smoke leaned into my touch. "Am I right?"

When he didn't move, I relented, breaking off a small piece of bacon and dropping it into his bowl. He leapt up, crossing the kitchen in a few steps as I took one of the mismatched mugs from the shelf and filled it with coffee.

The bacon was enough to entice him to eat the dog food beneath it, and I picked up my plate, going into the living room. The sofa was still draped with the quilts I'd found in the chest by the fireplace, my pajamas folded and stacked on one of the arms. I hadn't been able to bring myself to sleep in the bedroom. When we were kids, I'd had the bed in the alcove and Johnny had slept on the couch. But after Dad went to Oregon, I'd taken the bedroom for myself, and when I left it had finally belonged to Johnny. I hadn't even stepped foot inside; instead, I'd buried myself in the blankets on the sofa and watched the fire until I couldn't keep my eyes open, Smoke curled on top of my feet.

I followed the hall to where Johnny's makeshift office was tucked into the corner. The plate of food was still steaming when I set it down between the piles of envelopes, and the springs at the base of the chair screeched as I sat. But I froze when a rush of goosebumps raced up my arms, the quiet cabin coming to life. Almost immediately, the distant sound of fingers tapping on a keyboard drifted through the air. I could hear the drum of what sounded like a pencil's eraser on the desk. The rustling of papers. The hum of music. But all around me, the house was just a still life. A place frozen in time.

My eyes moved over the desk slowly, my mind trying to sift the sounds from the room. I knew the sensation. It was the same one I had every time the hollow space between me and Johnny bled together. When the feelings flooding his mind pushed into my own. I was usually good at drawing a clear boundary between what was him and what was me, but this was different. It was as if the hours Johnny had spent at this desk still hovered in the cabin like an echo of his existence.

Mentally, I was still waiting, breath held in my chest, for the thread between us to snap. But if anything, it felt stronger than ever. I pinched my eyes closed, pushing the sounds from my mind, and when I opened them again, I focused on the papers stacked in front of me and the patchwork of items pinned to the corkboard. There were notes and reminders overlapped with seemingly random contact sheets and pictures torn from magazines.

The workspace wasn't neat, but Johnny had had his own kind of chaotic organization that made sense to him. The trick would be decoding it. When I told Quinn Fraser I was coming up to Six Rivers to get Johnny's documentation for the conservation project, he'd offered to come with me. He'd even insisted that it would be easier to make sense of if he were here, and maybe that was true. But it wasn't the negatives and field notes I was after. The real reason I'd come to Six Rivers was to understand what exactly was going on here before Johnny died. To find some shred of explanation for the weight of dread I'd felt since that day standing outside the coffee shop. That wasn't something I could do from San Francisco. And I wasn't fool enough to believe that's all Quinn wanted.

I'd first met Quinn Fraser at a black-tie fundraiser for the city's art council at the San Francisco Public Library. In a way, that was where this chain of events began. Quinn had been seated next to me, and we'd spent the night trading polite small talk and bidding in the silent auction, but as we waited for the valet at the curb hours later, he'd slipped me his card. Flowers arrived at my studio the next morning and meeting up for coffee turned into dinner at Bar Nonnina. That's when I found out about the project he was heading up at CAS.

Since that night, we'd been walking the tightrope of our not-quite-official relationship, which had been made even more awkward after Johnny's death. He was Johnny's boss, but Johnny was my brother, and Quinn hadn't found a way to be there for me that didn't feel out of place. We weren't together, but we weren't not together, either. And I couldn't help but feel like it was all tangled up—me, Quinn, the project, Johnny.

I'd been compulsively following the train of thought back and forth since the day Johnny died. If I hadn't gone to the fundraiser, I wouldn't have met Quinn. If I had never met Quinn, I'd never have sent him the link to Johnny's work. If I hadn't sent the link, Johnny wouldn't have been hired on, and if he hadn't been hired on, he wouldn't have been in the gorge that day.

There were a thousand ways to divide and slice the timeline. Infinite variables and threads to pull. I'd broken the information down in every way I knew how, and each time, it only grew more maddening. If it had been any other day, if the weather hadn't been clear, if he'd been standing just eight inches to the left. But none of that mattered if it wasn't an accident. And that's what I was here to find out.

I took a sip of coffee and got to work, going through the piles on the desk. I didn't know exactly what I was looking for, but it seemed as good a place as any to start. I flipped through various pieces of mail, sorting them according to their importance. Once I was finished, I turned my attention to the laptop. It was still right where Johnny left it, and the screen came to life, the cursor blinking in the field for the password. I typed in our birthdate, the same password he'd always used for everything.

His email inbox was still pulled up on the screen, but the page took almost a full minute to reload. In the time since I'd lived in Six Rivers, the town had gotten internet connectivity, but it seemed to be almost unusable. I scrolled past the unopened messages from the last three months, a mix of junk mail, automated emails, and actual correspondence that looked like it was related to the research project. But when the first one I clicked took more than a minute to load, I gave up and minimized the browser, bringing the desktop into view. I'd have to wait until I had a better connection.

One of the generic Apple backgrounds was half covered by dozens of random files and folders visible on the desktop. The level of order matched the mess on the desk.

"Seriously, Johnny?" I muttered.

I had to skim the file names twice before I found the one I was looking for—*CAS*.

Johnny wasn't a scientist, but he'd completed a training series to become a certified research assistant, and his territory covered Six Rivers National Forest and into the remote stretches that lay north of it. The five research subjects he'd been monitoring over the last two years were documented somewhere in this maze of files and notebooks, and I was hoping that his records might give me some idea of what he was doing in the days that led up to his death.

I clicked the icon and a new window expanded, filled with more folders. Quinn had tried to give me a basic understanding of what he needed to compile, and after a few minutes, I was able to figure out that Johnny had the project sorted in a somewhat intuitive way. Each territory had its own research subject, a northern spotted owl identified by a two-digit number. Each of the five subjects Johnny was assigned to had their own folder, filled with the detailed records he'd been keeping over the last twenty-four months. Most of them still needed to be transcribed; others just needed to be compiled, formatted, and submitted along with the photographic content.

I glanced up to the metal shelf above the corkboard, where a series of filing bins were stacked side by side. I read each of the labels, taking down the one named *CAS NEGS/PRINTS*. The bin was organized into a series of sections, one for each of the locations that Johnny covered. Within their designated tabs, the negatives were cut and sorted into clear plastic sleeves with a selection of prints Johnny had developed.

I opened the section labeled *Subject 44* and pulled one of the prints from the top of the stack. My hand slipped from the edge of the bin as I sat back in the chair, staring into the pair of liquid gold eyes that seemed to be locked on me. The photograph was of an owl huddled on the branch of a redwood tree, its feathers puffed in the falling snow.

One of the reasons Johnny had been chosen for the project was his uncanny ability to get so close to the owls. Like they didn't realize he wasn't one of them. This photo was an example of that. The owl's gaze seemed to pierce right through the lens of the camera, as if it had been looking right at Johnny when he took the photo. There was a focused, soul-stirring look about the bird that Johnny always seemed to be able to capture.

I leaned in, studying the details. The color was so vivid, the flecks of snow so sharp. It wasn't until I brought the print closer that I could make out the misshapen form tucked beneath the bird. One perfect foot was clasped around the branch, talons shining, but the other was mangled. It was clutched in a tangle of bones under the feathers like it had been crushed and healed in all the wrong places.

The unsettling thought found me again, a nagging sense that I was looking at a picture of my brother. Johnny had always been the troubled one, the one no one understood. But no one *knew* Johnny. Not really. No one except me and Micah.

I flipped through the other sections of the bin, some of them labeled in more detail than others. Where a handful of negative sheets were identified with each subject's number, some of them had the number of the location. Others just had an abbreviation of some kind, like Johnny had never really developed a system to go by. That would be fun to figure out, I thought.

The last section seemed to be a kind of catch-all, with random incomplete film sheets, prints, and a few pages of scribbled notes. When I flipped past the glossy surface of a picture of Micah, I stopped, sliding it out from the others. My heart twisted a little in my chest when my vision focused on his face. He was lit in the warm glow of what looked like a fire, his dark blond hair falling into his eyes. In one of the shots, the image was blurred with the movement during the exposure, making him look like a smear of paint.

The corresponding negatives had the date *June 2* written on a piece of masking tape, and the entire roll was just variations of the same photo. Micah talking. Micah laughing. Micah's face turned into the darkness. I'd seen countless rolls of film just like it through the years because it was the kind of thing Johnny did when he was testing out some new piece of equipment. Maybe a lens or a new type of film he wasn't used to. Whatever was in front of him became his subject.

I reached into my sweater pocket for the roll of film I'd found in

Johnny's jacket, turning it over in my hand. My fingers stilled when I saw a black mark I hadn't noticed sitting in the dark car the night before. It looked like the squiggle of a Sharpie.

I flipped the canister over, realizing it was a set of letters and numbers. *TG 11/10.*

My brow creased. It looked like a date—November 10. That was just two days before Johnny died. And TG . . . was that Trentham Gorge?

Slowly, my eyes dropped to Johnny's camera bag, still tucked into its place beside the desk legs. I let out a long breath, staring at it.

It was one of the things that hadn't quite added up. If Johnny was out working in the gorge, he would have had his camera. But when he was found, he didn't have it. He also hadn't been wearing his safety gear, and that didn't track, either. We'd been raised in this forest and taught from a young age how to handle guns. Wearing safety gear was something ingrained in the culture of Six Rivers. Hunting season was knit into the fabric of this place, and there wasn't a single household that didn't have a gun collection full of firearms. But of all the unruly details, there was still one thing that unsettled me most. It was *where* he'd been found. Trentham Gorge. Of all places.

I reached out a tentative hand, letting my fingertips brush the canvas of the camera bag. Instantly, that strange, out-of-body sensation was back. I could feel the weight of the camera in my hands. The pull of the strap against my neck. I could hear the click of the shutter. The slide of the film being pulled from its canister.

I unzipped the bag and let it fall open. Johnny's lenses, batteries, and flashes were wedged into padded sections. Everything he needed on a shoot had its designated place, a far cry from the chaos of the desk in front of me.

It was evident that the gear had been meticulously cared for, in almost pristine condition despite its extensive use. And that made sense. The camera had been the eye through which Johnny saw the world. A window, where he could watch from a safe distance.

I zipped the bag closed and tucked it back into its place, then turned my attention to the desk drawers. The metal tracks of the large one on the left were stiff, forcing me to jostle it. When it finally slid open, a tall stack of notebooks was stowed inside.

I took them out and set them in my lap, thumbing through the one on top. It looked like Johnny had one dedicated to every subject in the study, with dates and times that labeled each observation. They were Johnny's field notes.

Smoke whined from down the hall, a high-pitched sound that made me lean forward to see the dog standing at the front door. I ignored him, setting the notebooks aside and reaching back into the drawer for several leather-bound notebooks that didn't match the others. It took only seconds for me to recognize them.

JG was imprinted at the top corner of the first cover—the initials I shared with Johnny. But these notebooks were mine. The last time I'd seen them was before I'd left Six Rivers for school in San Francisco.

Promise.

That's what the adviser who'd awarded the scholarship had said about me. That I showed *promise.*

I never went anywhere without one of my notebooks when I was a teenager, compulsively pulling out my pencils any time I had more than a few minutes to myself. And even when I didn't. By the time I made it to high school, my drawings had caught several teachers' attention. When I got to junior year, I was doing something I never dreamed possible—applying to art schools up and down the West Coast. I didn't really believe it could happen until I got the acceptance letter from Byron School of the Arts. But by then, I had a choice to make. One that felt impossible until the night Griffin Walker died.

I flipped through the pages of sketches, the smell of ink and lead swirling in the air. But my hands froze when I reached one that made my stomach drop.

It was a sketch of Trentham Gorge.

The gorge was deep in the heart of Six Rivers, at the end of a series of cliffside roads that were only drivable in the daylight. More than anything, it was just a steep, forested valley wedged between two small mountains, carved down through the rock over millennia by the twisting ravine at the bottom. But there was a stretch that was deep enough to dive into, and despite warnings from our parents and the people in town, most of the kids we knew hung out there on the weekends.

There was something both wild and protected about the place, created through the natural but unforgiving forces of persistent erosion. Even the meaning of the word *gorge* itself felt severe—it was French for *throat*.

My fingers ran over the drawing slowly, my eyes following the jagged lines. I'd sketched out the cliffs with lazy strokes, the ink smearing where the edge of my hand had brushed the paper before it had dried. It was probably the last time I'd drawn the place because after what happened there, I'd wanted to pretend it didn't exist. We all did. Which is why it never sat well with me that Johnny had chosen it as one of his research locations. And why it was too coincidental that it was the place he died.

Smoke's whimpering erupted into barking that reverberated between the walls, making me wince. When the sound gave way to howling, I shifted the notebooks to the floor.

"Cut it out, Smoke."

His shadow flitted across the wooden floor again, and I stood, coming around the corner. He let out another frantic string of yelps, and I realized his attention wasn't on the front door, like I'd thought. His eyes were pinned on the closed hallway closet.

I walked toward him, throwing a glance toward the living room before I looked between Smoke and the closet door, my gaze tracing its outline before I pulled it open. He instantly quieted, pacing back and forth behind me as it swung wide.

"What?" I looked at him, as if expecting him to answer.

It was just a coat closet, filled with pairs of boots, a few hats, and coats on hangers. The blue and black plaid jacket I'd hung there last night was among them, bullet hole and all. I stood still, listening to see if Smoke had heard something like the scamper of a mouse in the walls, but there was nothing.

He whined again, and I shifted some of the coats to the side, peering into the back. Johnny's neon-orange safety vest was hung on a hook, and I stiffened, my vision blurring just a little. I reached up, pulling the little string that hung from a bulb fixed to the wall, and the corners of the closet illuminated. The light gleamed on something glossy and black in the back, and I moved the safety vest aside.

It was a gun. A long barrel with a wooden stock and grip was propped in the corner behind the jackets, and my jaw tensed as I let go of the vest and it fell back in place. I didn't recognize the rifle as one of the ones Dad left behind when he went to Oregon. I'd grown up around guns, but I hadn't actually seen one in years, and they held a different kind of meaning to me now. There was no erasing that phantom pain that still throbbed in my chest. No way to unknow that a bullet had been the thing that stopped Johnny's heart.

I closed the door, pressing my back to it before I turned to face Smoke. He was panting, eyes still fixed on the closet with his head dipped low like he was hunting what lay inside.

"Come on."

I scratched behind his ear and took him by the collar, leading him back down the hallway. He stretched out on the floor when I sat back down at Johnny's desk. I returned my old notebooks to the drawer and closed it harder than necessary. The desk shook, making the pens in the tin cup rattle, and I rubbed at my temples.

Again, my eyes skipped over the contents of the desk, just as chaotic and cluttered as it had been an hour ago. I didn't know what I'd expected to find. I didn't even know what I was looking for. But that whisper at the back of my mind was still there.

My gaze lifted to the corkboard again, scanning the bits of Johnny's world that hung like a collage over the desk. I reached up, lifting the trimmings of a contact sheet, reading the page beneath it. It was a series of dates scribbled down on an envelope. But when I spotted a

piece of ruled paper half hidden at the bottom corner of the board, I
lifted the overlapping page to read it.

You changed my life. ✦

The unfamiliar handwriting wasn't Johnny's, scrawled in a hurried
script on a page that looked like it had been torn from a notebook.
The scribbled star that followed the words was almost unfinished, one
of the corners barely connected. My fingers slipped from the paper,
and it tucked itself back beneath the others. It suddenly sank in that
I'd been gone for twenty years. In that time, there was no telling how
many people had drifted through Johnny's life in Six Rivers or had
crossed his path through the conservation study. I was more than out
of my depth. The truth was, I knew almost nothing about Johnny
anymore. Nothing that really mattered.

The air around me suddenly seemed so stagnant and suffocating,
that oppressive feeling only growing heavier. As if at any moment,
I would look over my shoulder and see Johnny standing right behind me.

I'd underestimated what it would be like to be closed up in the
cabin with all of his things, the imprint of him touching everything
around me. I wasn't sure how many days of that I could take.

I closed the laptop and slipped it into my bag, getting back to my
feet. I was suddenly desperate for the fresh air, eager to escape the
skin-tingling sense that my brother was breathing the same air I was.

Smoke followed on my heels as I made my way up the hall, and I
couldn't help but glance back at the closet as I passed, remembering
the gun inside. I pulled on my jacket, and as soon as I was through the
door, my lungs inflated, fully expanding behind my ribs for the first
time since I'd woken. I could finally breathe.

I'd told myself for a long time that the past was the past. That there
was no coming back from it. That had been an easy lie to believe when
I was hundreds of miles away, but here, in Six Rivers, the past was still
living and breathing.

FOUR

Town was busier than the night before, with cars parked along the curb and the doors of the shops propped open. Smoke walked out ahead of me, knowing exactly where we were headed.

The signs that hung over the sidewalk identified the businesses that made up the little town of Six Rivers. The market was tiny, with produce stands out front that were filled with winter squashes, root vegetables, and bundles of fresh greens. It shared a roof with a tackle and bait shop to the right and the post office to its left, where a COUGAR LAND banner hung in the window.

The town's residents were fit into the scene perfectly, with their wool and canvas coats and lace-up boots. They were right out of the pages of one of the old *Field & Stream* magazines Dad used to have piled in the living room.

Two men standing beside one of the light posts on the street reached out to give Smoke a pat on the head as he passed, but their conversation was cut short when they saw me following behind him. Their heads tipped politely, gazes lingering on my face a beat too long, as if they were trying to place me. There was exactly one way into Six Rivers, and it was also the only way out, so seeing a new face in town wasn't usual unless you'd come for the hunting or fishing, or you'd taken a job at one of the logging outfits. It didn't take more than a glance at me to guess that I wasn't here for any of those things. And as soon as word got out that James Golden was back, I'd find more than one set of eyes following me.

I gave the men a polite smile as I passed, following Smoke until he reached the door of the diner. A metal bowl of water was set outside the entrance, and a thin crust of broken ice floated on the surface as he lapped it up. He plopped down, his long legs crowding the width of the sidewalk, forcing a passerby to step over him.

I caught my reflection in the diner's window, which had been fogged over the night before. It was clear now, and inside, most of the tables were full. Upholstered stools lined the long counter that stretched down one side of the stall-shaped restaurant, and old glass pendants hung from the ceiling. The place had always been alive in a way the rest of Six Rivers wasn't, buzzing with an energy that made it feel like the beating heart of the sleepy town, if it was possible for it to have one.

I pulled open the door and the bell on the other side jingled, making a few people turn in my direction. That same question was cast in their expressions, but this time there was recognition in some of the lingering gazes. Maybe word had started getting around quicker than I thought.

Many of them were faces I knew, though they were older now and their placement in my own memory was fuzzy, like they couldn't quite come into focus. The librarian from the middle school, the woman who ran the food pantry, and Harold, the only name I could readily pull from the ether of my mind because he'd worked with my dad as a logger. He sat at the end of the counter on the last stool, fork dangling from his fingertips as he chewed. He was the only one not outright staring at me. But the face *behind* the counter was easy to recognize.

Sadie Cross greeted me with a smile, but there was still a visible coldness to her that lay just beneath the surface. It had always been that way between us, a natural consequence of the cliché dynamics that often existed between a teenage girl and her boyfriend's sister.

"James Golden." Sadie said my name, wiping down the glass dome of a cake stand as she watched me. "You're maybe the last person I expected to see walk through that door today."

"Hey, Sadie." Even her name sounded strange as I spoke it.

She set the lid back down over a perfectly golden pie with a lattice crust missing a single piece. Her dark hair fell long over the shoulders of her blue sweater, covering the embroidered logo on her apron.

She glanced to the window behind me. "Saw Smoke out there, but figured he was with Micah."

She looked like the same girl I'd known all those years, but there was something just slightly hard-edged in her face now. Her on-again, off-again relationship with my brother had made her a constant in our lives in the years before I left. In some version of events, we'd technically been friends, but it wasn't until years after I left that I could see that my protectiveness of Johnny had made most of my friendships difficult. I'd never trusted anyone with him. The only exception there'd ever been was Micah.

I looked around me, searching for a spot along the counter to sit. The place was loud, filled with conversation, music, and the noise of the kitchen. Through the long opening in the back wall, I could see a man and another woman working back-to-back over the rising steam of a cooktop.

"I wondered if we'd see you after . . ." Sadie didn't finish, gesturing to the only empty stool. "But Micah said you were handling things from San Francisco."

I took the seat, wedging myself between two brawny men clad in flannel. I couldn't tell if Sadie was asking for an explanation or just talking in the nervous way people did after someone died.

"Just a few things to deal with up here," I said. "I'll only be in town a couple of weeks."

"Weeks," Sadie repeated, as if the idea didn't sit well with her. But the tone of her voice was quickly replaced by the smile returning to her lips. "Well, it's nice to see you. You look good, James."

"You too," I said, thinking that it was true. There was still a distinct look about her that was somehow compounded by the soft wrinkles that framed her eyes and the fullness of her figure.

"What can I get you?" She tucked the rag into the ties of her apron.
"Just a coffee."

I was glad she was willing to forgo the obligatory catch-up that I'd spent the entire drive to Six Rivers dreading. I didn't want to talk about life in San Francisco or anything else that had filled the time since I'd left this place. There had been an almost paranoid stirring in me that squelched the safe distance the miles between the city and Six Rivers gave me. I also didn't want to step too closely to the conversation about the fact that Sadie was still here, working in the diner and living the same life our mothers had, or the fact that I wasn't at all surprised by it.

She filled a mug from the full, steaming pot of coffee on the hot plate, and I let my eyes wander to the sea of framed photographs that covered almost every square inch of the wall behind her. The ones I'd seen a thousand times were still there—like a scrapbook of the idealized life in Six Rivers. There were pictures of the diner's regulars, kids at a picnic with balloons, a few people huddled around a fire on the beach. There were also several of hunting groups lined up beside rows of limp-bodied ducks or holding up the horned rack of a stag. Faces of every age looked back at me, some of the images posed and others candid.

Out of habit, my gaze found the one with me in it. It was a photo of a crowd of people standing out on Main Street, smiles wide in a sea of pale blue uniforms and team merch. What I remembered about that day was in splices of sound and light. The soccer team had just won regionals at a tournament in the Bay Area, and those who hadn't made the trip down to the game had gathered out in front of the diner to listen on the radio. The picture was snapped just after the

winning goal was scored. I was fifteen years old, beaming at the camera, and I could see Olivia's and Micah's faces in the crowd beside me.

I purposefully didn't let my eyes fall on the photograph of Griffin
Walker that still hung only a few feet away. He was handsome in an
all-American kind of way. Perfectly symmetrical and charming. He'd
been the town's golden boy, beloved and revered. That was never more
true than after he died.

The small bundle of dried roses that had been tied on the frame
after the funeral twenty years ago was still there, the petals now wrinkled and missing their color. There was a time when it wasn't possible
to go anywhere without seeing similar shrines, and that constant reminder had been the last thing to run me out of this town.

Growing up down the road from the Walkers had put Griffin into
our orbit at a young age, and when he became the star of the high
school's soccer team, it made him something like a god in this town.
That attention had changed him, and not for the better. There wasn't
anyone in Six Rivers who wasn't shaken by his death, and he was folded
into countless memories, some of them all but lost now. But there was
one I'd tried and failed to forget. I still remembered the crunch of ice
beneath my boots that night. The smell of woodsmoke and melting
snow. The way the firelight had gleamed in his open, empty eyes.

I forced my attention to the new photographs that had been added
to the wall, finding Johnny's face among them. Instantly, a sinking
feeling pulled in my gut. He was sitting in one of the booths by the
window with an arm stretched over the back of the seat. He had a
look on his face like someone had just called his name, his head half-
turned and eyebrows just slightly raised. The photo couldn't be more
than three, maybe five years old, but the picture of the young version
of him I had in my mind was flickering in and out of that image. To
me, Johnny would always be the eighteen-year-old kid jumping from
the cliffs at Trentham Gorge as I held my breath, watching from
below. I don't know if I ever let that breath go.

I scanned the room around me until I found the booth that was in
the photo. It was empty now, but as soon as I turned my head, I had

the faintest sense that I could see him from the corner of my eye. I shivered as Johnny's presence slowly leaked into the muggy atmosphere of the diner. The more it intensified, the more certain I was that I hadn't imagined it back at the cabin, and it was more than the thread of connection we'd always had. This was stronger—a palpable thing in the air. When a distinct shadow formed in my periphery, I instinctively turned my head back to the booth, where I was convinced Johnny would suddenly appear. But there was nothing.

Sadie set the cup and saucer down in front of me, snapping me back from the avalanche of thoughts tumbling through my mind. I looked up to find her studying my face.

"Can I get you anything else?" she asked.

I set my fingers on the edge of the saucer, still half-distracted by that shadow in my peripheral vision. "No, thanks."

Sadie moved as if to leave, but she hesitated. "I know there's not really anything to say, James, but I'm sorry about Johnny." Her voice was low now. Careful. Like saying my brother's name out loud was a spell that could wake the dead.

"Thanks," I managed.

Back in San Francisco, this was the part when the aura of feigned normalcy would typically be broken. The moment when someone heard about the death of my brother and the stilted grief descended between me and the world. But it was so much worse here in Six Rivers, where people had actually known Johnny. And not just the smiling, handsome man in the photo that hung on the wall. This town knew his shadows, too.

A bowl of sugar came down in front of me, followed by a tiny ceramic pitcher of cream, before Sadie's attention finally turned to a man waiting at the register. I curled my cold hands around the mug, hoping it would calm the trembling I could still feel in my fingers.

"Ben, can you grab another crate of those cups?" Sadie called out to the young man sweeping along the back row of tables as she absently punched the keys of the register. When he didn't look up, she tugged the rag from her apron again, tossing it at him.

He flinched as it hit his shoulder, pulling an earbud out of his ear as he looked up. "Huh?"

"*Cups.*" She motioned toward the empty shelf, and he answered with a nod before he leaned the broom against the wall. Then he was disappearing through the swinging door at the back.

"Can't take those things out of his ears for three seconds," Sadie muttered to the man at the register, half laughing.

She finished ringing him up, listening as he made a comment about the incoming weather, and I glanced around the diner, noting that people were dressed in warmer layers than I was. Hats and coats were hung from the pegs beside the door, and the temperature had already dropped several degrees in the time since I'd arrived. I'd forgotten how quickly the weather turned in winter, how suddenly, almost violently, the forest succumbed to the bone-deep cold. That wouldn't bode well for the incomplete job I'd done packing. I was pretty sure I'd brought exactly one sweater and was wearing my only jacket.

The swinging door to the back pushed open again, and the young man reappeared with a crate of steaming white porcelain mugs balanced against his hips. He slid them onto the counter and started stacking them.

"This is my son, Ben." Sadie was talking to me now.

The boy glanced over his shoulder, only half looking at us with a distracted expression that made his face appear blank. He was a handsome kid, with his mother's blue eyes, but he was at least six inches taller than her. Lanky in a way that reminded me a little of how Johnny looked at that age. But what age was that? This kid looked maybe seventeen or eighteen years old, and that math made me look at him a little more closely. Sadie would have been, what? Nineteen when she had him? Twenty?

That sinking feeling was tugging deep in my stomach again, and I immediately shot a look toward Sadie's left hand. If she was married, she wasn't wearing a ring. But the kid could have been from an old relationship, too. I tried to dismiss the possibility that he could be

Johnny's. He and Sadie had been involved for a long time before I left, even if they weren't exclusive or consistent. When we did talk, Johnny didn't say much about his personal life, but if he'd had a kid, he would have told me. Wouldn't he?

A dozen images flashed through my mind like a flip book as I studied Ben's face. I could see my brother up on the cliffs at the gorge. Moving like a shadow in the darkroom. Standing in the trees with a smear of blood at his brow.

Before that last memory could fully unfold, I shoved it back down.

"Ben, this is James," Sadie said. "Johnny's sister."

The kid's hands stilled on the mugs, his eyes finally focusing on me. "Oh." He stood there stiffly, looking from his mom's face back to mine.

I couldn't tell if there was something behind that look. Two women down the counter also discreetly leaned forward, catching my gaze, and I wasn't sure if I was imagining it or if the whole diner quieted just a little.

"Nice to meet you." I saved the kid from the awkward moment, giving him a smile.

Sadie pushed the drawer of the cash register closed. "He's a senior over at the high school. Video games for brains but manages to earn a few bucks here when he can be bothered." Sadie glanced at her watch and looked up at him. "Aren't you going to be late?"

Ben snapped out of his trance, finally pulling his gaze from me. "Oh, shit. Yeah."

"I'll finish that. Get out of here." Sadie jerked her chin toward the door, holding out a hand.

He untied his apron and balled it up, giving it to her. "Thanks."

She watched him round the counter and clumsily pull on a jacket. Then he was pushing out onto the street. "No such thing as a day off for some of us."

"Yeah, Micah told me you bought the place," I said.

Her eyes found me again, a glimmer of pride in them now. "Almost six years ago, but I'm almost always one employee short during soccer season. You know how it is around here."

I nodded in response, glancing again to the banner taped inside the post office window across the street.

COUGAR LAND

The entire town revolved around the team during soccer season. Because of it, the school was flooded with funds, despite its rural location, and businesses even shut down on tournament weekends. The headline of nearly every paper detailed a chronicle of the most recent game, and once the season was over, the town went back to being not much more than a supply stop for hunters and loggers.

I took a sip of the coffee before I pulled my phone from my pocket and unlocked it, opening the Wi-Fi settings.

"Looking for this?" Sadie pointed to a handwritten sign posted beside the coffee machine. It had the network name and password scrawled in marker.

"Yeah, thanks."

"You'd think in 2024 you'd at least be able to get those things to make a call, but service is still too weak in most places. But we put in one of those internet satellite systems a couple of years ago and business has never been better. Isn't that right, Harold?" She gave the red-bearded man at the end of the counter a wink before she moved back down to the register.

I typed in the Wi-Fi password and a series of email and app alerts stacked on the screen as soon as it was connected. There was a voicemail from my neighbor in San Francisco about picking up my mail and another from Quinn saying he'd give me another call in the morning to check in. I opened my email next, scrolling through a smattering of unread messages. The only one of consequence was from Rhia, the gallery curator at Red Giant Collective, where three of my pieces were being included in an upcoming show.

I pulled out Johnny's laptop, just barely finding the space on the counter to open it, and logged in to his bank account. I'd jotted down the list of photos I had to track down, followed by the records I needed

to locate for Quinn, which included financial reports Johnny was behind on. The portion of the grant money he had been issued had to be
accounted for on a quarterly basis, and Johnny hadn't submitted anything for the last two. That didn't surprise me. I couldn't imagine that
admin and red tape were ever something he'd managed to get good at.

I downloaded the statements from the last six months so they could
be printed out back at the cabin, and then started on the list I'd made
that morning. I hadn't found any files for Johnny's field notes, which
meant he probably hadn't started transcribing them. That meant that
someone at CAS would have to do it, but not before I had a chance
to take a look at the records from the days before Johnny's death.

I reached into my pocket for the roll of film that had been tucked
into his jacket and set it down on the counter, placing my chin in my
hand as I stared at it. If the numbers on the tube were a date like I
thought, the photos were from two days before Johnny died. The images on the negatives might even be the last photos he'd ever taken.

I unlocked my phone, finding the number Micah had sent me for
Olivia Shaw. But my fingers hovered midair, my mind turning with
what to say. The last time I'd seen Olivia, I'd lied to her, but that wasn't
why I'd never talked to her again. The reason was because she'd *known* it.

Hi Olivia, it's James Golden. Micah told me I could swing by.
Is now okay?

I hit send, and only a few seconds later, a reply made the phone
vibrate in my hand.

Hey James!! Sure thing. I'll be here until six. Can't wait
to see you.

I let out a steady breath, relieved, as my eyes lifted over the screen
of the laptop, finding Olivia's face in the framed photographs on the
wall. Her dark curly hair was escaping the ponytail it was pulled into,
and the lower half of her round face was hidden by a scarf around her

neck. But the movement of a shadow on the glass made me tense up again. I was almost sure that I could make out Johnny's reflection. His dark hair and wide shoulders took shape in the glare of light, but when I turned around again, the booth by the window was still empty.

I closed the laptop and reached into my coat, finding the few bills I had tucked into the pocket.

Sadie waved me off. "Don't worry about it."

"Oh." I glanced to the empty coffee cup. "I appreciate that."

"You'll be back. Don't worry." She smirked. "A couple of weeks is plenty of time to rack up a bill around here."

"Thanks."

She set both hands on the counter, watching me slip the laptop into my bag. Her mouth opened, then closed before she spoke again. "Micah's taken it really hard, you know—Johnny's death."

I was a little thrown by the sudden change in subject, my hands faltering on the zipper of the bag. I looked up at her.

"He's . . . he's not himself, James," she said. "I'd suggest treading lightly."

The words sounded like a warning, or a boundary she was making. It felt almost territorial. My smile tightened, and from the look on her face, Sadie noticed the change in the air between us.

I stood. "Thanks again."

"Sure thing." She fetched a new rag off the back counter and went back to wiping, but I could feel her gaze on me as I made my way to the door.

The six of us—me, Johnny, Micah, Sadie, Olivia, and Griffin—had been a kind of pack before Griffin died. But after his death, Johnny, Micah, and I became the subject of every conversation in town. After that, we'd formed a tightly closed unit to protect ourselves and one another from those whispers. The result was a separation between the three of us and Olivia and Sadie, and I imagined that when I left, a new line of alliances had formed. What Sadie wasn't saying was that I hadn't been in that circle for a long time. And she would close ranks if she had to.

FIVE

Six Rivers High looked more like a mountain chalet than a school. The original 1970s brick building was still partly visible behind the façade that had been added during the largest renovation, but the oiled wood trim and dark blue metal roof was the kind of modern architecture that didn't belong in a landscape as wild as this one. Large floor-to-ceiling windows reflected the trees like mirrors, creating an optical illusion that made it feel like the forest was inside the building. Sometimes it had felt that way.

The metal door sent a groan down the linoleum-lined hallway as I hiked my bag higher on my shoulder, trying to balance its weight. I followed the memorized layout of the school I still had filed away in the back of my mind, not bothering to look up to the blue-and-white signs that marked the corridors as I passed. When I reached the art wing, I was instinctively unnerved by how quiet it was. The school day had ended, but I could still hear a few distant voices and the faraway slam of a locker.

Large wood-framed windows looked into several studio-style classrooms that were brightly lit with afternoon light. For a rural public school, the workspaces were incredible, rivaling even the ones we'd had at Byron. It seemed that with every state championship won, the school got another grant or endowment. The art wing had been one of the first improvements and was a primary reason why I wound up painting the series that got me into art school.

I peeked into each of the classrooms until I reached the last door on the left, a long barrel-shaped studio that had three wooden work-tables in lieu of desks. Large papier-mâché sculptures painted in bright colors were suspended from the ceiling and several overgrown potted plants were stuck on the windowsills. I pushed the door open wider and stepped inside.

"James *fucking* Golden." I heard my name spoken in a soft kind of awe from the corner of the room, where Olivia Shaw stood with a plastic bucket in her hands.

Her dark curly hair was pulled back from her face in a long braid and thick-framed tortoiseshell glasses sat on the end of her nose. The yellow blouse she wore was tucked into baggy, high-waisted linen pants, and she had on a pair of cloth sneakers that were covered in specks of paint. Behind her, a messy, cluttered desk reflected the same creative chaos. Half-squeezed tubes of paint and different grades of charcoal pencils were strewn over a large desk calendar that was covered in frantic, looping writing.

She, too, hadn't changed. The Olivia Shaw I'd grown up with was cool, in a lazy kind of way. Pretty, but simple. There had also always been that innate sense that there was more going on behind her eyes than the echo of the smile on her lips.

She set down the bucket, rounding the corner of one of the tables before she threw her arms around me and squeezed, surprising me. "I can't believe you're here."

I tried to relax under her touch, keeping my balance as she pulled back to see my face.

"How do you look exactly the same?"

I smiled a little awkwardly. "I was just thinking the same thing about you."

"Wow." She let out a breath. "It's been a really long time."

The comment made me bristle a little because I knew that's what everyone was thinking. I was sure there were a number of theories about why I'd never come back to Six Rivers, and no shortage of judgments made about how I'd stayed away. But the curiosity and hurt I'd seen in Olivia's eyes the last time I saw her were gone now.

She folded her hands like she didn't know what to do with them, and then thought twice, absently picking up one of the colored pencils on the table and rolling it between her palms. It was the same fidgeting, excited energy she'd had as a teenager, too.

"Thanks for letting me come by," I said. "I don't want to keep you too long."

"Oh, it's no trouble at all." She gestured to a stack of cardboard portfolios on the table beside me. "I've got grading to do, anyway."

I studied the pieces that were already laid out. The assignment was a still life of three oranges in a bowl, and the students had used a number of mediums to capture it. It was the same assignment Olivia and I had when we were in art class here together. I distinctly remembered it, because our teacher had insisted that one of the great pursuits of an artist was to try to capture the color, shape, texture, and light of an orange every single day for an entire year. It was a challenge I'd taken on personally at Byron, but I'd made it only fifty-two days before giving up.

"It's weird, right?" Olivia laughed, reading my mind. "Bet you didn't think I'd wind up here."

I hadn't. At least, I'd hoped she wouldn't. Olivia had said for years that she would go to L.A. or New York—somewhere loud and bright, where buildings were covered in murals and you could sell your art on the street. And she could have. Olivia was talented, but she had never been desperate and hungry in the same way I was. She was more easily crushed by critique and devastated by rejection. I'd thought many times in my years at Byron that she'd never really had the grit it took to make it as an artist.

"When did you come back?" I asked.

Her smile fell a little before it righted again. "I never left. I mean,

I went to school in Redding, but I came back here after I finished and, a few years later, got my teaching certification. Then I just ended up here." She looked around the studio as she reached up, sticking the colored pencil into her hair. "I've been following what you've been up to in San Francisco. Keeping tabs, that sort of thing. It's been really amazing . . . just incredible, James."

I didn't know what to say to that, so I tried to soften the moment with a self-deprecating laugh, but it didn't quite land. The truth was, I was embarrassed. Olivia and I had been neck and neck in our pursuit of the fine arts as we came up through high school, and I knew there was a time when she'd believed she would be shooting for *National Geographic* or doing editorial work somewhere by now. If she was keeping tabs on me, it would all look very impressive. Press releases and collections and features in publications. But what people didn't know about that world was that it was mostly composed of smoke and mirrors. I was long past the point of rose-colored glasses.

"And Byron? Was it as magical as it seemed all those years ago?" she asked, voice wistful.

"Yeah, I guess it was." I smiled. "And you? Are you still shooting?"

"Oh, yeah. I mean, I'm not exactly working on my next series for an exhibition at the Met or anything." She laughed again, but this time it had just the smallest tinge of sadness. "But yeah. Still shooting."

I let my gaze wander to the corners of the studio. A lot of young artists with grand ideations of their future notoriety ended up as teachers in schools like this one or at the university level. For some people, it was a kind of settling they were glad to take in lieu of a dream that just never got closer, and I guessed that Olivia was in that camp. For others, it was a dangerous injury to ego that could poison your humanity. The same was true even for the professors at an institution as prestigious as Byron.

"I think it's really great what you're doing—finishing the CAS project for Johnny. It's been pretty wonderful for our little school in the middle of nowhere to be a part of something like that." She looked genuinely proud. "I mean, admittedly a very small part, but you know what I mean. The kids think it's exciting, and they just *adored* Johnny."

My mouth twisted involuntarily, threatening an ironic smile. *Adored* wasn't a word I'd ever really expected to hear in reference to my brother. *Intriguing,* maybe. Johnny's lack of interest in people had always seemed to make them that much more curious about him. In that way, he was magnetic, even. But not adored. No one knew what to do with Johnny.

Olivia laughed, as if tracking with the internal conversation I was having with myself. "I know. But he just had that thing, you know? That mysterious vibe." Her hands splayed out in front of her, illustrating the point like the slogan on a billboard.

"I get it," I said, though I wasn't completely sure I did. I was becoming increasingly uncomfortable with the familiar way people spoke about Johnny. Like they knew him better than I did. Like there had been more than just the miles of physical distance between us.

"Anyway, I don't want to keep you with all my reminiscing. Why don't I show you to the darkroom?" Olivia clapped her hands together.

"Sure." I adjusted the bag on my shoulder. "Thanks."

I followed her back out of the classroom to the single white windowless door down the hall. Above it, the telltale darkroom light was fixed to the wall—a red bulb caged in thick white wire. When it was on, it meant the door shouldn't be opened for risk of ruining the work going on inside.

Olivia turned the knob and let the door swing open, extending her hand with another flourish, and when I stepped inside, my throat constricted. The acrid scent of the processing chemicals was so nostalgic that it woke a numbed pain in me that I hadn't felt in a long time. Even after I'd left home for Byron, I made sure I was enrolled in a photography class every semester so that I'd have access to the campus darkroom. It wasn't just the comfort of the darkness or the familiar smells. It was the soft click of the egg timer on the shelf. The sound of the fan on the enlarger.

The tangible feeling of Johnny's presence was already beginning to take root from where it clung to the shadows. It drifted through the humid air, invisibly swirling around me as a string of memories skipped through my mind. Johnny had spent half of high school in this room, most of the time while he was supposed to be in some other class. I'd have to track him down after school when he didn't show up at the car, and I'd find him here, working away and completely unaware that the bell had even rung.

Olivia leaned into the doorjamb behind me. "I found a few things Johnny left behind. They're in his cubby there." She pointed to a row of built-in shelves that each had a set of initials assigned to them. It was the same one he'd had when we went to school there. "Put them in an envelope for you."

"Thanks."

"No problem." Her gaze dropped to the bag tucked beneath my arm. "What are you working on?"

I shook my head. "Just sorting through some of the negatives and prints. Trying to make sense of everything so I can get it all to CAS."

Olivia let her hands slide into her pockets, and I could see her struggling for something else to say. "Well, let me know if I can be any help."

I answered with a nod and she turned out of the room, but then she stopped herself.

"Actually, what are you doing later?"

I looked at her, a little caught off guard. "Nothing, why?"

"Do you want to grab a drink at The Penny?"

"The Penny?"

"Yeah, it's still around. Everyone's there on Friday nights and there's music. If you're not doing anything . . ."

"Yeah." I grinned. "That sounds great."

Olivia looked equally surprised and delighted. "Okay, perfect! I have your number, so I'll shoot you a text when I'm headed over there?"

"Sure."

She smiled even wider and then she was gone, her footsteps trailing up the hallway in a fading echo.

I let the heavy bag and stack of notebooks in my arms fall onto the worktable, trying to stretch out the tension that had seized my neck. The cubby with Johnny's initials had a manila folder slipped inside, and I eyed it, trying to decide if I had the energy to poke at the barely stitched-together wound in my chest. I didn't. Not after that conversation with Olivia.

I took off my jacket, finding the roll of film in the pocket and reading the date again—November 10. I peered down the hallway one more time before I closed the door and got to work. Everything I needed to develop the film was stocked, and I flipped the switch on the red light before I turned off the other.

It took a few seconds for my eyes to begin to adjust, but once they did, the rhythm of the darkroom came back to me. The crimson glow painted the shapes of the room in contrasting colors as I dropped the apron over my head and tied it. The room was colder than the classroom or the hallway, kept cool for the sake of the chemicals. It wouldn't take long for the temperature to make my hands stiff.

I developed the film and trimmed it, hanging it up on the suspended line over the trays. They would have to dry before I could handle them, but I could already tell that most of the negatives on the roll were blank. There were only eight photos, and I wouldn't be able to make them out until I could use the light box.

In the meantime, I turned my attention to the negatives I'd brought from Johnny's, situating myself on the stool and spreading out the contents of the bag before me. I'd gathered up all of the sleeves marked with dates that fell within a few months before Johnny died that also took place in the gorge. I still didn't know exactly what I was looking for, but I hoped I could at least get a handle on what his days out there looked like.

I flipped the switch on the light box and it came to life, filling the room with a soft, rattling buzz. I set the first sleeve of negatives on the surface, finding the date Johnny had written on the plastic label: *August 1, 2023*. I moved the magnifier from one photo to the next, but I couldn't identify many differences between the images, and from the thumbnails, the pictures looked like they were mostly of trees.

Then I opened the notebook for Subject 44, the owl Johnny had been tracking in Trentham Gorge. I skimmed through the pages until I found the correct date. Johnny's staccato, punctuated handwriting filled the pages, sometimes drooping off the lines as if he had his eyes on the trees as he wrote. The image of him hunched in an outcropping, hood pulled up over his dark hair with a pencil in hand, made the hole in me stretch wider than I thought possible.

There was something so fitting about it. My brother had always been pensive and serious, which made people inquisitive about him, and I think that's what Olivia had been getting at when she mentioned the kids in her class. Johnny had never cared for anyone's attention. He was content to be on his own, even if he didn't want to be far from me, and I imagined that he was truly happy out there alone in the forest for days on end.

The entries in the notebook were labeled by date, time, and location, beginning in September and October 2021. The notes were reports on the subject itself, but Johnny had also detailed his observations of the different locations in the conservation project, cataloging landmarks, erosion patterns, and even climate changes. On August 1, Johnny had seen Subject 44 only once and for a matter of minutes, jotting down a few almost code-like lines I couldn't totally make sense of.

There was nothing particularly helpful about the records. No mention of whether Johnny was working alone or alongside someone else, and other than what seemed like an irregular schedule, the dates were somewhat consistent with entries appearing at least once a month.

I cross-referenced each sleeve with the notebook until I reached the end so that I could make notes of ones Quinn might be able to use in the study. By the time I was finished, the processed film was dry enough to be touched. I cut the negatives and fed them into a fresh sleeve before I put them on the light box. The details of the images were more visible under the magnifier, and it looked like there was at least one where I could make out the speckled feathers of an extended wing. But it was the one of the rockface that confirmed it was Trentham Gorge. The distinct sediment stripes that marked the cliff face were clearly visible in two of the shots.

I slid the magnifier over the others, a series of tree lines and rock formations. The little thumbnails were a smear of gray and green, except for a little blot of pink in the last photo. Maybe from a lens flare or a speck of dust on the negative I'd missed when I was cleaning it off.

The enlarger thrummed on the counter as I filled the tubs with the chemicals, settling into the calming pattern of the movements. The walls around me felt like a protective casing that kept everything else out. I put the first negative into the carrier and turned on the lamp, adjusting the projection of the image onto the easel. I exhaled, relieved, when the image came into focus. Johnny had caught the owl straight on, eyes wide and intensely focused.

"Gotcha," I whispered.

I set the timer before I hit the button, and the lamp clicked on, exposing the image for seven seconds. When I pulled it out of the water bath a few minutes later, I smiled wide. The print dripped as I hung it on the line and turned on the gallery light, studying the details of the picture. Then I circled the negative number on my list and put a star beside it, going to the next. The last on the roll was the image with a blur of pink in one corner, a smudge of color that was starkly out of place in the thick overgrowth of green.

I lowered my face to the magnifier, squinting. It wasn't a speck of dust on the negative. The discoloration was exposed onto the film in a distinct shape, which meant it wasn't an imperfection in the film. It was something actually *in* the photograph.

I slipped the negative from the sleeve and loaded it into the carrier. When the lamp of the enlarger clicked on, I adjusted the projection, making it bigger until I was zoomed in on the corner of the image. My brow pulled as the shape came into focus.

The distant jitter of air vents and the resonant hum of the building filled the hallway outside the door as my fingers gently adjusted the focus.

The cold in the air around me sharpened, making me shiver. There was a sudden feeling in the room like it had grown smaller, like there was less space around me. I turned, eyes scanning the darkness. It was silent except for the sound of the enlarger and the trickle of the water bath in the sink.

I ran a hand through my hair, shaking off the feeling, and turned back to the machine. The timer and the light flicked on, making me wince against the brightness, and when it clicked off again, I opened the easel and took the paper out.

The image surfaced within seconds of me lowering it into the tray, and I pushed the print from side to side with the tongs as it darkened.

James.

My name filled the darkness and I jolted, bumping the developer in front of me. It sloshed over the edge of the tray, and I turned, scanning the small room. The red light was almost viscous, like if I lifted my hand into the air, I would feel it between my fingers.

My heart pounded as the developer dripped onto the floor, and I reached for the light with a shaking hand, flipping it on. I blinked furiously as my vision sharpened. The shadows were gone, that thick, muted sound dissipating as the seconds ticked by, but I could still *feel* my name buzzing in the air. I could still hear the voice that had spoken it. Johnny's voice.

The cramped walls of the darkroom felt too close now. The cold air too thin. I propped the door open and tore a handful of paper towels from the roll fixed to the wall, sopping up the mess on the counter and trying to dry the notebooks. Johnny's handwriting was already smearing on the pages of one of them. I absorbed as much of the liquid as I could, and once the mess was contained, I pulled the print I was developing from the water bath.

I sat on the stool, pushing my hair back from my damp forehead and willing my pulse to slow. The blob in the photograph was a backpack. The pink canvas was covered in winding doodles like the ones I used to draw on my Converse with Sharpie, making me think that it hadn't belonged to Johnny. He had either accidentally gotten it in the shot or he'd hit the shutter without meaning to.

It wasn't exactly evidence, but it did mean that only two days before he died, he was out in the gorge with someone else. And it was possible that whoever was with him that day could have also been with him on November 12.

The question was, who? My eyes trailed to the empty hallway, where the light was cast in beams from the windows. I knew so little about Johnny's life here in Six Rivers that I didn't even have a guess. But I had an idea of who would.

SIX

Every time I'd been to Trentham Gorge, it was with Johnny, and that's where we were the first time I remember it happening.

The memory was still so clear. The sound of our voices echoed down into the cavern above the cool blue-green water the first time we drove out to the swimming hole by ourselves. The ravine along the bottom of the gorge was rocky and shallow in most places, but there was one perfect pool deep enough to dive into just a quarter-mile hike from the trailhead.

Johnny, Micah, and I traversed the maze of steep rocky paths up the ridge, where there were at least six different heights you could jump from, and I'd taken the lowest one, watching from below as Micah and Johnny plummeted through the air, howling until they hit the water.

I could still see it, too—the view before I stepped off the ledge with my arms floating up over my head. I hit the water, my body piercing down past the surface, and my eyes opened just in time to watch the light race away from me the deeper I sank.

Johnny had already climbed back up the rocks to take another jump when I surfaced, and when I looked up again minutes later, my

stomach dropped. He was standing high up on the cliffs. Not on one
of the levels of well-worn jumps that looked out over the gorge. He
was at the very top.

There was a razor-thin silence between me and Micah as we looked
at each other, but Johnny's feet were already running toward the edge
when the scream left my mouth. His legs kicked as he flew out into
the air, and instantly, my heart was a metronome syncing to Johnny's.
That's when it happened. Not the third-eye sense I'd always had with
my brother—the undercurrent of awareness that had been there as
long as I could remember. No, this was something else.

The feeling of falling flipped my stomach on itself as the ground
disappeared beneath his feet, and suddenly, I was falling with him.
Sinking down, my head plunging below the water, and I couldn't
breathe. But the only thought taking shape as I sank was that I was
about to watch Johnny die. And when he did, my own heart would
stop beating.

He hit the water with a deep whoosh just before Micah's hand
found me and yanked me toward the surface. I was gasping for air,
coughing up the cold water, and when Johnny didn't come up right
away, I put my face back under, searching for him. The trail of bubbles
hid him in the deep blue for an agonizing, terrifying moment before
they began to clear. And then he was moving, his long legs kicking
him toward the surface.

I came up, the burn of tears exploding in my eyes and nose when
he finally appeared. He had an enormous smile on his face, his hair
plastered down the sides of his neck. My heart was still pounding so
hard that I felt like I was going to choke on it. It was several seconds
before I realized what was happening—that the chaotic race of my
pulse didn't belong to me. That the adrenaline I could feel coursing
through my body wasn't really there. My own paralyzing fear was
fused to it. I couldn't pull the two apart.

Micah pushed me toward the bank, and I was barely able to keep
myself afloat until I was climbing up the rocks. But Johnny was
laughing, the sound echoing through the gorge. He was completely

oblivious as I stared at him, trying to catch my breath. Behind him, Micah's face was red, his eyes furious. He shoved Johnny into the water, his own chest heaving, and it was the first time in my life that I really began to see my brother clearly. I'd always thought that we were the same. That we were two shades of the same color. But as I sat there, watching Johnny swim back to the bank, I had only one thought: that he was a storm in the clouds, just minutes away from breaking.

Now, sitting at the kitchen table, I was thinking the same thing. I studied the photograph again, tracing the contrasted lines of the rockface with my finger. The photo paper was still glossy and fresh, slick to the touch, and the reflection of light on its surface obscured the image just enough for me to imagine Johnny up on that ledge. He'd earned himself a reputation for being fearless, but that day was the first time I began to realize that we weren't immortal. That I could *lose* him. And that terror had opened a kind of doorway between us.

For years after that, the same link would wake from time to time, connecting us in an impossible, metaphysical way. I could feel what Johnny felt in those moments. Almost like I *was* him. Spaces and things that held on to bits of my brother felt like conductors. That, I expected, was what had happened in the diner. The darkroom. The first time I'd sat down at his desk. The traces he'd left behind were still alive all around me, and if I wasn't careful, I'd keep tripping those wires.

I set the photograph down, clicking my tongue, and Smoke leapt up from the heap of blankets on the sofa. He was out the front door as soon as I had it open, trotting down the drive ahead of me and turning toward town before I even had the door locked.

It was even colder than the morning, the cloudy sky painting everything in shades of dusty blue, and the thin jacket I'd brought was proving to be useless. I couldn't stomach the idea of taking one of Johnny's coats, and I wouldn't risk it now that I was convinced I was somehow connecting with him. I still hadn't even dared to step foot in his room.

I followed Smoke, tugging on the beanie I had stuffed in the pocket, but my steps faltered when I spotted the truck in the Walkers' driveway. The slow, creeping sense of dread I'd had since I arrived in Six Rivers opened its gaping mouth inside my chest and I picked up my pace, watching the house from the corner of my eye. It wasn't until I was past the turnoff that I saw the flash of a red checkered shirt beneath a pair of canvas overalls.

I nearly tripped over my own feet when Rhett Walker came into view. But it was the blood on his hands that made me stop breathing. Before him, a deer was strung up by its hind legs, its middle cut open over the dirt. The silver coat gleamed beneath the stain of blood painted over its body. The same blood that painted Rhett's forearms as he reached into the cavity and swept his hand from top to bottom.

I instinctively covered my mouth and nose, as if the scent would find me all the way out in the middle of the road, and a nauseous feeling swirled in my stomach. As if he could feel me watching him, Rhett's head slowly turned, eyes finding me over his shoulder.

He recognized me right away. I could see it in the way his pale, clear eyes sharply focused, his hands slipping from the carcass. The last time I'd seen Rhett Walker, he'd had a fistful of my hair, shaking me so hard that I'd bit my own tongue. Only a few days after his son Griffin died, he'd shown up at our door drunk, barely able to stand on his own two feet. Before I'd even known what was happening, he had his hands on me, his voice so loud it distorted in my ears. He wanted to know what I saw that night. What I knew. And if there was ever a moment that I was close to breaking the promise I'd made, it was then.

Ranger Timothy Branson had managed to haul Rhett off before Johnny got home, and I'd never told him about it. I was terrified of what he might do if I did. That was the same night I decided to leave—that I knew I had to. It was the very first time in my life that I'd admitted it to myself. That I didn't just love Johnny. I was scared of him, too.

Rhett didn't so much as blink as he watched me, and I forced my gaze ahead, walking faster. I had to resist the urge to keep checking over my shoulder as I walked, the unsettling vision of the man hovering bright and heavy in my mind. Like I was dragging it behind me.

Smoke didn't pick up his pace until the first sight of town came into view, and the sound of the music took shape in the quiet. Johnny Cash's "Cry, Cry, Cry" echoed out in the darkening trees, the lights of The Penny like glowing rainbow smudges in the descending fog.

The bar had been closed up and quiet when I'd walked past that morning, but now it was filled with people. Its windows were open to the street, the small parking lot packed with cars, and a few had their tailgates down, where several people sat with bottles of beer dangling from their fingertips. Their attention drifted in my direction as I came up the road, and I tried to ignore the way their voices hushed. A few of them gave me a nod as I passed and I returned the gesture, determined to make it through the door without having another stilted, half-true conversation about Johnny.

I ducked inside and the music exploded around me, twice as loud once I was within the walls of The Penny. It smelled like stale beer and old, unpolished wood. Bright lights washed over the little stage at the back, where a band was set up, and there wasn't an empty table in the whole place. License plates covered the walls, reflecting the neon glow of the beer signs over the taps, and it took several seconds for my eyes to adjust enough to spot Olivia sitting at the end of the bar.

As soon as she saw me, she sat up straighter, waving, and I followed the line of stools to the seat she'd saved for me. The lowball glass of whiskey that sat in front of her looked untouched.

"You made it." She was already flagging down the woman behind the bar, who was setting down two glasses of beer in front of the women beside us.

"What would you like?" She was looking at Olivia, but she tipped her head toward me.

"Go ahead," Olivia said. "I doubt I know your drink anymore."

Immediately, I was reading into the comment. Was it an attempt to make the point that I'd been gone for too long? Or maybe an implication that I drank something pretentious now that I lived in the city? But when I looked at Olivia, that innocent, sweet look was still in her eyes.

"Vodka soda, please," I said.

The bartender nodded, plucking a glass from the counter behind her.

"Okay, maybe I do still know your drink." There was a grin at the corner of Olivia's mouth now.

The cymbals crashed behind us, and all at once the music died out. It was replaced by the sound of the loud voices in the room. Laughter and shouting and the clink of glasses hitting the tabletops. The vodka soda landed in front of me and I thanked the bartender with a nod, lifting it to take a sip.

Olivia did the same with her whiskey, her glass drifting toward me in a mock salute. There were a few awkward seconds before she finally started talking. "Remember when we used to hang out in the parking lot and pay the loggers to buy us beer?"

I smiled, and this time it was a genuine one.

"Amazing what a ten-dollar bill and a pretty smile could get you back then." She snickered.

"To the loggers." I lifted my glass again, repeating the mantra we used to say.

Olivia clinked her glass against mine. "To the loggers."

We took a synchronized drink, and Olivia pushed her glasses back up her nose.

"Can't believe this place is still here," I said.

"Really?"

I laughed. "Yeah, maybe I can believe it."

"The Penny's an institution. Wouldn't be Six Rivers without it."

There was something nostalgic about the place that made it feel as if time had stood still. Like maybe all these years hadn't passed and when I stepped outside, it would be 2004 again.

I turned my glass on the counter, watching the light reflect off the ridges. "Ran into Sadie this morning at the diner."

"Yeah, she owns it now. Took over the place years ago, which no one complained about. Food's better, that's for sure."

Another song started and Olivia's shoulder touched mine as she rocked back and forth on her stool. The tension I'd felt when I walked through the door was slowly bleeding out of me, the vodka already warming me up.

"I saw Rhett Walker, too," I said in a low voice, eyeing the ring of condensation on the bar top before me. "Just now. On the way over."

Olivia stopped swaying, falling quiet for several seconds. Her fingers were tapping the side of her glass now. "Thought you might."

"Didn't know if he'd still be around."

What I really meant was that I'd *hoped* he wouldn't still be around.

"Did he say anything?" she asked.

I shook my head.

"He mostly keeps to himself these days. I don't think you have anything to worry about."

I tried to believe it. The thought of sleeping in the cabin knowing that Rhett Walker was next door was more than unsettling.

"He and Johnny still managed to get into it," she said. "That's for sure."

"What do you mean?"

She shrugged. "Just . . . about everything. The dog, a fallen tree on the property line, Johnny burning stuff out back. Always something. The guy is impossible."

I took another long drink. "Yeah, well, he's been through a lot."

"We all have, right?"

I didn't answer.

"I miss him," she said, more softly. "I got so used to having him around at the school that it's been strange. He seemed to really like it—being around the kids."

"Really?"

"Really. I asked him to come in and talk to my classes when he first started working with CAS. You know, like a visiting artist kind of thing, and they were *so* into it. I mean, like I said, the kids just loved

Johnny. They each did a project based on a photo from his Instagram feed, and you would have thought he was a rock star walking in here. They were so inspired. He actually mentored one of them last year—Autumn Fischer. She even wound up getting accepted to Byron, like you." She waved a hand in the air. "I'm sure you know all about that."

"Yeah," I lied, my smile growing heavy. That tight feeling had returned to my chest. "He talked about it all the time."

I couldn't remember the last time Johnny and I really talked. And when we did, it was almost always just a string of halfhearted updates about what I was painting or what shows were coming up. I'd never mentioned anything about my periodic dates with Quinn or anything else that fell outside the bounds of my work because sometimes, it was more like an interrogation than a catch-up. It always felt like I was reporting to Johnny. Like I needed to feel like he was proud of what I was doing. In some twisted way, it justified me staying in San Francisco.

The conversations were never long. When I asked Johnny about anything in his life, it was met with one-word answers and reasons he needed to go. For a long time, I thought it was because he was trying to protect me. Using himself as a shield between me and Six Rivers. But when he died, that nagging feeling that something had been going on with him made me wonder if his tendency to dodge my questions wasn't about me at all.

"I was really proud of him, you know?" she said. "It just seemed like things were finally lining up for Johnny. Like he'd found his thing. His purpose."

"Yeah," I replied. I had thought the same thing many times.

"Did he ever bring anyone else from the CAS project in to talk to the kids?"

She thought about it before she answered. "No, why?"

"Just wondering. I didn't know if he was working this area with anyone else."

"I mean, just Josie."

"Josie?"

"Another researcher out at the coast. Fort Bragg, I think. She was Johnny's counterpart, kind of overseeing his work for CAS."

I couldn't remember Johnny ever talking about her, but the name still felt familiar. I made a mental note to take a closer look at Johnny's records for any mention of her. If she was Johnny's counterpart, they'd probably worked together in person. She could even be the owner of the backpack.

"James?" A woman's voice called out from down the bar, and I looked up to see Amelia Travis.

It took a few seconds to place the forest ranger. She wore a long-sleeve denim shirt dress, her hair down and long, swept to one side. She looked almost a decade younger out of her uniform.

I waved in reply and she stood, making her way toward us, drink in hand. When Olivia's shoulders drew back, her lips pursing a little, I immediately clocked the change in her demeanor. She was watching Amelia's approach from the corner of her eye.

"I thought that was you." Amelia leaned in close, trying to raise her voice over the noise of the bar. "You settling in all right?"

"I am."

"Good. Heard you made it over to the school today."

Beside me, Olivia was pointedly staring in the opposite direction.

"Sorry, small town." Amelia laughed. "Just about everything is news around here. Wanted to make sure you hadn't run into any problems."

The way she phrased the non-question made me a little uneasy. "No. No problems."

She waited a beat. "Well, you just let me know if there's anything I can help with. Anything at all."

"I will. Thanks."

"You look after this one." Amelia was talking to Olivia now, gesturing toward me.

Olivia's placid smile was dismissive at best, but I couldn't tell if Amelia had picked up on it.

"You two have a good night." Amelia disappeared into the crowd, leaving an empty space between us.

"What's that look about?" I asked.

She shrugged. "Nothing. She's nice enough. Just a bit meddlesome."

"What does that mean?"

"Travis takes her job very seriously. She keeps a close eye on things, and you know how people around here are. They don't really like that."

I knew what she meant. With the exception of the loggers who moved through town periodically, new residents were few and far between. Even after decades, Timothy Branson, who'd had the office before Amelia, had been kept at arm's length. Especially after Griffin Walker died. People were devastated by what happened, but the moment Branson raised more questions about Griffin's death than could be answered, the town was quick to cut him out. Like if there was a lie to be unearthed, a truth to be discovered, it wasn't an outsider's job to do it. That's what had made Rhett Walker knock on my door that day.

"She said she was a friend of Johnny's," I said, meaning it as a question.

Olivia snorted. "I wouldn't say that."

"Yeah, I thought that didn't sound right."

What I was really thinking was that it seemed careless, considering the fact that he had secrets that wouldn't be safe in the hands of someone like Amelia. It wouldn't take much digging to begin putting pieces together that we'd worked hard to bury. But why would Amelia lie about her and Johnny being friends?

I took in the way Olivia shifted on the stool. She reached up, tucking the hair behind her ear. All at once, it dawned on me.

"Were you and Johnny . . . ?" I didn't finish.

Olivia's eyes widened, her cheeks flushing. "No!"

I stared at her, holding back a smile.

"No," she said again. "Are you kidding? I mean, Johnny? Interested in someone like me?" She looked genuinely embarrassed.

I was sure Johnny had relationships, but it was one of many territories that we didn't venture into when we talked. He'd never been good with women. He tended to get involved with women who fell hard and fast, but Johnny didn't get *close* to people. Sadie had been a good example of that. She'd spent our high school years at the mercy of his fickle attentions. And just like him, they were always shifting.

Back then, I didn't have any friends who weren't infatuated with my brother, and I'd decided a long time ago that it was because people were intensely drawn to the mercurial parts of him. As if the very things that made him so different were also the things that made him captivating. You never knew when Johnny was going to show up or disappear, what he was going to do or say. It had been an exhausting atmosphere to exist within and, at the same time, always made me feel singular. Like being one of the only people allowed in my brother's inner world meant that I was special.

I spent several seconds debating whether or not I wanted to ask the bigger question that had been eating away at me since that morning. About Sadie's son, Ben, and whether Olivia had any idea if he could be Johnny's.

Before I could make up my mind, Olivia turned on her stool to get a better view of the band and the drums picked back up, the music blaring through the speakers. I let the thought go and did the same, watching as the front man strummed his guitar and Elvis Presley's "Heartbreak Hotel" filled the place.

I had to willfully let myself sink into it. Nights like this one were rare for me, aside from the occasional drink with Rhia or the string of onetime dates with guys I met on dating apps. The Penny was nothing like the little neighborhood bar down the street from my apartment in San Francisco. The last time Johnny visited, I'd taken him there and he'd been personally offended by the fact that there was a lavender cocktail on the menu.

A smile stretched on my lips, remembering the way his face had looked.

"I know I already said it, but it's good to see you, James," Olivia said, suddenly.

I turned to look at her. "It's good to see you, too. Really."

The door to the street opened, making the heat of the room contract, and when my eyes flicked up, I felt my entire body still. Micah Rhodes shouldered past a few people in the doorway, tugging the beanie from his head. His hair fell into his face before he raked it back and made his way toward the other side of the bar. His gaze didn't land on me as he cast a few polite smiles to the people he passed, and when I felt Olivia watching me, I dropped my eyes.

"Have you seen him since you've been back?" she asked.

"Not really. He came by to drop off Smoke when I got in yesterday."

She drained her glass, lifting a hand to signal the bartender again, and then she leaned forward just a little to see Micah shrugging his jacket off.

I could admit to myself now that I'd underestimated what it would be like to see him again. To stand in the same room and chart the changes in his face since the last time I looked at him. It gave me a panicked feeling, like I needed to get into my car and drive back to San Francisco before it could wrap its hungry tendrils around me. Those memories were still floating just beneath the surface of my skin. His hands sliding up my back beneath my shirt, the humid air, the sound of breath against my ear.

I'd hoped that it was just yesterday, that after so long, it was bound to stir things up that I thought were long dead. But as I sat there in the red and orange lights of the bar, my eyes tracing his sharp angles in the dim light, I had that frantic itch again. Like being pulled and pushed at the same time. It almost made me consider getting up and leaving.

He took a seat with two other men, and as if he could feel my gaze on him, he suddenly looked up, meeting my eyes. I swallowed, fixing my stare back to the bar top, but now a slow, burning heat was moving over the side of my face, down my throat, and over my shoulder. Everywhere I imagined his eyes would land.

"How's he been?" I asked Olivia, keeping my voice low.

"Before all this? He's been good. He works as a fly-fishing guide on the rivers and stays busy during the season. One of the only guys we grew up with who isn't working as a logger, so that's something." Olivia paused. "But since Johnny? Honestly, I don't know."

"Sadie said he's not himself."

"That's putting it lightly." She leaned closer. "He took it hard. Of course he did."

I could hardly hear the words anymore, drowned out by the beat of the music. I resisted the urge to look back at Micah for all of five seconds before I finally gave in. He wasn't watching me anymore, but I could see his awareness of me in the stiff set of his shoulders.

"But he definitely isn't himself," Olivia continued. "Doesn't come around a lot. He and Johnny were on the outs for a while there, too, so I figured maybe that has something to do with it. Like he feels guilty maybe."

"On the outs how?"

"I don't know what it was about, but with Johnny? Could have been a million things. Those two were like family and family's like that. Just as likely to kill them as you are to kill for them."

The words made me suppress a shudder. She had no idea just how true that was. But she and Amelia both were right about Micah being family. It wasn't just the teenage angst and first love that had made him so hard to shake. It was everything else. Long before I was in love with him, we'd been threaded together in that permanent way that happened when your childhoods were interwoven. When you *grew* with someone. When they knew versions of you that no one else did. There was no erasing memories like that. There was no way to pretend that they didn't go right on living beneath your skin for your entire life.

I watched the way the amber light moved across his cheek, the muscle in his jaw ticking as he stared into his glass. Micah was the only person who knew my brother like I did. How to see his storms coming. How to weather them. How to protect him from himself. And that had been the biggest problem between us—Johnny.

I spent years after I left unraveling that thread, trying to follow it to its end. But the answer wasn't singular or simple. With Micah, nothing was.

SEVEN

I plucked yellow and green highlighters from the desk and set myself up at the kitchen table so I could start on Johnny's bank statements. They were surprisingly thin, with only a handful of deposits each month and a fraction of the transactions I usually had on my own accounts.

The payments from CAS were easy to find, two consecutive numbers that showed up regularly, and I highlighted them in green. The first was $1,200.00, the monthly stipend paid to Johnny for his position on the project. The second was $860.00, which was designated as grant funds to be used for research and issued quarterly. These were the sums Quinn needed documentation on, but there was a lingering worry in my mind that it wouldn't be that easy. That there would be some evidence of mismanagement or bending of the truth because, well, that was Johnny. Any missing funds, I'd cover or account for myself before the documentation went to CAS, because that's what I always did. I covered for my brother. I'd been doing it for my entire life.

Growing up, Johnny had gotten the bad-twin rap early on. More than once he'd been caught stealing something at the market, and when we were teenagers, he'd gotten fired from his first job because he'd swiped cash from the till.

I'd seen it in the way adults looked at us, and even talked about us. Like I was the good half and Johnny, the bad. But what people had never understood about my brother was that he was just willing to do what he thought he had to and there weren't many lines he wouldn't cross to make those things happen. He didn't care about perception or reputation. It was like he'd been born without that hardwiring the rest of us had—the instinctive fear that made you need to belong.

Once, I'd heard a teacher describe Johnny as a solitary species, like one of the animals who don't live in packs or exist in any kind of societal structure. To Johnny, life was very simple. He only belonged to himself, and his only job was looking after me. The problem was, at some point that became my only job, too—looking after Johnny. And that wasn't a simple task.

I worked my way through each of the bank statements, using the yellow highlighter to mark transactions that might have been project expenses. Some I'd have to run by Quinn to check their eligibility, but between the receipts I ran across in Johnny's email and what I'd found on his desk, I hoped it would get me in the ballpark of the amount that needed to be accounted for.

When I got to the July accounting, the largest transaction I'd seen appeared in the amount of $12,397.21. The yellow highlighter hovered in the air over the vendor's name.

BS 012001

I stared at the number, fixated on the discrepancy between this transaction and the others on the statements. The charge was more than the total Johnny usually had in his account by a significant amount. It was far too much money to be funds from the grant that he'd used for the project, which made me think it had been for equipment. A new camera and a couple of good lenses could easily amount to that much.

I tapped the highlighter on the table. The only person I could think of who might have an idea was also the only person I couldn't bring myself to pick up the phone and call.

I pulled it from my pocket and set it on the table, staring at the screen. Micah still hadn't texted, and while I wasn't surprised, I had a nagging sense of disappointment that I was ashamed to acknowledge. It had only been forty-eight hours since I'd first seen him, and already I was losing my resolve not to call or text him.

I picked up the phone, unlocking it, before I found the last text he'd sent me. I hadn't saved the number, which was just a pathetic attempt to ignore the fact that I had it. Sometimes, after a few glasses of wine or after hours of trying to fall asleep, I'd search his name on social media. But Micah had never made any accounts. I'd never asked Johnny for his contact information through the years, and that was intentional. Both because I didn't have a good excuse, and also because I didn't trust myself with it.

There was no getting around the fact that I would have to talk to him if I was going to answer the string of questions I had mounting about Johnny. He was the only person I could think of who might know whether Johnny was working with anyone out at the gorge. And if Olivia was right about Johnny and Micah having issues, I wanted to know why.

I'd half hoped Micah would be doing the same thing I was now, trying to find a good enough reason to call me or show up at the house again. But I'd also known in my gut that he wouldn't. Micah wasn't going to chase me. Not this time.

I changed my mind more than once before I finally opened the text thread. I changed it twice more before I hit send.

What are you doing tonight?

Heat bloomed in my face and I immediately regretted it. I pressed my hands to my cheeks, letting out a heavy breath. In some version of these events, Micah had just won. And if he didn't reply, I'd have the answer to the question I hadn't had the guts to ask for twenty years. Whether everything I'd done—everything I'd *not* done—had been enough to sever the ties that seemed to eternally bind us together.

My phone buzzed on the table a few seconds later and I dropped my hand, sucking in a breath. But it wasn't Micah's name on the screen.

"Shit."

It was Quinn.

I cleared my throat and impulsively pulled the elastic from my hair, shaking it out. I'd planned to take the call at the diner, but I'd lost track of time.

"Hey, Quinn," I answered, voice louder than necessary.

The line was silent.

I glanced at the screen, where the call timer was counting. It was connected, but I only had one bar of service.

"Hello?" I pressed the phone to my ear again and the staticky, broken sound of a voice cut in and out. "Hold on just a second."

I went up the hall, Smoke on my heels as I opened the front door and went down the steps. Another bar lit up, and I tried again.

"Hey, can you hear me?"

"There you are!" The voice cleared. "I've got you now."

"Sorry about that. Service is shit out here."

"No problem." Quinn's washed-out British lilt made his words bounce. "How are you, James?"

"Good. I'm good."

"You made it up there okay?"

"Yeah, everything went fine. Got in the day before yesterday and just getting everything sorted."

"Good, good." He paused, the next string of words clumsy. "I hope everything hasn't been . . . too hard. You holding up all right?"

The genuine, tender tone of his voice made me feel a little less balanced. One of the first things that had struck me about Quinn the night I met him was his uncanny ability to cut straight through small talk and socially acceptable pleasantries. He wasn't afraid to get to the heart of things and he didn't pretend not to notice people's vulnerabilities. There was no wondering what he really thought. Or what he wanted.

"I'm okay." I swallowed. "It's hard, but of course it's hard, right? I knew it would be."

He was quiet for a moment. "Yes, that's understandable. I hope it's an opportunity to get some closure."

My gaze wandered over the ground, my mind turning those words over. Closure was something I didn't even know how to wrap my head around. I didn't have any idea if it was even possible.

"And how are you getting on with Johnny's research? Making headway?"

I pulled the sleeve of my sweater over my hand and tucked my arm around me, shivering. It was freezing and I hadn't thought to grab my jacket. "Yeah, it hasn't been too bad. I've got most of the photographs together, just tracking down a couple more. I'm going through the field notes today just to make sure everything's there."

"That's great." The apprehension in Quinn's voice vanished, as if he'd been bracing himself for bad news. "Anything I can help with? I'd be more than happy to catch a flight up to Redding and come lend a hand."

I pulled the phone away from my ear, glancing at the call timer on the screen with a smile. It had taken less than two minutes for him to offer to come up. But the idea of having him or anyone else from my other life here made me squirm.

"That's okay. Really. I won't be here long."

I could hear the disappointment in the silence on the other end of the line, and I hated that feeling. Like every time Quinn tried to open a door, I was gently closing it.

"Right. Well, if you change your mind . . ."

I looked around me, realizing Smoke was no longer in view. The forest that surrounded the cabin was so thick that I could barely see a patch of sky through the canopy.

"I think I pretty much have what I need," I said, distracted. "I just have to go through some more records and get everything compiled."

"I'm relieved to hear that. I don't know how much Johnny told you about this project, but the purpose is to provide protection for vulnerable populations, and this species in particular has been more difficult to get the data on. Our job is to identify which of those populations . . ."

I rounded the corner of the cabin, only half listening as I scanned the trees out back. It was late morning, but the canopy was so thick that it was a few seconds before I spotted the dog. His pale gray fur caught the light beaming down through the branches.

"James? You there?"

"Yeah, sorry," I said. "I actually wanted to ask you. Johnny mentioned someone else on the project. I think her name is Josie?"

"Oh, yes. Josie. What about her?"

"I was wondering if she's in the area. I mean, in case I have any questions about Johnny's work."

"She's out in Fort Bragg. Not too far. What do you need from her? I could reach out."

"That's okay," I said, a bit too quickly. "I didn't know if she and Johnny worked together out here in Six Rivers."

Quinn paused. "Well, she is the one who trained Johnny at the start of the study, and I know they were friendly."

Again, I turned the woman's name over in my mind, trying to find some associated memory with it. I was almost sure Johnny had never mentioned her, but I couldn't shake my curiosity about whether the backpack in the photo was hers. Whether she'd been with Johnny that day in the gorge.

"Why don't I put you two in touch?" Quinn offered.

"Sure. That would be great." A frustrated exhale escaped my lips when I saw Smoke pawing at something in the fire pit.

"All right. Well, I've sent you a list of everything we need, the formatting, all of that. But honestly, I can take care of the finer details if you just want to compile everything."

"Okay, I can do that."

"Great. Oh, and just a reminder about those financial forms. I included what we need for those in my email as well."

"I'm actually working on it now."

A cloud of dust kicked up from the fire pit, where Smoke was digging, and I picked up my pace, trying to make it to him before he made an even bigger mess. When I reached him, I hooked a hand into his collar, pulling him away.

"Thanks. I really appreciate all of this, James." Quinn paused, and the line went quiet again. "I know it would mean a lot to Johnny, too. He really cared about this project."

I sat on the arm of one of the Adirondack chairs and my hand dropped into my lap, my eyes finding the trees again. "I know he did."

It was after Johnny started the project that I realized for the first time in a long time, I wasn't waking up in the middle of the night worried about him. He'd been so proud when he got the placement with CAS that he'd shown up in San Francisco the next day. Thinking about it now, I realized that was his last visit.

I didn't know if I'd ever seen him like that. At least, not since we were kids. It had been like watching a feather finally land, after floating a great distance. He'd found a purpose in the project. A sense of meaning. I even remembered feeling almost envious of him. Like Johnny had something that made him feel alive and connected to the world when I hadn't felt that in a long time.

"Well," Quinn said, "*please* don't hesitate to reach out if you need anything at all. I'm here, James. And my offer to come up still stands."

"Thanks, Quinn," I said, guiltily.

He was doing a poor job of hiding the fact that he'd hoped I would ask him to come, and I knew why. He wanted to connect with me in a deeper way than the periodic dinner dates and occasional nights I spent at his place. Quinn wanted to *be* there for me. But I didn't know how to let him do that.

He hung up and I stood, stuffing the phone into the pocket of my sweatpants. Smoke's muzzle was powdered white with ash, and I groaned, doing my best to dust him off. He was still tugging against my grip on his collar, trying to reach the fire pit again.

"Come on."

I whistled and his ears perked up before he loped past me, his long legs beating me to the cabin. I threw a glance at the Walkers' place, visible through the trees, and I was relieved when I didn't see Rhett's truck in the drive. I'd be lucky if I managed to dodge him the rest of the time I was here.

I followed Smoke up the steps, brushing the ash from my hands, but I jolted when a shadow of movement slid across the kitchen floor inside. I reached out to steady myself on the window frame as a figure came around the corner of the hallway, nearly toppling down the steps. When I had my balance, I looked up.

For a moment, I thought it was Johnny. Not the version of him I'd last seen, but the one I'd lived with in this very house. The tall, lanky teenager with a dark mop of hair and wide, brawny shoulders. My chest deflated, my face flashing hot as my vision swayed, and it took several seconds for my eyes to process the details enough to convince me that it wasn't him.

Standing across the kitchen, his hands lifted and eyes wide, was Ben Cross, Sadie's son.

"S-sorry!" he stammered. "The front door was open."

I let out a breath, pressing a hand to my ribs.

"I didn't mean to scare you," he said, apologetically.

I shook my head, a little embarrassed. "It's okay."

Smoke nosed Ben's hand until Ben reached down, scratching behind his ear. But he was still watching me with an expression I recognized. Guilt, or nerves maybe. It was almost as if he'd been caught. But when I looked around the room, glancing at the open front door, nothing looked amiss.

"My mom asked me to bring these over."

He motioned to a basket sitting beside the stove. It looked like a care package.

"That's really nice of you guys," I managed. "Thanks."

He shrugged, an awkward movement that told me the gesture had had little to do with him. His eyes moved around the cabin curiously, his hand still stroking down the back of Smoke's neck. I couldn't help but study the details of his face again, searching for some irrefutable trace of my brother. I couldn't tell which of the similarities were just teenage boy and which could be evidence that this was Johnny's son.

Ben's eyes drifted to the living room, and I watched as he studied the details of the place. Even if it hadn't changed much since I was a kid, there was something distinctly Johnny about it now.

"He wasn't much of a decorator," I said, trying to fill the silence. "But you probably know that, I guess."

"No," Ben said, flatly. His tone wasn't so much impolite as it was uncomfortable. "I didn't really know him."

That seemed strange, given the amount of time Johnny likely spent at the diner and the fact that Sadie and Johnny had been either friends or in a start-stop relationship for years. It also sounded like Johnny had worked at the school pretty regularly.

"Oh." I didn't know what else to say. There was something in Ben's manner that felt skittish. Edgy, even. Like his skin was crawling.

Again, I looked to the corner of the hallway, where I'd seen him coming from when I opened the door. It occurred to me suddenly that he might have been in Johnny's room.

"I gotta go," Ben said, suddenly. "But my mom told me to remind you that you can call if you need anything."

I nodded, a little stiffly. "All right. Thanks."

He didn't bother forcing another smile before he let go of Smoke and turned toward the door. Just before he opened it, he glanced down the hall, toward Johnny's bedroom. For a moment I could have sworn the expression on his face shifted, revealing a flash of something unreadable in his eyes. But when he stepped out onto the porch, giving me a final wave, the apathetic teenage boy was back.

I crossed the kitchen and peered into the basket he'd left. A crisp floral tea towel was nestled around a jar of honey, a few golden-topped muffins, and a small bag of coffee beans. I lifted the jar, turning it toward the light coming through the window. A perfect comb of honey was suspended inside.

The urge to glance at the hallway again made me turn my head, and I set down the jar, walking toward it. Johnny's door was still closed as I passed it, but I stopped in front of the desk, eyeing the stacks of papers and notebooks. I had tidied what I could, making piles to go through by level of urgency. And everything appeared to be in place, but something still didn't feel right.

I turned to the open bathroom door next, relaxing a little when I spotted the gleam of water drops on the edge of the sink. Maybe he'd used the bathroom. Or maybe he'd just been looking for me, ducking his head into the other rooms since the front door had been left open.

I let myself sink down into the desk chair, eyes dropping to the camera bag on the floor. It was still zipped closed, but it wasn't perfectly squared with the legs of the desk. Had it been before? I wasn't sure.

I reached down and unzipped it, taking a quick look at the bag's contents. Everything was in order, right where Johnny left it.

A pitiful laugh escaped me as I put my face into my hands and rubbed at my temples. On top of everything else, I was getting paranoid.

My phone buzzed in my back pocket and I let myself draw in another breath before I pulled it out. This time, Micah's name was on the screen.

Address is 8 Overlook. 6pm okay? You'll have to drive the 4Runner. That car won't make it up the ridge.

I exhaled, emotion welling in my throat.

I wanted to pretend that there was a universe where I wasn't so relieved he replied that I could cry. And he probably knew it. He'd probably been waiting for me to text, knowing it was just a matter of time before I crossed the line I'd drawn.

That was one of the reasons I'd dreaded seeing him. Because when

I did, he knew exactly how to get his fingers beneath my scales and peel them back. But if he did that this time, I didn't know what he would find.

My thumbs hovered over the screen. When I texted Micah, I'd imagined making plans to meet him at the diner or even The Penny. I hadn't expected him to invite me over, and the idea of going to his house made me feel jittery.

I hesitated before I typed a reply and hit send.

Sounds good.

I waited to see if the trio of bubbles would appear, indicating that he was sending another message, but there was nothing. I imagined him standing there, staring at his phone exactly the way I was now, debating whether to say anything else. Whether another message would make me change my mind. But Micah wasn't just good at wearing me down. He also knew exactly how to not scare me away.

EIGHT

I stared at myself in the little bathroom mirror, reaching up to give my cheeks a gentle pinch. The cold had all but drained the warmth from my skin, but there was also something about the light in Six Rivers that seemed to suck the color out of things.

I loosely ran my fingers through the length of my hair, giving my reflection one more glance. I hated that I was nervous. That I'd even felt the need to look in the mirror in the first place.

I'd stopped by the diner that afternoon to look up the directions to the address Micah sent and jotted them down before I left, not willing to risk losing the GPS mid-drive. It was less than four miles from town, but on these twisting, steep roads it was more than a fifteen-minute drive. I'd stared at that little red pin on the screen, thinking about the fact that I was about to drive to Micah's house. The place he *lived*. I couldn't help but marvel at the fact that this spot on the map, right *here*, was where he'd been all this time.

For so long, it seemed impossible to imagine that he, Johnny, or I could exist anywhere without one another. Like removing one of us from a specific time and space made the others vanish, somehow. But in the years since I last saw Micah, he had, in fact, gone on living. We both had.

I stood in Johnny's driveway with his keys clutched in my hand for several minutes, staring at the 4Runner.

The old truck had a story, just like we did. It had belonged to the foreman at the logging outfit before Dad bought it, and when he left for Oregon, he gave Johnny a ten-minute driving lesson before he handed him the keys. Only a year later, I'd be sitting in the cab surrounded by shattered glass, blood pooling on the carpet and the flash of police lights reflecting on the wet street.

Within the decades of memories I had of this place, the 4Runner felt like a time capsule that concealed the life I'd lived in Six Rivers. Like it had been sitting here waiting to be opened at this moment. By me.

I went over it again in my mind. The cabin, the darkroom, the diner—there was a pattern taking shape. It seemed like every time I fit myself into the spaces Johnny had been, I was plugging into an outlet. Like I was suddenly reanimated into a scene of his life. That made this feel like an experiment.

When I finally got up the nerve to open the door, it popped with a familiar sound that loosed a shaking breath from my lips. Smoke jumped in and I reached up for the handle, lifting myself onto the step below the driver's side door. I lowered myself in, and the soft, ripped beige seat gave beneath my weight. When I looked up, my line of sight just barely made it over the steering wheel.

Within seconds, I could hear it—the sound of the engine roaring to life before I even had the keys in the ignition. The sticking sound of the gear shift and the echo of music—what sounded like an indie folk jam. The click of a seatbelt.

The smell of exhaust drifted through the air, and I closed my eyes, trying to chase down the vision. Carefully, I tried to let it unfold, sinking into the seat until the sound of the guitar came more sharply into focus. Soon, I wasn't in my own world anymore. I was in Johnny's.

I didn't know how, but it was working. It was even clearer this time, more distinct than the slivers of moments that had found me in the cabin and the darkroom. Almost as if Johnny *wanted* me to see this.

Where are we going?

My eyes popped open, the sound of a voice making me jump, and the keys slipped from my fingers. But the voice wasn't Johnny's. It wasn't a man's at all.

I sat up straight, eyes shooting to the passenger seat, but only Smoke was there. Slowly, the remnants of the moment were bleeding away. So quickly that I couldn't grab hold of them. Within seconds, the emptiness of the space around me returned and it was just me sitting in the cold truck. Alone.

I swallowed hard, fist clenching tighter around the keys before I finally started the engine and turned on the heat. I had to consider the possibility that I was the one creating these visions, these moments. If I was, there were a number of explanations, grief being the most plausible. But I'd lived my whole life with a supernatural connection to my brother and there was a part of me that believed, or wanted to believe, that all of this was him. And if I was right, I didn't know what that meant. Was I was simply crossing into currents of his energy or—I hesitated before I let myself think it—was he trying to tell me something?

I stared at the windshield, carefully letting the thought settle in my mind. The question had been like a slowly building fire inside of me. Johnny wasn't *gone*. Of that, I was sure. But whether he was capable of communicating with me from the other side of whatever this was, I had no idea.

The truck took a while to warm up, but a few minutes later, I was putting the gear in reverse. My hands gripped the leather-wrapped steering wheel, and before I let my foot off the brake, my eyes turned to the scar that wrapped around my forearm, down to my wrist. My own memory was hovering in the cab now. I'd been sitting in this same spot, my hands on the wheel, watching the shining red drip from my elbow. That was the first time I'd started to understand just how far I would go to protect Johnny. Just how fast I'd take the fall.

I leaned forward, reaching down to lift the floor cover beneath my feet. The bloodstain was still there.

Overlook Road climbed the ridge with sparse views of the twisting canyon below, and the farther from town I got, the more treacherous it became. I'd learned to drive on roads just like this one, which made the famed steep city hills of San Francisco easy to handle when many refused to drive them. You didn't realize just how much this forest was trying to kill you until you got out. The skyscrapers and bridges I saw out my dorm window at Byron had felt safe compared to this wild, unruly place.

Smoke hung his head out of the passenger side window as I took the truck up the bumpy dirt track until the road came to a crude fork, and my headlights landed on a small wooden stake marked with the number eight. It had been driven into the ground on the left-hand side, and I turned, flicking on the brights. The cabin looked to be the only one on this vein of the road, and its lights were like amber orbs in the growing darkness. Thick mats of moss clung to the roof, where a few fallen twigs were scattered across the shingles. The trees were more spread out than the ones that encircled town, and the blaze of the sunset in the distance cast orange beams between the trunks as the sun descended toward the ridge.

I parked beside Micah's truck, and Smoke was climbing over me before I'd even made it out myself. He jumped down, bounding up toward the front door, and it opened, flooding the small porch with light.

Micah stood inside, wearing a green half-zip sweater and jeans. When Smoke reached him, he jumped up, paws landing on his chest, and Micah gave him a rough scratch behind both ears before he pushed him back down. The smile on his face made the clock rewind ten years. Twelve. Fifteen. Until the man standing in that rectangle of light was the first boy who loved me. The first and only one I ever loved back.

Smoke disappeared inside the house, and Micah leaned into the doorframe, waiting. "It's too late, James. No going back now," he said, cracking another smile.

It wasn't until then that I realized I wasn't moving, one hand still on the car door like I might duck back inside. I rolled my eyes, trying to bury my own smile as I grabbed my bag and closed the door. I was a few minutes late, and he'd probably spent them convincing himself I wasn't going to show. Another few seconds, and he might have been right.

His eyes moved over me as I made my way up to the porch. "Hey," he said, the low timbre of his voice nearly lost beneath the sound of the wind in the trees.

"Hey," I echoed.

He stepped back, gesturing for me to come inside, and as soon as I did, I could feel my heart coming up into my throat one agonizing centimeter at a time.

His place was . . . perfect. Beautiful in a rugged way that I couldn't quite find a word for. A plush, deep-set sofa faced the stone fireplace, where a fire was crackling, and most of the furniture looked old. Antique. Mission-style wooden chairs were pushed up to the dining table, where an open-shelved farmhouse hutch reached almost to the ceiling. But the little things that colored in the corners of the room were full of character. A blanket thrown on the worn leather armchair. The southwestern woven rug. The clay pot on the kitchen counter. There was a record player turning on the cabinet in the living room, playing something acoustic and slow.

He closed the door behind me. "You find it okay?"

"Yeah." My voice sounded strange.

I picked up one of the blush-colored stones that were arranged along one side of the fireplace mantle, turning it over in my hand.

"Petrified wood." He answered my unspoken question, hands sliding into his pockets. "I run across it on the beach or along the rivers sometimes."

I glanced down at the striped wool socks that covered his feet. This was the same Micah I'd known for most of the first half of my life. The same one who spent the better part of our junior and senior years crashing at our place. But something about the sight of those socks felt more intimate and vulnerable than all the mornings he walked around our house in his boxer shorts.

The look on his face made me think that he was struggling with that feeling, too. Like he was both relaxed and uncomfortable at the same time. That was us, I thought. Snapping into place so easily and then struggling to just be still there.

I set the stone back down.

"Can I get you something? A drink?"

"Sure," I answered, letting the bag slide down my shoulder.

Micah went to the cabinet against the wall, pulling two glasses down before he filled them. The smell of whiskey slowly distilled in the air as I took a seat at the table.

"You want to talk about it?" he asked, keeping his back to me.

The sheer number of possible things he could be referring to almost made me laugh. There was a long list. "About what?"

"About whatever made you text me."

He picked up the drinks, setting one in front of me before he pulled out the chair next to mine. He was only inches away, and I instinctively inhaled, catching his scent drifting between us. He still smelled the same, and I didn't know how that was possible.

He raked his hair back carelessly, not bothering to mess with it when it fell back into his eyes. It took a moment for me to realize that he was still waiting for my answer.

I hadn't figured out exactly how I wanted to do this. I hadn't even let myself imagine how this first conversation might go. There were countless unfinished things we could discuss, and I wasn't prepared for most of them.

"I want to talk about Johnny," I said, finally.

"Okay." Micah's tone was careful. "What about him?"

"I want to know what was going on with him before he died."

Micah's eyes moved over me again, as if he was trying to read me.

After a long moment, he picked up his glass and took a drink. "All right. But it's probably all stuff you know."

"I want to hear it from you."

"Hear what, exactly?"

I let out a frustrated sigh. "Anything. Everything. I show up here, and it feels like he had this whole life he didn't really tell me anything about, and I just . . . ."

Micah cut me off. "This was his home, James. Of course he had a life."

I gave him a look that bordered on exasperation. "I get that. I just— I've been back for barely forty-eight hours, and that's all it's taken to make me feel like my own brother was a stranger. It almost feels like he was . . . like he was hiding things."

"That's Johnny," he said. "That's what he did."

"He didn't used to hide things from me."

This time, Micah said nothing. But the set of his mouth told me that he wanted to.

"What?" I prodded him.

He shrugged. "Maybe there were things he thought you didn't want to know about."

In an instant, a swift and familiar anger rose up in me. "What the hell does that mean?"

"Come on, James. You left Six Rivers the second you could and you never looked back."

"Are you serious? You're going to make it about me?" I gaped at him.

"I'm not the one who made it about you." Micah's tone took on the slightest edge. "You show up in town after all this time, pretending to give a shit about this project he was working on—"

"I *do* give a shit about it."

"But that's not why you're here," he said. "You tell me what you're really doing in Six Rivers and I'll tell you what you want to know about Johnny."

We stared at each other, and I fought to push down that rising heat that ignited when he looked at me. I wasn't about to tell him about the pain still throbbing in my chest or the voice I'd heard in the dark-room. I wasn't going to tell him that I was convinced that the Johnny we knew wasn't quite gone from this world or that he might actually be trying to communicate something to me. That was a bridge I didn't want to cross. Not even with myself.

"I think there was something going on with him," I breathed.

"What do you mean?"

"I don't know. Like something was off. I've just had this feeling since he died that maybe there's more to it than a hunting accident. Like maybe there's something missing."

Micah's expression changed a little, his eyes softening.

"And for it to happen out *there*." I swallowed, careful not to touch too closely to the memory we'd both worked hard to bury. "I mean, that's just a coincidence?"

Micah leaned back in the chair, saying nothing, and I didn't know if it was because he didn't want to revisit the night Griffin Walker died any more than I did, or if he'd thought the same thing.

Griffin had been our friend. Never as tightly pulled into the cir-cle as me, Micah, and Johnny, but, living next door, he was always around. I would never have pegged him as a kid who would turn out to be remarkably talented, but the entire town revolved around him for the few years before he died. Even then, to us, he was still just Griffin.

Things didn't really change until he was recruited by Stanford, and overnight, it was as if he suddenly believed everything everyone was saying about him. I'd had the same experience when I got my accep-tance letter and scholarship to Byron. Like before that moment, it hadn't been safe to really buy in to what other people said about me.

That's also when things changed between *us*. I still don't know why, but Griffin was the first person I told about the news from Byron. I didn't know how to tell Johnny, or Micah for that matter, and I wasn't sure I could really talk myself into going. Maybe the reason I told him was because Griffin was the only other person in town who was leaving. Or maybe it was because I wanted someone to give me permission to actually do it. But what I didn't know was what would happen once there was a secret between us.

Stanford was only a short drive from Byron, and it wasn't long before Griffin was talking about when *we* went away. When *we* went to the city. Weeks went by, and I still hadn't told my brother. Not because I was afraid that he would stop me from going. The real reason I didn't want to tell him was because I knew he would make the decision for me. He would pack my things himself. Drive me down to San Francisco, even if I didn't want to go. And I was ashamed to admit that I was terrified to leave him behind.

By the time I realized that Griffin had feelings for me, it was too late. And that night in the gorge, when he'd tried to kiss me, he was drunk. I couldn't tell him that I was with Micah, because no one knew. Not even Johnny. And I had no idea when I put my hand on his chest and pushed him away, what was going to happen next.

"I'm just trying to understand what exactly was going on before Johnny died," I said.

Micah finally exhaled. "Honestly, things were going . . . really well. Once he got hired on to the CAS project, I felt like that was it for him. Like he'd finally found his way in the world. He really believed in what they were doing, and he was well suited for it. I could tell that he was dreading it being over."

"And he seemed . . . normal?"

"Normal?" Micah almost laughed.

"I mean, was he himself?"

"Being himself wasn't exactly . . . You know how he was, James."

I did. And that was the whole problem. Johnny had always been a burning fuse, even when we were kids. I'd spent years feeling like it was my job to tamp it out, but eventually, I'd had to accept that there was no controlling him. No predicting him, either. It was that burning fuse that had resulted in me leaving.

The mistake I'd made was thinking that I knew the limits of what he was capable of. And I'd also been wrong about the lengths *I'd* go to protect him. In the end, Johnny wasn't the only one with blood on his hands.

"I just want to know that he was okay," I said.

"Sometimes he was. Sometimes he wasn't."

"Come on, Micah."

"What do you want me to say? You want a detailed timeline of Johnny's moods for the last twenty years? I can't give you that. Was he always kind of a mess? Yeah, he was. But he'd made a life for himself. He was happy. And you would know that if you'd bothered to come back."

As soon as he said the words, I could tell that he wanted to pull them back into his mouth. But it was too late. It had taken all of three minutes for us to fall back into the same gaping wound that had always been there.

"Look, I don't want to fight with you, James."

I swallowed past the pain in my throat. "I don't want to fight, either."

"That's a first," he muttered.

I shot him a look, my temper ready to flare again, but it fizzled out when I saw the small grin pulling at his mouth. He was teasing me now.

"How about we try this again." His eyes lifted from his glass to meet mine straight on, but it looked like it took effort. "It's good to see you, James. Really."

I let my fingers tap against my glass, emotion curling in my throat. "Yeah. You too."

The words were hard to say, but not because they weren't true. It was good to see him, but it hurt, too.

He licked his lips, hesitating. "And I know I owe you an apology."

"For?"

He leaned forward, coming closer, and one of his knees came between mine. I looked down at it as another song started on the record player. It was a stripped-down folk ballad that swelled softly in the air. That little bit of physical contact made me feel like a channel of electricity had opened in my veins.

"I should have been the one to call and tell you what happened," he said.

The weight of the words bore down on me as he spoke them. It's not what I had expected him to say. I may have been Johnny's next of kin, but I knew that Micah was probably the first one they called when they found my brother. He'd been told before me. Maybe even hours before. But when the call finally came, it was a stranger's voice on the other end.

"I should have told you myself. I should have gotten in the car and . . ." He trailed off.

"I'm glad you didn't," I whispered.

He nodded, and I could only assume that he knew what I meant. The only thing I could imagine being worse than feeling the kind of pain I did in that moment was the idea of touching Micah's pain at the same time. I didn't know if either of us would have survived that.

"We haven't talked about a funeral or anything," he said, changing the subject. Though it didn't feel any easier than the last. "We didn't arrange anything after Johnny died because I wasn't sure what you wanted to do. But Sadie offered to host something over at the diner. A memorial."

"That would be nice." I took another long drink.

He nodded, as though he was thinking the same horrible thought I was. That a memorial made all of this feel so final. So real. It was like an acceptance of what couldn't be true.

I cleared my throat. "Amelia Travis asked about the ashes, and I told her she could send them to you."

Micah stayed silent.

"I'm leaving soon. Thought it would be easier," I offered as explanation.

"I'll take care of it." His words were a little hollow now. He didn't sound angry, exactly, but I had a feeling that I knew what he was thinking. That I was putting it on him. That I wasn't willing to deal with things. And I wasn't. I couldn't.

Micah stood, and as soon as the press of his leg against mine was gone, I found myself aching for it. He went to the dying fire, stoking the flames before he put on another log.

"So, how's it going with the project?" he asked.

"Fine, I guess. I'm making my way through the paperwork and reports, and I'm still missing some of the images."

"What are you missing?"

"A few photographs of one of Johnny's subjects. I'm sure they're all there, but his stuff is kind of a mess, like you said. I'm just narrowing down which images go to which location and all of that. I might have found a few I can use, but I need to compare them to other negatives and figure out where they're from."

"I don't know if I'd be any help, but let me know if you get stuck on something."

"Yeah?"

"Yeah," he answered.

I gave him a grateful smile, relaxing into the almost normal feeling between us. Even if it was fleeting.

"That reminds me." I pushed the chair back from the table and went to the front door, where I'd left my bag. When I returned, he was back at the table, refilling our glasses.

I thumbed through the negatives and prints, pulling free the one I was looking for. Micah's brow pinched when he saw it. It was the photograph of him I'd enlarged from the negatives I'd found at Johnny's. Micah's face was illuminated in shadowed angles, the edges of him gently blurred in the firelight.

"I found it in Johnny's things. I thought you might want it." I slid it across the table.

The muscle in his jaw ticked before he picked it up, face paling just a little. Maybe because of the strange sense I'd gotten when I saw it, too. Like I was looking through Johnny's eyes.

"Do you remember it?" I asked.

He stared at it, thinking. "Maybe. We were probably just out at the fire pit behind your place having a couple of beers. There were a lot of nights like that." For a moment, it looked like he was going to say something else but thought better of it.

"What?" I said.

Micah cleared his throat, shaking his head. "It's nothing. He just had a way of seeing things, you know?"

I watched the light in his eyes shift with the tone of his voice. "Yeah."

"Thank you." He set the photo down on the end of the table, making a concerted effort not to look at it. The warmth and humor that had made him feel so familiar to me a moment ago was gone now. The thought that maybe the photo would graze the surface of something in him that still hurt too badly to be touched hadn't crossed my mind, and now I wondered if it should have.

I studied him, watching the tendons in his neck flex beneath the collar of his sweater. "What's wrong?"

He shook his head. "Nothing."

I hesitated before I set a hand on his arm, and immediately his hand closed into a fist. "Tell me."

"It's just hard to think about."

"What is?"

His face flushed a little. "Just, sometimes when I think about him, I can't forget seeing him like that—when we found him."

I froze.

Found.

That word was like an expanding pinprick, conjuring that image of the sun-spotted treetops from the forest floor. The one that had been branded into my mind. Immediately, that pain in my chest was back, an echo of the rib-splitting hole that had ripped through me. I reached up, pressing two fingertips there and trying to push the feeling down.

"What do you mean, *we?*" I said.

Micah's hand dropped from the table and he turned toward me. There was a question in his eyes.

"You were there when they found him?" I rasped.

Micah nodded, confused. "Yeah, I thought you knew."

I leaned back in the chair. Amelia had never mentioned it.

He rubbed at his brow. "He'd been gone a couple of days, and I was worried when he didn't come back. Amelia and I went to look for him."

I shifted the stack of photos until I found the one I'd enlarged of Trentham Gorge. My gaze traced the shape of the rocks, following the white diagonal sediment lines until they disappeared into the lush green. The picture I had of those treetops in my mind flickered back to life. That window of light through the branches—what I imagined was the last thing Johnny saw as blood pooled on his chest. I could feel the heat of it on my own skin, beneath my shirt.

"James?" Micah's voice was like a fading light.

I stared at the contact sheet, eyes on the thumbnails. That buzzing in the air was back—the same one I'd felt in the truck. At the cabin. Anywhere Johnny had left his trace. Is that what I'd find in Trentham Gorge, too?

I'd been looking for evidence that there was more to all of this. I'd come all this way, back to Six Rivers, because I needed to make sense of the fact that Johnny wasn't gone. And now, I suddenly had the overwhelming need to see it for myself. To stand on that circle of earth where Johnny took his last breaths.

A bone-chilling, stomach-turning thought snaked through my mind. That if I could find the exact place he'd been, the exact spot they'd found him, maybe I'd be able to connect with the part of Johnny that had refused to leave. Maybe there, in the gorge, there was something to find.

"James?" Micah tried again, and this time his hand came down on my arm, his fingers lightly resting on my wrist, where my pulse was racing.

My eyes lifted from the table, finding him. "Micah, I need you to take me there."

NINE

It had taken some convincing, but Micah agreed to go with me to Trentham Gorge.

He was booked for a guide trip on the Klamath River that would last the entire day, and in the meantime, I'd set myself up at a small booth in the back of the diner. The morning rush was clearing out by the time I arrived, with the exception of Harold, the red-bearded man who'd been seated on the same stool every time I'd come in. His bulky build hunched over the counter as he sipped his coffee, a ring of keys dangling from his pocket, and I listened in to the meandering trails of conversation between him and the other customers who came in throughout the morning.

I'd had an email from Rhia waiting when I opened my inbox, going over the details for the show that was opening when I got back. I was the only female artist in the lineup, and there was a magazine that wanted to interview me for a profile on working women artists in the city. It was the kind of thing that had once excited me. When I was fresh out of art school, any spotlight on my work felt like an opportunity to be seen and discovered. A way to become known. But I'd been a *working artist* long enough now to know just how quickly art was consumed and forgotten. The glimmer of being a Byron graduate had all but faded, my own idealistic view of my work whittled down to the nubs. Now, I mostly painted what people wanted.

Unfortunately, I'm unavailable. Please politely decline.

I typed the reply and hit send, dedicating the rest of the day to Johnny's field notes. I'd made my way through only about half of them, and it was evident that he'd taken the work seriously. There was special attention given to the accuracy and details he was relaying and there were times that I almost couldn't believe the writing in the notebooks was his. He sounded so . . . scientific. So specific and technical. I imagined his voice speaking as I skimmed his notes, but I struggled to hear it.

The places I *could* hear him were in the entries that meandered from the default voice of the scientist. He sometimes rambled into more than just what he saw in a way that felt almost strange. Two notebooks in, I was picking up on a pattern that suggested that the longer Johnny observed his subjects, the more attached he appeared to get. His handwriting became increasingly illegible as he teased out his theories about how the birds might be related to one another, or how they *seemed* to him. Every few reports, it almost sounded like he was talking about the feelings, struggles, and circumstances of people, not animals.

That was Johnny. That was Johnny through and through. And it was nowhere more apparent than in his recorded observations of Subject 44. The owl in Trentham Gorge.

The entries began officially on October 11, 2022, when Johnny first documented the subject. Only a few entries in, it was apparent that the bird had been an elusive one. There were fewer negatives in Johnny's files for the owl than any other, which meant he hadn't had much luck when he went out to get photographs. Most of the entries in the field notes revealed that Johnny had been fixated on the owl's defective foot, taking detailed notes on 44's health, mobility, and any other perceived areas of concern he wanted to compare notes on.

His visits to the gorge were spread out over the next two years, and unlike the other subjects, 44 was spotted fewer than half of those times. That explained the lack of film.

I unearthed the contact sheet for the roll I'd developed, setting it beside the laptop. If he was in Trentham Gorge on November 10, the date that had been written on the canister, then Johnny was a few weeks past the designated CAS observation window.

Knowing Johnny, the looming project deadline might explain why he'd been out there that day, and he'd obviously had his camera then. He'd probably been trying to get more images before he had to submit everything to Quinn. Why he hadn't even finished the roll of film he was shooting, I didn't know. Maybe a storm had blown in or something else unexpected had forced him back to town. But two days later, he would return to the gorge. This time, without his camera. Or his notebook.

I stared at the open page, trying to make sense of it, but the flicker of movement in my peripheral vision interrupted the thought. My gaze lifted to the booth across the diner—Johnny's booth. But it wasn't empty anymore.

The blurred, shadowed shape sharpened more with each second. A head of dark hair. A set of square shoulders. As each detail solidified, it was harder and harder to deny what I was seeing. It was him. It was Johnny. Slowly materializing before my very eyes.

He sat with his back to me, his elbows on the table and his attention cast to the window. I felt cold suddenly, my throat closing. The lights of the diner seemed to dim, the sounds quieting around me as I stared at the back of his head, waiting for him to turn around. Like at any moment, he would feel my gaze on him.

"No rest for the wicked."

I jumped when Sadie appeared at the edge of the table, a pot of steaming coffee in each hand. She followed my gaze to the empty corner booth I'd been staring at with a faintly puzzled look.

When I blinked, Johnny was gone.

"You all right, James?"

I could hear my own breath loud in my ears, the cold on my skin replaced by a sheen of sweat. "I'm fine," I choked.

Sadie's expression was shifting now. She eyed my empty coffee cup. "Should we switch to decaf?"

I glanced at the clock, rubbing at my temples. It was already almost five P.M. "God, I didn't realize it was so late."

"You've been sitting here for hours." She turned to shout at Ben, who was standing behind the counter. "Get her some soup, Ben. A slice of cornbread, too."

"That's okay. You don't have to—"

She ignored me. "The eggs you had this morning are only going to take you so far. And the longer you sit here without eating, the more anxious it makes me."

That warmth and tenderness wasn't something I'd expect from the old Sadie. She'd always been defensive, like she needed to prove something. And maybe she did, with Johnny. With a guy like that, I wondered if it was possible to ever feel good enough. But now, there was a warmth in Sadie's eyes, and I wondered if it was a characteristic that came from motherhood.

"I wanted to say thank you, actually. For sending Ben over yesterday. That was really . . . sweet."

"No problem." Sadie filled my coffee cup just as the door to the diner opened, making the bell jingle.

Rhett Walker stepped inside, making me go stiff. He pushed the hood of his jacket down, revealing a head of wild dark hair, and his mustache twitched as his icy gaze scanned the diner.

I impulsively glanced down at his hands, half expecting them to still be covered in blood. But now, they were clean.

"Hey there, Rhett." Sadie lifted one of the coffeepots in greeting, and he grunted in return. When his eyes landed on me, he stopped short.

I tried to smile. "Hi, Mr. Walker."

But he just stared at me, those glassy eyes not breaking from mine.

The rigid set of his jaw was turning more severe by the second. When he finally spoke, his voice was like crushed stone.

"Better keep that grim away from my property line."

My brow creased. "What?"

It took a few seconds for me to make the connection. He was talking about Smoke. Calling him a grim—a specter or a haunting spirit. The reference made my blood run cold again.

He tipped his head toward the window, where we could see Smoke sprawled out across the sidewalk. "I've got venison curin' out in the shed, and I warned your brother what would happen if—"

"Okay, Rhett. Go on and get your seat before someone takes it." Sadie tried to smooth it over with a placating grin, but Rhett's gaze was still fixed squarely on me.

"Been sayin' it for years. Got no business keepin' a wolf as a pet. That animal will tear your throat out if he catches you not lookin'."

"All right, that's enough," Sadie said, more firmly.

Rhett's lips pursed before he finally relented, his knobby hands reaching up for the zipper of his coat. He was shrugging it off a moment later, boots shuffling toward a table along the wall.

I looked up at Sadie, eyebrows raised in question.

"Probably best to steer clear of him." She sighed. "He wasn't too happy when he heard you were coming back to town."

I watched him from the corner of my gaze. It was no secret that we were all there the night his son Griffin died—me, Johnny, and Micah. I'd been the one to leave the gorge, driving the treacherous roads back to town to get Timothy Branson. And while the story we told had been accepted by everyone else in Six Rivers, Rhett had never believed us. Not really. For months after I left, I had nightmares about waking up in my dorm to find him standing in the dark. Watching me. He had that same look as he eyed me now. Like he still hated me for what happened.

Ben appeared beside Sadie, breaking the spell around us, and he slid the bowl of soup across the table. It was followed by a small plate of cornbread. I'd convinced myself that I was being paranoid about Ben snooping in Johnny's cabin, but the way he avoided my eyes now made that sense of disquiet resurface. Ben wasn't comfortable around me, and I didn't know why.

"Thanks," I said.

He gave me an almost imperceptible nod and Sadie watched him go.

"I swear to you there are *some* people in this town who have manners. Unfortunately, none of them can be found at present." She gave me an apologetic smile before she moved to the next table.

I took a sip of my coffee and closed the notebook before I opened Johnny's email inbox. It was flooded with unread messages, and I scrolled, looking for one that mentioned the name Josie. When I didn't readily spot it, I typed the name into the search field at the top of the page. A few letters in, the email address populated.

Josie Garver [j.garver@ncowlproject.org]

I hit enter and a series of emails filtered from the inbox and archived messages. None of them appeared to be unread. The most recent was from August 4, but there was nothing in the subject line.

I opened it, eyes scanning the one-sentence message.

Stop or I'll report you to CAS.

I read the message again, staring at it for several seconds, unease gripping my stomach. What could that mean? Stop *what*?

I clicked back to the search results and skimmed the other emails from the same address. They all looked like they were related to the project, arranging meetings, or exchanging information on different sectors. But there were no more emails after August 4.

My mind jumped from one possibility to the next, trying to place the missing context. The other messages were all professional, familiar, and friendly, but the last one had a tone that felt pointed. In fact, it was threatening.

I scrolled to the bottom, copying down the phone number under the signature of the email. It was possible Johnny had gotten involved with Josie outside the bounds of a professional relationship, but Micah hadn't alluded to anything like that.

I typed a quick message from my own account, asking if Josie would be willing to meet and copying Quinn so that it looked like official business for CAS. When I hit send, I sat back in my seat, fingers slipping from the edge of the table.

My eyes lifted to the booth across the diner, half expecting to see Johnny again. I waited for him to take shape, piece by piece, like the strokes of a paintbrush. But there was only the bend of evening light on the table. The shadows of passersby on the street. Now, I wasn't even sure of what I'd seen. I wasn't sure of anything anymore.

TEN

⊱══════⊰

I could hear the old Ford Ranger before I could see it. The rumble of the engine broke the silence of the forest, growing louder until the light reflected off the windshield like a spark in the trees. Smoke's head lifted from my lap, his ears perking up before the truck pulled into the drive.

I stood from the top porch step and slung my bag over my shoulder as Micah shifted the gear into park, resting one hand at the top of the wheel. His beanie was pulled low over his ears, making the ends of his hair curl along his jaw, and he hadn't shaved since I last saw him, making him look gruffer than usual. I was still trying to get used to the ways he'd changed. Knowing him at eighteen wasn't the same as knowing him at thirty-seven. The kind of shifts that happened in that time were more felt than seen, but there were some things, like the width of him or the look of his hands, that were different now. They were details that measured time, and that was something I tried not to think about.

I opened the door and Smoke jumped into the cab, finding a spot where he could look out from between the driver's and passenger's seat. The truck was a model from the nineties with a topper on the back, and it was surprisingly well-preserved for its years in the unforgiving landscape. It had been converted into a camper, so the backseat was gone and the entire space all the way to the tailgate had been retrofitted with a pallet bed and several compartments fixed to the inside frame.

"Morning," Micah said, voice rough with cold and sleep.

"Morning." I lifted myself inside and he took my bag, setting it in the back. "One of these for me?" I asked, eyeing the two coffees in the cupholders.

"Picked them up at the diner on the way."

"Thanks." I lifted one from the holder, curling my cold hands around the warm paper cup, and took a sip.

We sat there for a few seconds, the truck idling with Micah's hand paused on the gear shift. "Thought it was worth asking one more time if you're sure you want to do this."

I could see in the way he was looking at me that he didn't think it was a good idea. For him or for me, I didn't know.

I thought about it, keenly aware that I'd asked myself the same question several times throughout the night. But I felt like I'd already made the choice back in San Francisco. The moment I decided to come home. Since I'd arrived in Six Rivers, the connection I had to Johnny had grown like a wild vine, snaking around my existence. I wasn't only *sensing* him anymore. I was hearing him. Maybe even seeing him, and there was a part of me that didn't want to find out where all of this led. But there was also a more desperate part of me that had to know.

"I'm sure," I answered.

A steady breath filled Micah's chest and he pushed it out. "Okay."

He reversed, taking us out onto the road, and I reached for the seatbelt, watching the cabin disappear in the rearview mirror. We were headed away from Six Rivers, back toward the main interstate.

"I hope you didn't have to shift too much around to do this," I said.

"It wasn't a big deal." He shrugged, but his eyes avoided mine, making me think it was. "Sadie said you were working there all day yesterday."

"Yeah. I was."

The image of Johnny in the booth flickered back to life in my mind. That flutter was still in my chest, the anxious anticipation of waiting for him to turn around and look at me. It had been like a splice of film playing on repeat all night as I lay awake in the dark.

Micah turned off the main road, and Smoke's face came up to rest on the back of the seat between us, eyes fixed on the view out the windshield.

"Micah . . . I don't know how to ask this. . . ."

He turned to look at me, waiting.

"Ben—Sadie's son." I paused. "He's not Johnny's, is he?"

Now Micah was the one who'd fallen quiet. I studied the immediate change in his demeanor, his hands gripping the steering wheel tighter. His eyes focused on the road.

When he finally spoke, it was through a sigh. "Sadie says he isn't."

"That's not really an answer."

"Then my answer is I don't know. She's always said it was a random hookup with a logger who was passing through. It happened after I left, and when I got back, she was pregnant."

"Johnny never said anything?"

Micah shook his head. "He wondered, sure. But Sadie said the kid wasn't Johnny's. She was adamant about it. He asked for a paternity test years ago and she refused."

I let my weight sink back into the seat, watching the light flit through the trees. "What if he is?" I asked, softly. "What if he *is* Johnny's?"

Micah didn't answer, and I wondered if his mind was turning with the same thing mine was. If Ben was Johnny's son, that meant I had a nephew. I had family. It also meant that my brother had left something physical—something flesh and bone behind in this world.

"Sadie could be telling the truth," Micah offered. "I don't know what reason she has to lie."

But I did. Johnny had strung Sadie along for years when we were teenagers, and I knew enough to guess that he'd done the same after I left, at least for a time. Sadie wasn't the kind of girl to get pregnant for the purposes of pinning a guy down. But she was the type to create her own reality. And if she'd decided that Johnny would never want her, I could imagine her cutting her losses and lying about Ben.

"Wait." My train of thought caught up with me, rewinding back to what Micah had said. "What did you mean *after* you left?" The truck jerked to the side as the tar gave way to gravel, and I reached up, holding on to the handle over my head. "Left where? Six Rivers?"

"Yeah."

"You didn't tell me that you left."

"You didn't ask," he said.

I finally turned to look at him. "I'm asking now, Micah."

His hand was tightening on the wheel again, eyes catching mine for a fraction of a second before they returned to the road.

"After—" He stopped himself, jaw clenching.

I didn't know what he was about to say, but there were several things that could finish that sentence. *After you had left. After what happened to Griffin. After everything changed.* Apparently, he didn't want to go there any more than I did because he didn't finish.

"I packed up and I used the money I had saved to buy this truck. And I just . . . started driving."

"Where'd you go?"

He shrugged. "All over. Drove up the West Coast first and didn't stop until I got to Seattle, then started east. Stopped in Montana for a while, and that's where I learned to fly-fish. Spent a month in Colorado, then Texas. Over time I started outfitting the truck into a camper, and after that, I really didn't have a reason to stop driving."

A reason. The choice of words haunted me. I couldn't help but wonder if he was thinking that *I* hadn't given him one.

"Johnny didn't go with you?"

"No."

The single word felt incomplete. Like there was a longer explanation he didn't want to give me. But when I left Six Rivers, I'd thought I was leaving Johnny with Micah. That after I was gone, he'd take over. It was the only way I'd been able to stomach the thought of going to Byron. If I'd known that Micah wasn't here, that he'd left Johnny, too, I would have come back. Something told me that both Johnny and Micah knew that.

"By the time I made it to New Mexico, I'd been on the road for more than a year. Then I just couldn't stop thinking about coming home. I realized it was the only place I didn't want to leave. Or maybe just the only place I felt like I *had* to leave," he amended.

I tried to analyze the tone of his voice, looking for any hint of his meaning. Did he feel like he had to leave because of me? Or because of Griffin?

"When I got back, I started picking up odd jobs, trying to avoid having to take work at one of the logging companies. And then one day someone came into the diner asking about a fly-fishing guide and Sadie gave him my number. Just kind of accidentally started doing it and never stopped."

"I didn't . . . ." I searched for the words, unsure what to say. "Johnny never told me."

The fact that Johnny never mentioned Micah was intentional for a number of reasons. I didn't have to hear it from Johnny to know that. He'd never liked the idea of me and Micah being together and he didn't want me to have any reason to stay in Six Rivers. He definitely didn't want me to have a reason to come back.

"You think you'll ever leave again?" I asked.

Micah shook his head. "No. I'm made of this place."

It was such a simple way of saying it, but the meaning was anything but. That's what Johnny had always believed, too. That we were made in the dark. Forged from the shadows of this forest as creatures that were created to survive only here. I'd felt that, too. In fact, I was sure that was what was wrong with me. Why I'd never been able to feel like I belonged anywhere else.

"I haven't asked you . . ." I hesitated, fumbling over the question.

"What?"

"If you're with anyone. If you *have* anyone, I mean."

He smirked, side-eyeing me.

"I know it's not any of my business. I'm just curious." I rubbed at the place between my eyes, embarrassed now.

"I'm not with anyone," he said.

I didn't know what kind of reply wouldn't sound strange, but before I could manage to say anything, Micah was already talking again.

"There aren't exactly a lot of options in a town this small," he said, setting the cup back into its holder. "And trust me, no one wants this baggage."

He gave me a knowing look, like I knew firsthand what he was talking about. But we were already much too close to wading into the unknown waters of a conversation like that.

"I'm not judging you, Micah. It was just a question." I impressed myself with how true it sounded. I knew I had no right to jealousy, but it was still festering. I'd never liked the idea of Micah with someone else.

"When do you have to be back in the city?" He tried to ask the question nonchalantly, but I could hear an undercurrent of tension.

"Next week. There's a thing I have to be back for."

"A thing," he repeated.

"A show," I clarified. "There's a show coming up featuring some of my work."

"Why didn't you just say that?"

I ran a hand through my hair, casting my gaze out the window. "I don't know. I guess it just feels kind of stupid."

"Stupid how?"

I shrugged. "Just, everything is different there, you know? What people do, how they act, what they think is important."

"It's not stupid, James," he said, sounding serious. He waited for me to look at him, and when I did, he said it again. "It's not."

I didn't say anything because there was nothing to say. Trying to save me from my own embarrassment was a kindness I wasn't sure he owed me.

"You like it? The shows and all of that?"

"Yeah, I mean, it was my dream, right?"

He nodded slowly. "Right."

For a moment, it felt as if everything that happened before San Francisco blinked out like a dying star. There was a comfort in the familiarity of just existing in the same place at the same time. If I was being honest, that's one of the reasons I'd texted him. But then my smile fell a little. Eventually, that fading light would reignite. Too much had happened for it all to just . . . disappear. And I'd learned the hard way that wishing things were different only drove deeper how unfair it was that they weren't.

"So, what exactly are we looking for out in the gorge?"

I let my head fall back to the headrest, shooting him a look. I'd wondered if he was going to let me off the hook, but he wasn't. "I just . . . need to see it. I need to try and understand what he was doing out there."

Micah gave me a perplexed look. "He was working."

"I don't know," I said, softly. "I've been through all the negatives, and the last photos I have from the gorge were taken on November tenth."

"Yeah?" It sounded like a question.

"But there aren't any from the day he died. Why?"

Micah shrugged. "Maybe he was just doing more observation. He wasn't always shooting."

"But there aren't any entries in his field journal for that day at Trentham Gorge, either. And wouldn't he have at least *taken* his camera?"

The set of his mouth straightened. He was thinking through it.

"He didn't mention anything about what he was doing out there to you?" I asked.

"No."

"Nothing seemed . . . different?"

"Not that I remember."

"You said it seemed like he was dreading the project being over. Was he stressed about the CAS deadline?" I tried again.

"I would think so."

The rapid-fire, vague answers made me study him more closely. "You would think so?" I repeated the words so that he could hear how incomplete they sounded.

He was annoyed now. "It's not like we sat around talking about this stuff all the time. We were both busy, and especially in the fall I was booked so much I was almost never home. You had to really know what questions to ask if you wanted answers from Johnny. You know that."

I did know. Sometimes it felt like having a conversation with a Rubik's cube.

Micah's hand drummed on the steering wheel as he thought. "Honestly, I don't know. It was always hard to tell with him."

"Yeah, I guess," I admitted.

We fell into a pensive silence, and for the thousandth time, I tried to think back to my last conversation with my brother, replaying it in my head over and over and trying to sift the last words he ever spoke to me from the broken memories.

"Can I ask you something else?" My hands tightened around the coffee cup, but I could hardly feel its heat anymore.

Micah pulled his gaze from the road again, eyes running over my face. Like he was trying to guess what I was about to say. "Yeah, sure."

"What happened that day?"

I watched as, inch by inch, Micah's shoulders went rigid, the tension traveling down his arms, into his hands. His knuckles paled as his grip on the wheel clenched again.

"When Johnny went missing," I said, more softly. "When you found him."

He took one hand from the wheel, propping his elbow in the window of the driver's side door. His fingers brushed over his mouth like he was thinking. Maybe remembering. I could see a flush blooming beneath his skin.

"A couple of days before he died, he borrowed the truck to go out to the gorge."

"November tenth," I said, looking for confirmation.

"It was the ninth, actually. He only shot at dawn, before the sun was up, because that's when the owls are still active. But the gorge is so remote that he'd leave the night before and camp."

I waited.

"So, he went out that day and I was expecting him to return late the next night, but then he was back a lot earlier than usual. He dropped the truck off and picked up Smoke, then the next day, he showed up at my place again saying he needed to go back. He was in a hurry, so he just grabbed my keys and went."

"Did he usually do that? Just show up last minute and go?"

Micah hesitated. "No, it was usually a planned thing. But I think he was just behind schedule and trying to fit it in."

"When exactly was that?"

"The day before he died. He left that afternoon, and when he didn't come back the next day I started getting worried, but I figured maybe he'd had to stay an extra night or go out to one of the other locations. I couldn't call him because there's no cell service out there. Amelia was out of town, but she got back that next day, and when Johnny still hadn't shown up, I called her. We drove out together to check on him, and we found the truck, but no sign of Johnny." He paused, swallowing. "We split up to start looking for him, and"—he exhaled—"I found him across the ravine, halfway up the ridge."

The flush in his skin deepened, and I wanted to reach for him, but I couldn't make myself do it. The small thread that was holding me together was about to break. I could see that was true for Micah, too.

"He was gone. Had been gone since the day before," he said.

I tried to breathe through the tight feeling in my chest. That vision of the treetops, sunlight blinking through the leaves, was there again, stretching wide over my mind.

Micah cleared his throat, as if trying to squelch the emotion in his voice. "I know what you're thinking."

"What?" I blinked.

"That I should have gone sooner. That first day that he didn't come back, I should have gone to look for him then."

My mouth dropped open wordlessly for several seconds before I could speak. "Micah, I don't think that."

His jaw clenched.

"Micah." I did reach out for him then, taking a firm hold of his arm.

He looked down at my hand.

"I *don't* think that," I said again.

"Then what are you thinking?"

"I was thinking that I'm sorry," I whispered.

I wasn't sure he could hear me over the roar of the truck, but he looked at me, his expression saying what he couldn't. I could guess that it had been the worst moment of his life. And somehow, I was still glad that it had been him. That after Johnny had lain there alone for an entire day, it had been Micah who'd found him.

If there was fault to be had, I knew where it would land. Johnny never would have been out there if he hadn't been working on the CAS project. He never would have been on the project if I hadn't gone to San Francisco. And I wouldn't have left Six Rivers if that night with Griffin Walker hadn't happened.

It didn't matter how we divvied up the blame. In the end, it landed on me.

ELEVEN

The rest of the drive to Trentham Gorge was quiet. Micah kept his attention on the road, driving the unpredictable route by memory. I surprised myself by realizing that even after all this time, I could have done the same.

He hadn't said much after telling me about the day he found Johnny, and I didn't ask more questions. I was afraid that his answers might give teeth to the pain already writhing inside of me. I was already walking a tightrope of what I wanted to know and what I didn't. But it seemed to change by the day, the hour, even the minute. That was the way of grief, I was realizing. It was a barrage of pain that was so unbearable that it made you numb. And then out of nowhere, something made you feel again and the cycle started over from the beginning.

Raindrops dotted the windshield as we drove deep into the gorge, and after a while, I noticed Micah giving a series of concerned glances up to the darkening sky. I followed his gaze to the gray clouds visible through the canopy. If the weather didn't hold, we'd have to stay the night. The roads we'd come down weren't safe when there was runoff, and it wouldn't be the first time we'd gotten stuck out here.

"Just like old times, right?" I said, my voice a little uneven.

The gorge was something like a rite of passage for teenagers in Six Rivers. Once you got to high school the legends about the place found their way to you, and before long a new generation of kids with their driver's licenses were spending their Saturdays making the trip to the swimming hole.

I looked into the back of the truck, where Smoke was still curled up on the pallet bed that took up what little space there was. It looked like Micah had the camper stocked with gear and food, but that's not what made me uneasy.

I reached over the back of the seat, my hand sinking into Smoke's fur in an attempt to anchor myself. I'd honestly never liked the idea of being way out here in the middle of the night. The forest seemed to come alive in the dark, like I could feel its eyes following me. Hear its thoughts. That had been one of the things I was glad to leave behind.

When the rocky walls of the landscape began to pull apart outside my fogged window, I reached up, wiping it with the sleeve of my shirt. The cliffs that hugged the road gave way, opening into a huge, gaping vein chiseled into the earth.

From what I'd learned about the CAS project, this place made sense. Owls needed vast, biodiverse hunting grounds with plenty of prey and cover, and the gorge was just that. Towering walls rose up from the narrow ravine with a sea of trees on either side. Ferns grew in the maze of cracks on the cliff face, with boulders peeking out of the brush. The enormity of it all only grew greater the deeper we descended down the muddy road, the stones and tree trunks getting wider and taller by the second. It was beautiful, but that word in itself didn't do it any kind of justice. The gorge was like an unraveling seam in the universe, a portal to a new realm where nothing else existed.

The farther we maneuvered down the switchbacks, the more I could feel it. Johnny seemed to press through the cracks in the truck, like the pressure of water leaking in. Way out here, there wasn't a single soul to feel it, except me. I glanced at Micah from the corner of my eye, watching him carefully for any sign that he could sense it, too. But his attention was on the road.

He steered around the little rivulets dragging divots in the mud, and I tried not to count them as they multiplied, ignoring the fact that the rain was falling harder. Micah seemed to be doing the same, not bothering to acknowledge it when he finally had to turn on the windshield wipers.

Once the road began to level again, he pulled off at a gravel turn-out, where a wooden marker was driven into the ground. When the engine cut off, the sound was replaced by the patter of rain on wet stone and the babble of water in the ravine. I stared out the window, eyes fixed on the trailhead.

"You want to wait and see if it lets up?" Micah leaned forward to look up through the top of the windshield. The fog was thickening, curling in the air until the deep, saturated colors of the forest paled.

I opened the door of the truck in answer, afraid that if I had any more time to sit and think about it, I might change my mind. My boots hit the ground and my eyes slowly lifted to the cliffs far above. They only seemed to reach farther away the more I looked at them.

When the crack of gravel sounded behind me, I flinched, turning to see Micah standing at my back. There was a blue raincoat in his hands, and he was already wearing his own black one, the hood pulled up over his beanie.

"I had an extra in the back." He held the blue one out to me.

I took it, slipping my arms into the sleeves and zipping it up. The smell of him wrapped around me, like the warmth of summer piercing through the cold.

"Thanks."

The rain was still picking up, the incessant tap of it hitting the canopy high above us in a sound that reminded me of waves pulling from the sand on a beach. Micah and I looked at each other, both thinking the same thing. There was no way we were getting out of here before nightfall.

There were many times that we'd either chosen to spend the night or were forced to, drinking around a fire and camping in our cars. A night just like that one was when Griffin Walker died. That's why I'd been so unnerved when Johnny had told me that this was one of the locations he had included in the project. I hadn't understood why he'd ever want to return to this place.

I looked at Micah. "Did you ever come back here? After what happened to Griffin?"

His mouth pressed into a straight line. "Just once."

I nodded, understanding. The day he'd come to find Johnny had been the first and only time he'd ever returned.

"Ready?" he asked.

I nodded. "Take me to where you found him. The exact spot."

Micah started up the trail without a word, and I couldn't tell if he was afraid for me or for himself. Smoke stuck close to my side as I followed, and we walked down into the open mouth of the gorge until we reached the water. We took the trail that ran alongside it, crossing the ravine at the enormous skeleton of a great fallen redwood. All around us, the brilliant greens glowed bright where they were interspersed with red bark and jet-black rock. I found my hands instinctively reaching toward them as I passed, pressing a palm to the rigid skin of an ancient tree or letting my fingers graze the delicate fronds of a fern. Everything was so . . . *alive*, making it feel impossible that anything could ever die here. But maybe, in a way, nothing did.

Johnny was steeped in the descending haze, gathering like a storm in the narrow valley as we walked. As soon as the black-and-white marbled cliff face appeared, my heartbeat picked up. My feet stopped midstride, eyes following the veins of brilliant color. At the top, a gnarled oak tree was growing, roots exposed, into the crevice of stone. Small clusters of leaves adorned the dwindling branches like last, gasping breaths.

The longer I stood there, the smaller I became, until the vision of them cracked and shifted, replacing the memory of the first day the channel between me and my brother broke open. I could still see Johnny up on those cliffs, dropping down to the ravine below as the steep walls of the gorge flew past. I could still feel my pulse sync with his, the stomach-dropping feeling pulling me beneath the surface of the water.

The sweet smell of earth filled my lungs and then I exhaled, breath fogging in the cold. With it, the memory faded, but I could feel Johnny so close now that at any second, I was sure that I'd catch another glimpse of him in the trees.

Micah turned with the ravine once, then again, before he parted from the trail. The rush of water grew dim as I climbed the slope after him, and his steps finally slowed. My feet stopped a few paces behind his, and the icy air seemed to suddenly rush beneath the rain jacket, finding my skin.

Micah reached up, rubbing his face before he cleared his throat. He kept his back to me. "This is it."

I stepped around him carefully, my gaze falling on a patch of sagebrush that stretched through the trees.

"This is where I found him."

That single word punched a hole in my chest again, breathing back to life the gaping cavern within me. They'd *found* him. Because he'd been lost. Alone. Because he was gone. The singular, all-consuming gravity of the fact that Johnny was dead came rushing back, like a wave that had pulled far, far from shore.

My eyes moved over the trees, the sound swelling in my ears. From this position, there didn't seem to be a good vantage point of the gorge, and if anything, it was heavily obstructed. It might make sense if there was a specific subject that nested in this area, and it would be difficult for me to locate with my own naked eye, not knowing what to look for. But Johnny hadn't had his camera or his field notes that day. That was still the thing that didn't add up.

Maybe he'd gotten into an argument with a hunter out here. Maybe he'd stumbled upon someone poaching or won a hand of poker against the wrong group of loggers. The scenarios had been running through my mind for months, like flipping through a deck of cards.

There had to be more to all of this. There had to be some kind of explanation.

"Can I have a minute?" I said, hoarsely.

Micah didn't look sure that he should leave me, but his arm brushed mine as he turned back toward the trail. I waited for his steps to get farther away, and when I couldn't hear them anymore, I walked toward the tangled underbrush, eyes fixed to the spot Micah had pointed to. There was an almost indiscernible shape there, like the forest had grown back over the imprint of footsteps and cracked twigs and crushed ferns.

I knew the exact place that Johnny had lain, because the earth under my feet was drumming with it. Like the steady but quickening beat of my heart. I could almost hear it.

Slowly, I sank down to my knees, finding the soft, damp soil. My hands pressed into it, the smell of sagebrush breaking open in the air. *This* was where my brother's soul had been loosed from his broken body.

I lowered down in the shallow depression, chest rising and falling as I turned onto my back and let my gaze lift to the towering treetops. It was the same. The same image that had blinked open in my mind the day he died. A patchwork of swaying light breaking through the canopy. I hadn't imagined it. It was real. That flicker of sun beyond the branches was the last thing Johnny saw. And somehow, it had traveled through time and space to find me.

Slowly, the rest of the picture was filling in. The pressure in my chest, the sound of footsteps. A distinct, metallic click. I could hear breathing. Deep, labored breaths as the feeling of warmth pooled on my skin. And when I heard the voice, it was threaded in the wind.

Johnny.

The warped, distant tenor of a woman's voice sounded in my ears as my body became heavier. And that was all. The crunch of footsteps trailed away, the light above blurring, and my hand found the phantom hole in my chest. I pressed my fingers there, feeling the exact place the bullet had struck him. How long had he lain here? How long had it taken for his heart to stop? For his vision to go dark?

A hot tear slid down my cold temple, disappearing into my hair. I could feel him in the dirt. The wind. The piney scent of the trees. Johnny was gone, but he hadn't left this place. He hadn't left *me*. Not yet.

TWELVE

I pulled the collar of my sweater up beneath my jacket, watching
Micah set another piece of wood on the fire. The stone outcropping at the trailhead was curved enough to provide shelter from the
rain and wind, and with Smoke curled up beside me, the trembling in
my body had begun to slow.

He was doing his best not to be obvious about it, but every few
minutes, Micah's gaze found me in the darkness. I'd returned from
the other side of the ravine with my eyes swollen, so cold that I
couldn't feel my fingers. Micah had pulled off his gloves and handed
them to me without a word, taking a blanket from the truck and
wrapping it around me.

He'd already started a fire, resigned to the fact that we wouldn't
make it out of the gorge in the rain. Looking at the cascade of water
coming down the slope and spilling into the ravine far below, I was
glad we weren't going to attempt it. I didn't have the energy to climb
out of this hole in the earth. I didn't know if I ever would.

Micah stoked the flames until the heat was hovering in the air
again, and he sat down beside me, propping his feet up on his pack.
He looked so at home in the consuming darkness, relaxed in a way that

reminded me of all those nights we'd spent out here. But the memories inevitably led to the one that I couldn't stomach revisiting—the night Griffin died.

That single moment hung like a black cloud over everything that came before and after. We'd all lied about what happened that night, a choice that had haunted me since. We'd never discussed it again, never rehashed the events or tried to talk it through. We'd made a decision, we'd stuck to it, and we'd done it for Johnny. Looking back, everything we did was for him.

I looked up at the dark treetops, where I could still feel his presence hovering over us. Coming to the gorge had been another twisted kind of experiment—a way to test the live-wire connection between me and Johnny. I didn't know what I had expected to happen when I lay down on the earth where he'd died, but he seemed to be even more tightly coiled around me now.

That voice I'd heard saying my brother's name was still echoing inside my head. Too deformed to be recognizable, but it had definitely belonged to a woman. My mind had been jumping back to the November 10 photographs for the last hour. The pink backpack. The blank images that followed. Now I was convinced the voice belonged to whomever had been out here with Johnny that day.

"Do you want to talk about what happened out there?" Micah asked.

I swallowed. "No."

What would I tell him? That I was beginning to think I was being haunted by my brother? That I'd come to the gorge with the disturbing hope of somehow communicating with him? I knew how it sounded. The last thing I needed was for Micah to think I was losing my mind.

He didn't argue or press, instead taking something from the chest pocket of his jacket. It took a moment for me to realize what it was. He held a joint up in the air with a question in his eyes. An involuntary smile broke on my lips before I nodded, and he grinned, fumbling with a lighter until its end was aglow. He took a steady drag before he leaned back over the fire, offering it to me, and I sat up, taking it between my fingers.

The sweet, potent smell of the weed was another one of those things that reminded me of before. Skipping class with Micah or coming home to him and Johnny smoking out at the fire pit was synonymous with those nights in the parking lot of The Penny with Olivia or the weekends at the swimming hole.

I set the joint on my lips and inhaled the smoke, letting the taste swirl in my mouth and down my throat, into my chest. It burned before it began to numb the ache that lived there. After I exhaled, I took another to chase down that dull stupor.

I passed it back to him, watching the flick of the flames between us. It only took a few minutes for the erratic jolt of the fire to slow in my vision, mimicking the movement of water. I sank into that feeling, burrowing down into the blanket until it covered my chin.

The joint glowed bright between Micah's fingers as he took another drag. Once the smoke had left his lips, he let his head fall back to rest against the stone wall.

"You still have it," he said.

I blinked slowly, his words taking their time to land.

"That thing with Johnny. It's still there, isn't it?"

I let my eyes run over his face, the shock I felt not fully taking shape through the high. "What thing with Johnny?"

"Are you really going to act like you don't know what I'm talking about?"

"I didn't know you knew about that," I said, throat tight.

"I watched you almost drown that day, James."

The memory came flooding back again, rushing ahead of my sluggish thoughts. Johnny up on those cliffs. The way my heart had nearly stopped. That falling feeling that pulled me under the water.

"And that wasn't the only time. I was around you guys long enough to see it. Even if you didn't want to tell me." His eyes were on the fire now.

I hadn't ever considered whether Micah had really thought about what he'd seen that day. I hadn't even figured it out myself for a while after. Once I did, the strange link between me and Johnny wasn't something I'd talked to anyone about. Not even Johnny.

"You could have, you know," Micah said.

"Could have what?"

"Told me."

I exhaled, shivering beneath the blanket. There was a part of me that knew that. There was almost nothing I felt like I couldn't tell Micah back then, but in the end, it was that very secret that had made me leave.

"I can still feel it," I said. "I can still feel that connection between us. Like it's not gone."

"He's a part of you, James. Maybe it won't ever feel that way."

"That's not what I mean." I shook my head. "This is different. It's worse since I got back. Like I'm somehow tapping into his mind. His memories. I can hear him sometimes. The other day, I thought I . . ." I didn't finish. "What do you think that means?" I breathed, the fragrance of the weed still potent around me.

The calm that had settled in me moments ago dissipated just a little. I was suddenly desperate for him to put words to this. To validate this inexplicable, unquantifiable feeling I'd had since we were kids.

"I don't know."

"Do you believe in anything?" I asked. "Like about what happens when we die?"

His head lifted back up so he could look at me. "What?"

"Seriously, what do you think happens?" It was almost all I'd thought about since Johnny died, but I couldn't remember the three of us ever talking about it. I had no idea what Johnny had really believed.

Micah took his time in answering, putting together the words with care before he spoke. "I mean, I guess I've always felt like it makes the most sense that we would just . . . become a part of everything else, you know?" He waved a hand at the surrounding darkness, where the sound of the rain and wind still swelled. "This can't just all be for nothing, right?"

Those words unearthed ones that Johnny had once spoken to me.

What the fuck are we even here for?

It was one of the only times I remember really feeling like Johnny and I weren't on the same side. It was the fight that would change the trajectory of our entire lives, we just didn't know it yet. And I did understand what Micah meant. Standing in the belly of the gorge felt almost spiritual. There was a transcendence to the moment that couldn't be explained, and it was impossible to be in a place like this and not feel it. More than that, I *wanted* to believe. I wanted to believe that we didn't just stop with our pulse or our brain waves, and that there was more to all of this than the carbon and water that made up our skin and bones.

"What are you thinking?" he asked.

I pressed my lips together, staring into the flames again until my eyes burned. "I just don't feel like he's gone." I heard the words leave my mouth, but I hadn't planned to say them. When my eyes focused past the fire, to Micah's face again, he didn't react. "There's this unbearable pain in knowing that he *is* gone, but it also seems like it should feel different somehow, like there should be this absence. But there isn't. He's still here, Micah."

Micah watched me, unblinking.

"Sometimes I think he's trying to tell me something," I whispered.

His gaze grew subtly more focused, as if the words concerned him. It only made me more afraid of what he was thinking.

"Like what?"

I inhaled past the splintering sting reigniting in my chest, waiting for the words to find my lips. But they didn't. I wasn't ready to say out loud what I could feel in every bone of my body—that it wasn't an accident. That I'd begun to believe that he wanted me to know that something happened out here that day.

"It went both ways. You know that, right?" Micah said. "He always knew when something was going on with you or when you were lying about something. He knew about us. Long before you told him."

I sat up, looking at him. The day I finally admitted to Johnny that Micah and I were together was the same day we'd had that fight. I'd kept it from him for months because I knew my brother. I knew that Johnny would ruin it. Burn it all down. And the day he found the acceptance letter from Byron, that's exactly what he did.

Finding out that I'd lied about the letter was one thing. Leaving Six Rivers was everything Johnny had ever wanted for me, and that was mostly because he knew it's what I wanted for myself. But it wasn't just Johnny I was afraid to leave behind. It was Micah, too. He was the one who'd been the most hurt about Byron, because he knew I wouldn't have hidden it if I hadn't already decided I was going.

"I get it now. I understand why you lied," Micah said.

His words fractured in my mind as the weed bled deeper into my veins. "You do?"

He passed the joint back to me. "That's how you and Johnny worked. You made your own reality. Sometimes that meant distorting what was real so that the other one wouldn't have to know the whole truth. You protected each other. That's why you left, right?"

I met his eyes, catching his meaning. "I don't want to talk about Griffin," I said, in a tone that was more pleading than angry. If we pulled at those stitches, I would come undone.

Micah nodded. "I know you don't."

Mercifully, he let it drop, and I realized that while I'd come to Six Rivers armed with my yearslong anger, I was now mostly just bracing myself for his. But whatever tension that had materialized in the darkness slowly waned with the passing silence, and that white-knuckle feeling began to fade.

That was like him, I thought. Micah was never one to hide things, like the rest of us. He didn't pretend.

"Why didn't you ever tell me any of this?" I asked.

"Come on, James."

"What?"

A long, exhausted breath escaped his lips. "We could fill the fucking ocean with the things we never said to each other."

That pinch behind my ribs twisted tighter. There was more behind that statement than I wanted to absorb, because it was unbearably true. Now that ocean was so deep and wide that I couldn't even begin to make sense of it.

"I'm sorry about that," I said, finally.

The shadow of a warped smile changed the shape of his mouth. "Me too."

I waited for him to look at me, and when he finally did, the Micah I knew best was there in his eyes. The high from the joint had given me a reprieve, but that one look was enough to push the simmering pain over the edge of that numbness.

I opened the blanket wrapped around me, letting one hand extend toward him, and after a moment his hand found mine. I pulled him into me, and the ache was there before he even got his arms around me. Like every ounce of pain and fear and sadness we'd known had been a mere harbinger of this. And on the other side of it, I didn't know if there would be anything left. I was so tired of all the remembering.

Micah's warmth enveloped me and I let myself press into it, inhaling the smell of him. His face turned into my hair, and that one, simple touch held so much tenderness that all the tears I'd cried across the ravine were there again, tucked just beneath the surface. But I didn't feel like crying now. A different, more desperate feeling knotted in my stomach. It was a heavy weight that I could feel all the way into my legs.

I tipped my face up to look at him, and the firelight moved over his cheek, reflecting in his eyes. They didn't leave mine, and I could feel him searching for an assurance that I knew what I was doing. That I had some kind of awareness of how close I was to tipping over this cliff between us.

Slowly, his hand came up and grazed my jaw until his fingers slid into my hair, and when my mouth was only inches from his, I could hear my own breath coming faster. Like I could feel the seconds ticking down to the moment he closed the distance. But Micah didn't move. He was waiting. For me.

His fingers tightened in my hair, igniting a chain reaction that pulled me closer, and as soon as I pressed my lips to his, his hands were on me. Opening my jacket. Tugging at my jeans. I leaned into his weight, the blanket falling to the ground, but almost as quickly as he'd kissed me back, he was pulling away from me, his mouth breaking from mine.

My chest rose and fell between us and I stilled, watching him swallow.

"I don't know about this, James."

Emotion curled tight in my throat. Because neither did I. Things with Micah had always felt like a riptide, and once I was in its grasp, there'd be no escaping its pull. I didn't know if I was trying to find a home inside of it, or if I needed to break out of its orbit, once and for all.

The first time Micah kissed me, I'd felt like I'd been waiting my whole life for it. And that's what this felt like now. Like the entire world was rotating around *us*.

Before he could decide to pull farther away from me, I kissed him again. This time more slowly. It was several agonizing seconds before his arms tightened around my body. And then we were swallowed by the firelight. I lifted the sweater over my head, not thinking about what we were doing or why. I was just chasing anything that didn't hurt.

He pulled me onto his lap, sliding my legs around him, and a rush of gravity swept through me. The moment froze, the seconds static as my stomach dropped. It felt suddenly like I was falling again. Like I was moving through the air, about to slam into the ground. I could hear the sound of my heartbeat, taste him on my tongue. Micah's hands found the old, worn paths they'd once taken, and I let myself pretend we were still those kids. Before I left. Before Griffin Walker. Before everything changed.

THIRTEEN

ven before I'd opened my eyes, I knew it was a mistake.

Pale gray light streamed through the truck window, the soft, deep sound of Micah breathing beside me. I was pressed against him, clinging to his warmth beneath the sleeping bag, with Smoke stretched out on the other side of me with one leg kicked across my body.

I'd fallen asleep in the haze of the dwindling high, listening to the vibration of the rain on the roof of the truck. I could still smell Micah's scent on me, feel him between my legs. And I didn't want to move for fear that the spell would be broken.

I gently shifted onto my back, letting a hand fall into Smoke's fur, and I let my gaze follow the curve of Micah's freckled shoulder to the line of his neck and blond stubble on his jaw. He was still deep beneath the surface of sleep when I slipped my arm around him and pressed my face into the soft skin of his back. The smell of him was still the same. The eyes and the voice. But he was different now. We both were.

The flicker of movement outside made my eyes lift to the window. The condensation on the glass blurred the shape of whatever was there, but the low-hanging branches of the white fir at the trailhead were rocking with the weight of it.

I sat up slowly, the cold air kissing my skin as I reached over Micah and wiped at the moisture fogging the window. I exhaled heavily when my eyes focused on what was there.

Two wide black eyes stared back at me as the fluttering wings of an owl tipped and swayed, trying to balance on the branch. A shower of rainwater shook from the needles as the bird settled, the white specks of its body curving around its shape. When my eyes traveled down to the twisted lump that was one of its feet, my lips parted. The gnarled bones and upturned talons were the same as the owl I'd seen in Johnny's photographs. The same one I'd seen documented in his field notes.

It was Subject 44. Johnny's owl.

I leaned forward and its head careened toward the truck, like he was trying to see me, too. Frantically, I reached into the front seat for my bag and unzipped it. My hand found the folder inside and the pen that was clipped onto it. I tucked my legs beneath me, trying not to make any sudden movements, and when I took the pen into my fingers, a desperate, urgent rush flooded through me.

The owl's glassy eyes met mine and the pen touched down, arcing over the thick paper of the folder in a sweep of motion that happened more by instinct than intent. I knew this feeling, the mind-clearing connection between my eyes and my hand. I hadn't felt it in years.

The heart-shaped face of the owl came together, its liquid eyes catching the rising light as I drew. My hand brushed over the folder quickly in a movement that smeared the ink, but I didn't care. The urgency had gripped me, taking me by the throat, and I could feel it the moment the bird tipped forward, shifting its weight to take off. I had seconds. Less than that.

The lines became more fluid as my hand jerked over the paper, and just as I finished the tangled contour of the foot, the owl's wings unfurled, catching the air. I froze, watching its feathers stretch wide, and before I'd even let the breath in my chest go, it was gone.

I blinked, dropping my gaze down to the folder in my lap, where the pen was still pressed heavily to the surface. The ink was gathering there in a shining pool.

Micah shifted beside me, dragging my mind from that bright light and back into the shadows of the truck. But that seemed just as impossible. When I looked down, he was watching me. He propped himself up on his elbow, the warmth of him filling the space again as his eyes dropped to the folder.

His mussed hair fell into his face as he sat up and he pushed it back, attempting to tuck it behind one ear. He reached toward me, setting a hand on my wrist and moving my arms so he could see.

The owl was hidden there in the blur of lines, but I could make it out. Its form had just been beginning to take shape, its eyes like two empty puddles. But Micah's face didn't betray what he was thinking as he looked at it. His gaze just moved over the page slowly.

"What?" My hand fidgeted nervously with the pen.

"Nothing."

"What?" I pressed, heart sinking.

"I just haven't seen you draw in a long time," he said, his voice so deep with the morning cold that it made me shiver.

His focus moved from the drawing to the pen in my hand, and he reached out, taking hold of my wrist and turning it over so that the scar was visible between us. The pale, rope-like mark had faded over the years, but it was still raised on the skin. Micah had been standing only feet away when I dragged the broken glass over my arm, and I could still remember that look of horror on his face.

Now his eyes traveled up from the scar to his soft, thin cotton T-shirt I was wearing. I'd pulled it on last night before we'd climbed into the truck and now I was drowning in it, the fabric clinging to my naked body underneath. His gaze lingered on the shape of my breasts, and I could see that it was sinking in for him, the memory of what happened last night. His hands touching my bare skin. The broken sound that had escaped my lips.

He let me go and sat all the way up, sending his gaze past me, toward the window. "Last night . . ."

"Was a mistake." I said it before he could. At least one of us had to have the guts to admit it, and this way, we shared the burden.

He let out a long breath. "I don't know what it was."

That wasn't what I'd expected him to say. He ran both hands through his hair again, taking the sweatshirt from the front seat, and I tried not to watch the muscles move beneath his skin as he pulled it over his head. I didn't know how I was going to put that part of me back to sleep.

"We should head back," he said.

I nodded, trying not to show that it hurt when he wouldn't look at me. I could feel him putting more than just physical distance between us. He was shutting down, the Micah from last night disappearing before my very eyes.

He opened the back of the truck and Smoke jumped out. Micah tugged on his jeans and boots, and by the time I was untangled from the sleeping bag and dressed, Micah had his keys in hand. He got into the driver's seat without a word and started the truck.

I knew he was thinking the same thing I was. That we'd done something that couldn't easily be undone. We'd crossed thresholds like that in the past, and we'd be paying the consequences for the rest of our lives. I'd known that leaving Six Rivers would be hard. That's why I hadn't told him when I was accepted to Byron. But what I hadn't known—what I'd underestimated to my core—was how hard it would be to stay away.

Micah had the engine running when I opened the door and let Smoke jump back in. Then I climbed into the front seat, buckling my seatbelt as he put the truck in reverse.

"Thank you for bringing me out here," I said.

He turned toward me, waiting to take his foot off the brake. "All you had to do was ask."

That was truer than maybe I even knew. Micah had been offering to help me, trying to get me to open up about what I was doing here, since I arrived. But I'd shut him out. Mostly because I was afraid of what opening the door between us would do. Last night had been a perfect example of that.

"Micah?" I breathed, staring out the windshield.

"What?"

"I don't think it was an accident," I whispered.

He went still before he shifted the gear back into park. "What? Johnny?"

"Yeah."

"Why do you think that?"

"I don't know. I have these flashes, like remnants of what happened, and I just feel like he wasn't alone out here that day. That he was scared."

His voice lowered. "That's why you wanted to come out here?"

I nodded.

Micah let his hand fall from the steering wheel. I could see him considering it, his mind racing with the thought.

"Is there anything you can think of that was going on before he died? Anything that could have gotten him killed?"

Micah went stiff, as if the idea made him tense up all over. "No. I don't think so."

"Was he involved with anyone?"

Micah didn't react, but I thought I could see just the slightest ripple of something beneath his calm expression. "Why are you asking that?" He sounded almost a little defensive.

"I'm just trying to put together what was going on up here."

"Did someone say something to you?"

I narrowed my eyes at him. It was a strange thing to ask. "No. Should they have?"

Micah rubbed his face with both hands.

"What about Josie?" I pressed.

"The CAS girl?"

"Yeah."

"I have no idea. I mean, maybe."

"Do you know her?"

Micah shook his head. "No, not really. Met her once when she was here getting Johnny set up for the project."

"Was she around in November?"

Micah licked his lips, frustrated now. "What are you getting at, James?"

"I don't think he was really alone out here when it happened. Is it possible that Josie was in town?"

Micah considered it. "I don't know. Maybe."

"Would he have told you?"

Micah let out a heavy breath. "What does that mean?"

"Olivia said there was something going on between you two. She implied that you were fighting about something."

"That's just Olivia being Olivia. We were fine, okay?"

I waited, and when he didn't say anything else, I gave in to the temptation to push even harder.

"Then why do I still feel like there's something you're not telling me?"

"Look, is it possible he had someone with him? Maybe. But there was no one here when we got here, and the truck was left behind. Where did they go? How did they get out of the gorge?"

"Maybe he met someone here."

I reached for the bag at my feet, pulling out the folder with the prints. When I found the one I was looking for, I set it on the seat between us. It was the photograph of the pink backpack.

"This was taken out here just a couple of days before he died."

He went still when he glanced down. I could see right away that he was tempering his reaction, reeling back the look on his face.

"What? What is it?"

"Nothing," he said, but the word was only half formed, buried in thought.

"Do you recognize it?"

Micah tucked the photo in with the others. "This is from the gorge? You're sure?"

"Yeah, it was on a roll of film from November tenth." I studied him, asking the question again. "Whose is it?"

"Maybe he labeled it wrong. Or maybe you misread the numbers? The guy had shit handwriting."

"Micah, whose backpack is it?"

He leaned back against the seat, eyes still on the photo. "It's Autumn's."

"Autumn?" I struggled to place the name.

"A kid from the high school. Johnny was teaching her some photography stuff. Helped her get into Byron."

My conversation with Olivia came back to me in broken fragments. She'd said that Johnny had mentored a student there.

"How do you know it's hers?" I said.

"The drawings—she marked it up like that. She carried that backpack around everywhere."

"So, what are you saying? That Johnny was out here with that girl?"

"I'm not saying anything." He was definitely avoiding my gaze now. "I'm just telling you whose backpack it is."

I shot a glance out the window, to the dense forest that surrounded us. Micah told me that when Johnny shot in the gorge, he always spent the night. And that's what he'd done on November 9.

"Didn't you say he spent the night out here that night? That he didn't come back until the next day?"

"Sometimes he let her help out on his shoots," he thought aloud.

"But she's like, what? Eighteen?"

Micah didn't answer, but I was still confused. "I thought Olivia said she was away at school."

"She is. She left back in the fall."

"But he wouldn't have done that, right? Spent the night all the way out here in the middle of nowhere with a teenager?" I asked.

"No," he said, dismissively. "No way."

"Then how do you explain this?"

He sighed, agitated now. "I don't know, James. I don't know anything."

The number of things that didn't add up here were multiplying by the second. If Johnny was out here on a shoot on November 10, how and why had that girl been with him? And did that mean that she was here when he returned a couple of days later? I didn't like how that looked. How it felt.

I slipped the photo back into the folder, letting it rest in my lap. The idea was still pricking my thoughts. None of this was sitting well with me.

My hands curled around the folder in my lap and the eyes of the owl in the drawing bored into me, two ink-black pools that made me shiver. There were so many ways that Johnny and I were the same, and this was one of them. Both of us had always been trying to capture moments and keep them. Him with the camera, me with my pen. But in the end, we somehow always saw things differently.

FOURTEEN

I tapped my phone to wake up the screen, checking to see if Micah had texted. I hadn't seen or talked to him since he dropped me off at the house after the gorge, and I was beginning to worry that I wouldn't.

Over the last forty-eight hours, I'd had the list of reasons I shouldn't have slept with him scrolling through my mind on repeat, and he was probably doing the same. I didn't know if it was this place or if it was me, but sitting out there in the firelight, the rain falling in the gorge, I'd been sixteen again. Seventeen. Eighteen. I'd been every version of myself that was in love with Micah Rhodes.

I traced the scar that curved up my wrist, remembering the way it had felt when Micah's fingers had done the same thing. I had seen in his eyes how the memory played out the morning we woke up in the truck.

We were seventeen our first time. The house was empty and our secret was becoming harder to keep. I don't know which of us first said out loud that we wouldn't tell Johnny—not yet. But according to Micah, Johnny had known. I suppose I knew that, too.

Things had changed between all three of us, as if the closer we got to finishing school, the closer we came to nothing ever being the same. It didn't take long for me to realize I was in love with Micah, but when it came down to it, I was afraid of any feeling of permanence. Any chance that I would be grafted into this forest like my mother, like so many other women who married loggers and had babies and erased themselves. I was even more worried about how Johnny might mess it all up. And in the end, he did.

Micah and I were lying tangled in my sheets when the landline rang, and a few seconds later, I was frantically pulling on my clothes, snatching Micah's keys from his hand. We spotted the beams of the headlights cast across the road just outside of town, and I was already opening the door before Micah had stopped the car.

Johnny stood almost invisible against the trees, blood snaking down his neck in a sticky stream, but his eyes were strangely vacant, his movements limp under my touch. He was wasted.

The 4Runner's windshield was busted, the passenger side scraped and one of the mirrors dangling from a single rubber cord. It looked like he'd sideswiped something, and when I looked back to see Micah climbing out of his truck, his eyes were pinned across the road, to the glow of light down in the ditch. Another car.

What scared me, even now, was how quickly I'd done it. How instantly I'd made the decision. One second I was standing on the side of the road, and the next I was climbing into the 4Runner and telling Micah to take Johnny home. Only an hour before, I'd been kissing Micah in the dark, giving my body to him for the very first time, but even that, I couldn't have. Everything always came back to Johnny.

I hadn't even blinked as I pulled up the sleeve of my shirt and dragged my arm across the broken glass. It was an impulse. A deep-rooted instinct in me, like I had no choice in the matter. It was up to me to protect my brother. To save him from everything, even himself. And the only thing that had given me pause, had made my trembling hand hesitate, was that look on Micah's face. He stared at me through the shattered windshield, like it was a terrifying thing to watch, and I remember feeling like I was looking in a mirror. That *Micah* was that mirror. It was a moment that marked a change in him. After so long of everything revolving around Johnny and whether Johnny was okay, Micah suddenly became the only person in the world who seemed to be worried about *me*.

It didn't really hit me until the fire truck arrived. Until they were pulling the man from the car in the ditch. I remember staring at the linoleum floor, barely feeling it as the doctor stitched up the cut on my arm, and Timothy Branson's voice was a faraway sound in the room.

Micah and I met eyes over the paper-lined tray of sutures as Branson told me that the man driving the other car had been drinking. He was a logger from out of town, on his way home from The Penny. His legs were broken, but he would live, and according to Branson, we'd all been lucky that night. No one but me and Micah ever knew that Johnny was even there.

I pulled down the sleeve of my sweater, covering the scar. Then I turned my phone over to hide the screen, in an attempt to ignore it.

There was a reply from Josie waiting for me when I got back to Six Rivers, and she'd offered to meet me in Fort Bragg. In my mind, I was still trying to draw a line from the voice I'd heard out in the gorge to her. It had sounded almost like it was underwater. Drowned and buried, but it was there. I could still hear it, like a ghost I'd woken in the gorge. If Micah was right and the backpack belonged to Autumn, maybe there was no real reason to believe that Josie was there that day. But I didn't know if I was ready to consider that Johnny had really been out there with that girl. Just thinking about where that possibility could lead stoked a heavy sense of dread in me.

I made the walk to town by myself, and when I got to Main Street, it wasn't the sleepy downtown I'd seen in the days before. Cars were parked in every space available along the shops, engines running and a few stereos playing. There were people everywhere, meandering along the sidewalks and huddled up beneath the awnings, with the blue and white team colors painting everything from car windows to letterman jackets to ball caps. It was a scene I'd witnessed many times growing up in Six Rivers. The team was caravanning to a game.

A banner that read GO COUGARS was strung up between the two light posts, and a man with a clipboard was standing in front of the market, caught up in conversation with several people who were gathered around.

Walking into the crowd was like stepping back in time. The picture of me in the diner had been taken on a day just like this one, when we'd come to see the team off before a game in Crescent City. It was the last one they played with Griffin. When they went to state a few weeks later, it was without him.

I stepped off the curb, finding an opening in the crowd toward the market. When I went inside, the smell of soil and floor cleaner stirred in the air with the scent of winter, making it still feel like I was in a time machine. I picked up one of the baskets stacked at the crowded entrance, eyes roaming the narrow aisles stockpiled with groceries and a limited number of household goods you couldn't find anywhere else in town. George Harvey, the man who'd worked behind the counter since I was a kid, was even posted at the register.

A few teenagers were in line with sodas in hand, and one of the store's patrons clapped them on the back as they passed with a *good luck* murmured. When one of the kids glanced back toward the door, I realized it was Ben, Sadie's son. He didn't notice me, giving the man a half-conscious but polite nod before he went out the door. As I watched him go, I couldn't help but search for another trace of Johnny.

I filled my basket with a few things to hold me over for the next couple of days, and being ignored in the midst of the commotion felt good. The list of dreaded reunions I had to make was dwindling now, and ripping off that Band-Aid had been the hardest part of coming back. Now, I found myself counting down the days until I left, and the feelings that accompanied that idea were becoming more confusing. Mostly because every single one of them led back to Micah.

I wasn't surprised that he was keeping his distance, but if I was going to get to the bottom of my questions about Autumn, I needed him. What happened at the gorge between us had made that more complicated.

When I made it to the register, George was waiting to scoop my half-dozen eggs from the basket. "Was wondering when you'd wander in."

"I was wondering if you'd remember me." I smiled, a little embarrassed as I took out the rest of the items for him to ring up.

"Oh, I remember you, James Golden."

His tone implied that the name brought with it a number of memories, and I wondered which they were. We'd been in the market almost every day after school, and half the time, Johnny was swiping something from the shelf. I didn't know if George really didn't know, or if at some point he'd just decided to pretend not to.

I eyed the small jar on the counter that Ben had dropped his change into, stiffening when I read the wrinkled laminated sign taped to its front: GRIFFIN WALKER SCHOLARSHIP FUND.

There was an old faded photo of Griffin in his soccer uniform above the words, and several folded bills and coins had been stuffed inside.

I looked away, sending my eyes to the store window as George punched the register keys, totaling up the items by hand. The number of people outside on the street had already multiplied twice over.

"Game this weekend?" I asked.

"Yep. The boys are off to Whitehorn."

"The whole town still comes out to see them off?"

"There's always a decent showing. A lot of them still go along, too. Should be pretty dead around here this weekend."

"Are you going?"

He huffed. "Of course! Last one of the season!"

"Glad I came in then."

He finished packing up the groceries, propping the head of lettuce on top so that the tender leaves could stick out beneath my arm.

"You be sure to winterize that cabin, now. Those pipes won't stand a chance when the freeze comes in a couple of days." He waited for me to nod in answer before he ran my credit card and pushed the filled tote back to me with a smile. "You have a good one."

"You too."

The door to the street opened again as a woman came in and I caught it before it could close, recognizing a face farther up the sidewalk. Amelia Travis was dressed in blue and white, the hood of her team hoodie untucked from her U.S. Forest Service jacket. She stood on the curb with a steaming paper cup in hand, and after a few seconds of indecision, I made my way toward her.

I waited for the line of teenage boys in front of me to file out onto the street before I crossed the jammed parking spaces. When she spotted me, she cut her conversation short, coming to meet me.

"You going with them?" I asked, looking around us.

She lifted a walkie-talkie into the air. "You're looking at this weekend's caravan captain."

I followed her gaze to the boys kneeing a soccer ball in the street, completely unaware that a car was trying to pass them. "Which one's yours?"

She pointed at a kid with red shaggy hair. "That one there."

The driver of the car gently tapped the horn until the boys moved and Amelia gave an exasperated sigh.

"I know this probably isn't the time," I said, wrapping my arms around the bulging tote. "But since you'll be gone for the next few days . . ."

Amelia turned to me, giving me her full attention. "What is it?"

"I just wanted to know if you had any reason to think that Johnny wasn't alone out at the gorge when he died?"

I managed to get all the words out in one go, but the question clearly caught her off guard. She tucked the walkie-talkie under her arm, taking a step toward me.

Her voice lowered to a discreet volume. "How do you mean?"

"I'm not really sure, I guess. I've just been going through every-thing for the CAS project, and I'm having a hard time accounting for what exactly he was doing out there."

"From what I've gathered, Johnny made pretty regular trips to the gorge for the study."

"He did. But he didn't have his camera or his field notes. They're all still at the house."

She fell quiet, eyes focused on the pavement beneath our feet as she considered it. "Do you have reason to believe he *wasn't* alone?" She turned the question back to me.

I bit the inside of my cheek. I wasn't willing to tell a law enforce-ment official that I thought my thirty-seven-year-old brother might have had the habit of taking his eighteen-year-old protégé out to a remote location overnight to work with him.

"No," I lied. "But if there's any chance that someone saw what hap-pened, or . . ."

Amelia didn't quite look convinced. She was watching me more closely now, her eyes roaming over the details of my face.

A horn honked behind me and she sighed, giving someone a dis-creet wave. "Why don't we sit down and chat when I get back? How's that?"

I nodded, but that curiosity in her gaze made me uneasy.

"Thanks," I said, a little unevenly. "I appreciate it."

Amelia's walkie-talkie beeped before a pulse of static came through and a man's voice cut in and out. She frowned, staring at it.

"Sorry." She gave me an apologetic look. "I think they're rounding everyone up."

I managed a smile. "No problem."

"I'll give you a call in a few days."

I watched her go, clutching the tote to my chest before I took out my phone, checking the time. It was only a little after three P.M., which meant that the school was just about to get out. I pulled up my text messages with Olivia, fingers fumbling over the words as I typed.

Hey, are you still at the school?

I hit send. It took only a few seconds for the three dots to appear ahead of Olivia's reply.

Yep! Need something?

Do you mind if I come by?

Not at all. See you in a few.

I slid the phone back into my pocket, finding Amelia in the crowd again. I was suddenly unsure if I should have said anything at all or if I hadn't really said enough. There was part of me that felt like I'd just walked into some kind of trap. Something about Amelia's response felt as if she *knew* I was hiding something, but I wasn't ready to tell her about the photograph of the backpack. Not yet.

My mind went back to the night I'd gone to her office, replaying that conversation in my mind. What was it she'd said? That she had a *working theory*? Now that I thought about it, I couldn't remember her actually saying that *she* believed Johnny's death was an accident.

FIFTEEN

The halls of Six Rivers High School were still filled with students when I arrived, and I found Olivia standing in a sea of paintings that stretched like a patchwork blanket across her classroom.

The tables were covered in large sheets of paper that had served as the canvas of what looked to be a landscape assignment. The paint was still wet on many of them, and the earthy smell of it filled the air, transporting me right back to the studios at Byron. Those two images in my mind, the overlap of before and after, gave me an almost out-of-body experience. The girl I was in this classroom and the one I'd become at Byron were like two different species. I didn't know anymore which I really was.

Olivia's hair was pulled up into two buns on top of her head and her thick-rimmed glasses were swapped out for a funky green pair. It would be easy to confuse her with the kids out in the hall.

The smile on her lips made the glasses cinch up on her nose when I came through the door. "Hey!" She had one of the paintings balanced on her arms, trying to find space at the end of the table for it.

"Hey, need a hand?"

"That would be great." She tipped her chin at the other paintings, motioning for me to slide them over.

I set the tote of groceries on one of the chairs and shifted the pages down until there was enough room. Olivia carefully situated the piece beside the others, making sure the edges weren't touching.

"Thanks."

"No problem."

I took a step closer, studying the landscapes more carefully. There were definitely ones that didn't show any promise or skill, but to my surprise, there were several that did.

"Some of these are actually quite good," I said.

She came to stand beside me, looking over the table. "They really are, right? I think we'll have a few in this class that stick with it. I hope they will, anyway." She turned to look at me, setting her hands on her hips. "So, what's up?"

I hesitated, hands nervously fidgeting with the edge of the painting I was still looking at. I wasn't totally sure that what I was about to do wasn't a mistake. If Johnny had been in the gorge with Autumn that day, it would open up a whole host of questions. Ones that would need to be answered. But that didn't change the fact that it still felt like a kind of betrayal.

I cleared my throat, going over what I'd planned to say. This was delicate, and I didn't want to imply anything to Olivia that would plant an idea in her head that wasn't already there.

"I wanted to see if you could tell me more about Autumn, the student Johnny was working with?"

Olivia's head cocked to the side. "Oh, sure. Why do you ask?"

"No reason, really. Micah mentioned her the other day and I guess I'm just . . ." I shrugged. "Curious."

Olivia leaned one hip into the counter behind her, pushing the glasses up her nose. "Well, Autumn is one of those kids who got dealt a bad hand. But she also happens to be immensely gifted. Her mom's a mess, and no one seems to know anything about her dad, which means she basically brought herself up. People around here tend to try and look out for one another, but there's only so much you can do, you know?"

"Sure."

I did know. It was one of the double-edged swords about this town. Johnny and I had pretty much been on our own for most of high school, and people had mostly looked the other way. But I'd known even then that if we'd needed something, they would have come through.

"The art teacher at the middle school had given me a call about Autumn before she started as a freshman here, because he saw something in her that he thought was special. As soon as I met her, I could tell that he was right. She was just . . . *extraordinary*," she said, a little breathless. The look in her eyes changed, as if she was remembering the exact moment she first thought it. "She was drawing mostly at that time, and it seemed like the art just came easily to her. She was immensely dedicated for someone her age, and photography became a focus for her sophomore year. Johnny started working in the darkroom around then, and Autumn had been learning what she could from YouTube videos and that kind of thing, but Johnny saw her work and took a genuine interest in it. I asked him to come by because I thought it would be inspiring for her to meet a working artist, and they just hit it off."

Hit it off. Those words rubbed me the wrong way.

She pointed behind me, getting back to her feet. "This is some of her work here."

I followed Olivia to the glass case fixed to the far wall, where a row of black-and-white photographs was on display. The subject of the images was the same in each one—they were trees. But not just any trees. These weren't like the lush, life-filled giants that filled Six Rivers. They were bare-branched and gnarled. Strangled, even. One was blackened, split down the middle like it had been hit by lightning. But the photographs themselves had an almost human quality about them, as if they were portraits of people.

A cardstock marker that read *SRHS Alum Autumn Fischer* was mounted beneath them.

"Incredible, right?" Olivia's voice was almost a whisper.

"Yeah."

I meant it. They were good. Better than a lot of the self-indulgent, overdramatized work of the students I'd been surrounded with at Byron. This was a unique point of view. The photographs felt inhabited, somehow. Lived in. To be honest, it reminded me of Johnny's work.

But when my gaze focused on a small mark in the corner of each of the photographs, my stomach twisted. It was a five-pointed star with looping ends, just like the one that marked the note I'd seen pinned above Johnny's desk.

You changed my life.

I could see it now, the distinct way the proportions of the shape were intentional. It was a star, but it wasn't. It was an *A*. An artist's signature for *Autumn*.

Slowly, the words I'd read became misshapen, contorting themselves into a number of possible meanings. But in the context of what I'd learned in the last couple of days, they felt intimate. *Too* intimate.

"This series got her an interview for a grant program at Byron, and Johnny pulled some strings through CAS to get her considered for a scholarship."

That made me pause. If Johnny had wanted to pull strings, why hadn't he done it through me? I was an alumnus. I'd even served as a visiting artist for a stint a few years ago. But Johnny had never mentioned a thing about it.

"We were *so* excited when she got accepted. All the teachers took up a collection to buy her bus ticket and the other stuff she needed to get started—prepaying her cellphone for the next year and getting her books. All of that."

"That's . . . incredible."

"It is. Like history repeating itself, you know?" She pushed her glasses up again, her eyes locking with mine.

She was talking about me now, but the turn of phrase was a little too close to the unnerving feeling I'd had that day in the gorge. Like this place—this forest—was telling the same stories over and over again.

"Some people are just lucky," she said, a little more quietly.

I stared at the lightning-struck tree, emotion gathering in my chest like a storm. Autumn's life and mine felt uncomfortably similar.

"Does she come back much to visit?" I asked, trying not to sound overly interested.

"Oh, no," Olivia scoffed. "Honestly, I doubt we'll ever see that girl again. She couldn't wait to get out of here. I'm sure you know what that's like. And really, Autumn doesn't have anything to come back for."

But that didn't line up with the story that Johnny's photographs told. She'd been in the gorge in November.

"So, she hasn't been back at all since she left?"

Olivia's gaze grew more focused on me, as if she was trying to puzzle me out, and I instantly regretted pressing the question. "No. Why?"

I let my eyes wander over the paintings on the wall next to me, trying to appear distracted. Like my insides weren't twisting with the uncertainty of what all of this meant. If Autumn hadn't been back since she left for school, then how could she have been with Johnny that day? Unless she'd never come back to Six Rivers. It was possible she'd made the drive from San Francisco and met Johnny at the gorge.

"I was just thinking maybe I'd get a chance to meet her while I'm here."

"I'm sure she's got herself very busy down there in the city. I mean, Autumn is really just a typical teenage girl. Emotional, passionate, looking for adventure. During high school, she spent pretty much all of her time out shooting or in the darkroom, and if she wasn't doing that, she was with Ben."

That got my attention. "Ben?"

"Yeah, she dated Ben Cross for a couple of years before graduation."

"Sadie's son?"

Olivia nodded. "Yeah. Kind of a fragile kid. I never understood what she saw in him, honestly. Autumn was such a . . . force. But he was crazy about her and absolutely devastated when she left."

The fact that Autumn had a boyfriend was at least some comfort, but I still didn't like the way things looked. Judging from Micah and Olivia's casual take on Johnny and Autumn, I seemed to be the only one concerned about it.

Olivia's phone chimed and she went to the desk, picking it up. She hissed, wincing. "Sorry, I gotta go."

"Oh, no problem. I appreciate you letting me come by."

"Of course." She smiled, reaching for the ties of her apron. "Any time."

I picked up the tote and crossed the room, my steps slowing as I passed Autumn's series on the wall. The fluorescent lights bounced off the glass, distorting my reflection. I looked at each of the photographs once more, eyes lingering on the dead, gnarled branches.

When I started for the hallway again, Olivia's voice stopped me.

"He really helped her find her voice, you know. Encouraged her to pursue this series she was doing with the trees." She gestured to the mounted images on the wall. "It's pretty rare to have a mentorship opportunity like that, particularly at that age."

You changed my life.

I smiled, but it was heavy. "Yeah, it is."

I pushed through the double doors that led to the parking lot, starting the walk back toward town. But my curiosity about Autumn had only intensified now. I only made it a few blocks before I couldn't resist the urge any longer. When I had enough bars of service, I ducked into the little alleyway behind Main Street, leaning my back against the brick wall as I pulled out my phone. I opened the Instagram app, finding Johnny's account, and his photos populated in the grid.

I clicked on his followers and the list of handles popped up, all

34,000 of them. When I typed the name *Autumn* into the search, only one was filtered out. I tapped it.

The screen loaded and I stared at the profile picture at the top. A girl with wide, round eyes looked into the camera, the waves of her chestnut hair falling over one shoulder. Beneath it, only a few words were written in the description.

Give me donuts or give me death!

I bit down on my bottom lip, scrolling down to the grid. The photos were a mix of artistic and candid, a few of them featuring dead trees similar to the series I'd seen displayed in Olivia's classroom. Others featured ordinary things like coffee cups or an ice cream cone. There were really none of people, which I thought strange for a teenage girl. Where were the selfies or pictures from parties? Where were the group photos with friends?

The posts were inconsistent, some of them months apart, with the last one being a kind of farewell post before college. It was a photo of her reflection in the window of a car, but the phone was lifted up, hiding her face. The caption read, *Last party in Six Rivers. At dawn, we ride.*

There were only a few comments.

@g4life231 Gonna miss you girlie
@firstfrostchronicle Bright and early!

The last one from @marimarimayhem was just a motorcycle emoji followed by a fire emoji.

Only a few of the posts featured Autumn herself. I clicked on one of them and it filled the phone screen. She was sitting on a curb with her hands in her lap, legs extended out into the street. The background was only partially visible, but it looked like the downtown strip. Her long hair was in a thick, messy braid and the gleam in her eyes was bright. She was beautiful. A sweet kind of beautiful. There was no denying that. The curve of her cheek was sharp, the angle of her jaw severe, but it balanced the softness of her face perfectly. She had a mysterious look, like there were secrets folded behind those eyes.

There were twelve likes on the picture, and I couldn't help myself. I clicked on them, looking for Johnny's handle, but it wasn't there. When I went to the next, I didn't find his name on that one, either. Of the several I randomly chose from the grid, many of the same handles appeared in the likes and comments. @firstfrostchronicle, a @sooziekyoo, and @marimarimayhem were among them, but Johnny hadn't liked or commented on any of the posts.

When I went back to Johnny's page, the opposite was true. Autumn's handle showed up on the likes of every photo I clicked on.

I let out a breath, ashamed of the relief I felt. Like somehow, I'd been afraid that Johnny was about to let me down in a way that I didn't think I could come back from. But if there was anything going on between Autumn and my brother, it could have been no more than the infatuation of a young girl, cast on an older man. I remembered what it was like to be on the edge of adulthood. How tiny the steps were between one thing and another. You could just wake up one day and be standing on the other side of a line you didn't remember crossing. For Johnny, I'd done it many times.

SIXTEEN

I leaned back in the booth, nervously biting down on my thumbnail as I stared at Johnny's phone. It sat on the table in front of me as I talked myself through what I needed to do, but that feeling of guilt was growing into a heavy thing inside my chest.

He was there across the diner again, in the booth against the window. His back was to me, his face turned toward the street, and I waited, heart pounding, for him to turn and look at me. The vision of him was so clear now. Less like a painting, more like a photograph. His shadow moved over the tile floor beside the table, the sunlight catching his hair. He looked so real. So . . . alive.

Look at me.

I willed him to turn his head. To cast his gaze over his shoulder and warn me to stop. To stop digging. Stop asking questions. But Johnny didn't move.

Slowly, my eyes dropped to the dark screen of the phone again.

There was no question that it was an invasion of his privacy, even if he was gone. But the unknown variable of it was like a monster hiding in the dark. I could feel it, but I couldn't see it. And I needed to turn on the light.

As soon as I made up my mind, I pulled the charger from the bag and plugged it in. The battery icon illuminated on the screen a few seconds later, and I turned my attention back to the laptop.

I opened Johnny's email inbox while I waited for the phone to turn on, typing the name *Autumn Fischer* in the search field. Only one email address auto populated, an *afischer24@outpost.com*. I clicked it, bracing myself as the results loaded, but it came up empty. There wasn't a single message.

I was struck by the unnerving thought that it wasn't quite believable. If Johnny's email had the address saved, it meant that at some point, he'd either sent her a message or received one. And if the conversations were archived, they would still come up in a search. The only reason there wouldn't be any found was that they'd been deliberately deleted.

I pulled up Johnny's bank account next, but this time I wasn't looking at the abbreviated records that appeared on his statements. I went line by line, inspecting every transaction going back from the day before he died, opening each one for the vendor's information and location. I couldn't prove whether or not Autumn had been back to visit Johnny, but I could get a sense of whether he'd been to see her in San Francisco if I was looking in the right places.

With every link I clicked on, Johnny's presence grew heavier and heavier around me. It was enough to feel so suffocating that I finally fished my earbuds from my bag and put them in. I tapped the first song in the first playlist I found, turning up the volume until my senses were flooded enough to drown him out. He was still there, in the middle distance, but I could almost ignore him.

Going back to the summer before Autumn would have left for school, there wasn't a single purchase on the account that I could narrow down to San Francisco or anywhere else in the Bay Area. It seemed the only time Johnny had left town was to head out to the coast, where I assumed he'd been meeting Josie.

I scrolled back and forth through the dates, stopping when I ran across the twelve-thousand-dollar transaction that was still a mystery.

I highlighted the vendor ID BS 012001, copying and pasting it into a Google Search. The moment I hit enter, I saw Sadie moving toward me from the kitchen. She had a plate in one hand, a pot of coffee in the other, and her eyes skipped over the laptop and papers on the table as she set a stack of waffles down in front of me.

"I see you have your battle station up and running." She refilled the coffee mug. "I think we can safely say this booth is officially your spot."

"Sorry, I don't mean to keep camping out here."

She set the coffeepot down, leaning into the table. "Believe me, you and everyone else in this town spend a minimum of two hours a day in this place, and that's how I like it. Full, busy, loud."

"Are you sure?"

"Very sure." She gave a single nod. "Pretty quiet around here this weekend, though."

It took a moment for me to understand her meaning. "That's right. I saw everyone heading out of town for the game. Couldn't make this one?"

"No. I go to the home games and the ones that aren't too far from here, but the weekend ones, not so much. The fate of a small-town business owner with next to no employees, I'm afraid."

I gave her a sympathetic smile.

"What're you workin' on today?"

She glanced at the laptop, giving me the sudden urge to close it.

"Paperwork. Financial stuff. Just trying to tie up loose ends, that kind of thing."

"I'm sure that's easier said than done." She looked at me, coffeepot still hovering over the table, as if she was waiting for me to continue. Again, her attention found the laptop screen, and my fingers itched to reach for it. When her eyes finally traveled back to mine, her blue irises seemed to have paled a few shades lighter. "Stay as long as you like," she said, finally.

"Thanks."

She gave me another gentle smile before she went to the next table, and I sighed, staring into the plate of waffles she'd dropped off. I'd barely eaten in the last few days, my mind constantly turning. But the smell of the syrup and butter was making my mouth water. I picked up the fork and knife, letting myself take a few bites before I turned my attention back to the screen.

The search results for the vendor ID were accompanied by a few image thumbnails at the top. One of them looked like a crest I thought I recognized. I took a sip of coffee as I pulled the laptop toward me, but I nearly spilled it on the keyboard when I started reading. The vendor associated with the ID was listed in multiple search results, one on top of the other: BYRON SCHOOL OF THE ARTS.

"BS," I whispered, putting it together.

I clicked on the link to the school's website, eyes jumping over the banner at the top. The transaction on Johnny's account was a payment made to Byron. *Autumn's* school. And the only possible explanation for that was that the money had been for Autumn.

The fact that he'd paid such a large sum that he didn't really have was suspicious, but it wasn't proof of the intention behind it. He'd never been materialistic or proud. It was entirely plausible that the money had been a generous gift meant to support a deserving pro-tégé. But twelve thousand dollars wasn't the kind of money you gave to a friend.

My fingers tapped on the edge of the keyboard nervously, my mind fixated on what it could mean. But when Johnny's phone finally turned on, the screen lit up on the table beside me and my fingers froze in the air.

The background image made my heart come up into my throat. It was a picture of Johnny and Smoke. He was smiling with a cascade of mountain peaks visible behind him, and the dog was tucked under his arm, tongue hanging from one side of his mouth. I'd never seen the picture, which made it sting in a fresh way.

I stared at Johnny's face, asking myself one more time if I was really going to do this. Getting into his email was one thing. His phone felt like another.

My eyes lifted to the booth in the corner, where I could still see him. Again, I waited for him to turn around, as if giving him one more chance to stop me. But he didn't.

My fingers typed in the passcode—0914—Johnny's and my birthdate.

I stabbed another bite of waffle and shoved it into my mouth before I opened Johnny's text messages. I stopped mid-chew when I saw my name at the top. Johnny had our conversation pinned so that it wouldn't get buried beneath the others. A small picture of my face looked back at me—an old photo he'd taken years ago.

I didn't tap it open because I knew what I'd find there. I'd reread our last text conversation over and over in the last few months. It was mostly about nothing, and every time I looked at it, I found it even more devastating. A TV show Johnny was watching and recommending, a picture I'd sent him of a Chicago-style hot dog, and him letting me know he was planning to come for Christmas. I'd thought a lot about that last one on Christmas Eve, as I finished off a bottle of wine sitting out on the freezing-cold balcony of my apartment. Alone.

The texts had been so mundane. So simple. I wondered now what I might have said if I knew it was the last thing I'd ever say to him. I had no idea.

There weren't any messages on his phone with anyone named Autumn, so I went to his contacts, thinking I'd at least find her information there. But I didn't.

I opened Johnny's Instagram app next. If they weren't communicating on email or text, maybe they were talking in DMs. As soon as his profile loaded, I tapped on the messages, looking for Autumn's name. It wasn't there.

How was it possible that Johnny had been the girl's mentor for over a year and yet they'd only ever spoken in person? Micah said Johnny took her out on shoots, and Olivia said he'd helped her with getting into Byron, so they had to be communicating somehow.

I ran a frustrated hand through my hair. This was what I'd wanted, right? To *not* find anything? So, why did it feel like I'd stumbled upon some kind of irrefutable proof?

I opened the call log, finger pausing on the screen when I saw Micah's name at the top in red. There were sixteen missed calls from him the day they found Johnny's body. There were twelve the day before.

A tingle rushed over my skin as I imagined him dialing Johnny's number over and over. How many calls had it taken for Micah to call Amelia and decide to drive out to the gorge? At what point had he really started to worry? When had he *known,* like he said?

Beneath my and Micah's missed calls was the last call Johnny made. The phone number wasn't saved, but the date was the day he died. And he'd called the number three times.

The next call on the log was to Amelia Travis, but that same unsaved number was there again and again in the two days before. I added them up, biting my lip. He'd called it thirty-six times, and it looked like they'd all gone unanswered.

"James."

A deep voice beside me made me knock the fork off my plate, and I looked up to see Micah standing only feet away. His face was flush from the cold, a few snowflakes dusting his shoulders, and as soon as my eyes met his, that tight feeling in my stomach returned.

He gave me a peculiar look as he crouched down, picking up the fork. "You okay?"

I pulled Johnny's phone from the table, wedging it beneath my leg on the seat. "Yeah, sorry. You scared me."

"I said your name like four times."

I glanced at the door, then behind him, to the line of barstools. I hadn't even seen him come in.

Sadie came out of the kitchen, giving Micah a wave when she saw him. "Hey, Micah."

"Hey."

He gave her a nod when she lifted an empty paper coffee cup into the air and then he slid into the opposite side of the booth, surprising me.

He looked over the contents of the table. "You've been busy?"

"Yeah." I could feel the burn of the omission on my tongue.

The question he was really asking was why I hadn't called or texted him since we'd returned from the gorge. But that wasn't an easy answer, and to be fair, he hadn't reached out, either. What was I going to tell him? That I hadn't called him because I could still feel his hands on my skin and that even now, sitting across the table, mine itched to touch him? How did I tell him that I was afraid I couldn't rebury things once they'd found the light?

Sadie made a quick pass by the table, setting down the to-go coffee cup, but Micah was really studying me now, and I could feel him plucking the thoughts right out of my head. Like he'd listened to me say them out loud.

He set his elbows on the table. "How are you?"

"I'm okay," I said. "I thought maybe you were avoiding me."

He didn't deny it. He leaned forward, pulling at his bottom lip with his teeth, like he was trying not to say whatever he wanted to next. "I don't know how to do this version of us, James."

"I know."

That was the only reply I could muster, and it seemed to be enough. A long silence stretched out between us as we looked at each other, and Micah seemed to relax a little, as if just admitting it made things a little easier.

His attention fell to the laptop in front of me. "Did you find anything?"

"I don't know," I said. "I've been sitting here looking through his email and texts and everything, trying to . . ." I rubbed my temples. "Did you know that Johnny paid for part of Autumn's tuition?"

Micah's brow furrowed. "No. You're sure?"

I nodded, dropping my voice. "He made a payment to Byron in July. Over twelve thousand dollars."

He looked concerned now, and that worried me. I picked at my fingernails in my lap, trying to determine the cost of saying out loud what was already so hard to even think about.

"What exactly was Johnny's relationship with this girl, Micah?"

An unreadable expression crossed his face. "James . . ."

"It just doesn't make sense. There's not a single text, email, or even DM between them. Almost like he—" I paused, swallowing. "Almost like he erased it."

Micah stared at me.

"You don't think that's strange?" I pressed.

"Johnny did a lot of things that didn't make sense to me."

"That's not an answer."

Micah's jaw clenched. "Is it strange? Yeah. Strange for Johnny? I don't know."

I wished that wasn't true. It was hard to measure Johnny by what other people did or how they acted. In so many ways, he couldn't be calculated or analyzed. Everything that felt true to me about my brother had been based on feeling. On instinct.

I closed the laptop, slipping it into my bag. "I'm going out to Fort Bragg tomorrow to meet Josie."

"Did you talk to her?"

"Not yet."

Micah watched me, teeth scraping his bottom lip again. "Why don't I drive out there with you?"

I searched his eyes. I didn't know how to do this version of us, either. I didn't know if it was possible. But before I could even answer, he was already standing.

"Text me what time we leave." He waited to see if I would argue, but I didn't.

A subtle smile tugged at his mouth before he started for the door, but I stopped him.

"Hey."

He turned back. "Yeah?"

"Are we okay?" I asked.

He gave me one of his *I know you, you know me* smiles. "We're okay, J."

J. That's what he'd called me when we were kids, and I had to swallow down the untethered feeling hearing the nickname he gave me.

I waited until he was out of sight before I picked up Johnny's phone, punching in the passcode. The call log was still pulled up, and I reluctantly copied the unsaved number, typing it into my own phone. Slowly, I lifted it to my ear. It took a few seconds for it to start ringing, and I licked my lips, pulse climbing. It rang again and again, until finally the voicemail picked up.

The high-pitched, melodic voice was like a siren in my ear.

"Hi, it's Autumn! Leave a message!"

SEVENTEEN

The road to Fort Bragg was like a rope pulling me from the dark.

An hour and a half in, I was grateful that Micah had offered to come. Every few minutes, I had the impulse to turn my head and look at him, as if to prove to myself that he was really there.

The twisting route carved through the thick forests all the way to the coastline, where the sea battered the land into jagged, sharp-toothed cliffs. The farther we drove, the less I could feel Johnny. The more I could breathe.

There was an almost-comfortable quiet between Micah and me that kept me from getting lost in the labyrinth of my thoughts—Johnny. Autumn. Josie. The backpack. Each question was like a brick stacked on another. The weight of it all was proving too much to bear.

The last few days had felt like years, and having a ticking clock on my time in Six Rivers made me feel anxious. Like the stirring, penetrating energy that saturated the old-growth forest was already getting its tentacles around me. It was something that just sucked you in.

"Let's go over it again," I said, waiting to see if Micah would argue.

He didn't, giving me a nod. We'd spent half the drive nailing down the timeline until it was in an order that made sense, and each time I repeated it, the events felt a little less convoluted.

"Okay," I began. "Johnny borrows your truck and heads out to the gorge on November ninth. He would have arrived there in the late afternoon?"

"Early evening. Enough time to make camp."

"Okay, so he stays the night and shoots the next morning, November tenth—that's when Autumn's backpack shows up in the film."

"So, she could have met him out there, like you said. But for whatever reason, he returns to Six Rivers earlier than he planned," Micah thought aloud.

"So, what? Why does he go all the way out there just to leave suddenly?"

"Maybe he forgets something or the weather turns."

I shook my head. "I checked. There wasn't a storm that day. There wasn't even a drop of rain."

"Okay, so if he's out there with Autumn, maybe they get in a fight?"

"Maybe . . ." I murmured, still thinking. "And she goes back to San Francisco? There's nothing to suggest that she came back to Six Rivers."

"That would explain why Johnny would have been calling her. Maybe she leaves the gorge angry and he's trying to get ahold of her."

"But he didn't say anything to you when he got back?" I turned to look at Micah.

"I wasn't home when he dropped off the truck. I just came back and it was there."

"And you didn't talk to him at all before he went back out to the gorge?"

"No. I was booked solid that whole week and I was barely in town. But I came home that day and the truck was gone again. He'd dropped off Smoke and just took off."

"November twelfth," I said. That was the day he died.

"So, he goes back out to the gorge without telling anyone. Doesn't take any of his gear. He's up on the ridge on the other side of the ravine, and . . ." He didn't finish.

"Was he going back out there to meet her again?"

Laying out the facts did little to ease my mind. There was no evidence that Autumn had ever answered Johnny's calls, and there were no other communications I could find between them. Maybe the most concerning part of all of this was that Autumn seemed to have been meticulously scrubbed from Johnny's life, but I was far beyond trying to dispel my own suspicions about what Johnny was hiding. The bottom line was that if Autumn was there that day, then she was the last person to see Johnny alive.

"And when you found him—" I paused. "He didn't have anything with him? Nothing that indicated why he'd been up on the ridge or what he was doing out there?"

"No, nothing. He was just lying there. He looked like . . ." Micah swallowed. "He almost just looked like he was asleep."

That image alone was enough to make a cold silence settle back in the car. Micah's eyes were cast out the window, but I could see the tension of the memory in every inch of him. Like remembering it was physically painful.

"Let's say Johnny did go out to meet Autumn on November ninth," I said. "There's something wrong about that, am I right?"

I waited for Micah to look at me as confirmation. When he finally did, it made my heart sink. There was no getting around the fact that Autumn was an eighteen-year-old girl and that Johnny was a significantly older man who was in a position of power and influence over her. And I also couldn't ignore that Autumn was both beautiful and talented.

"Maybe he had a good reason." Micah's voice lowered.

"Can you think of one?"

Micah was quiet for a long moment. "No."

We didn't talk for the rest of the drive, which allowed the possibility taking root. I had to acknowledge that the way this all looked, it was plausible that Johnny had gotten himself into an unforgivable, inexcusable situation. And when Johnny got himself into trouble, there was a protocol. Micah and I took care of it. We covered for him. But if Johnny had done what I thought he'd done, I didn't know if I could do that this time.

Once the forest finally thinned and the land turned into steep shoreline, we took curve after curve until town appeared in the distance. The sky was cast over with a gray haze when we arrived in Fort Bragg, and the air was full of mist, making my hair curl up with damp the moment I got out of the car.

The colors of the seaside town looked almost washed out, as if the salt in the wind had diluted their hues. It didn't matter how many times I saw the Northern California coast. There was always something that felt unknown about it, even when it was familiar. The way the waves climbed hungrily up the beach and then tore away. As if the sea was writhing with anger.

"You sure you don't want me to come with you?" Micah said, watching me stare out at the water.

"Yeah, I'm going to do this alone."

He nodded, catching my hand with his as he passed, and he gave it a quick squeeze before starting up the street. The gesture was so easy and warm that I was tempted not to let his fingers slip from mine.

He didn't look back as he headed toward the beach, and I went in the opposite direction, where the string of pastel buildings climbed the hill. Josie was based in Shasta-Trinity National Forest, and according to the emails I had seen between her and Johnny, the little coffee shop in Fort Bragg was where they met every three months for a check-in.

I'd gone through the inbox again for any sign of more messages like the one I'd found, where Josie had threatened to report him to CAS. Johnny hadn't replied to the message, and no others had followed it, making me think that things had still been strained between them when he died.

I stopped beneath the sign for Headlands Coffeehouse that hung over the sidewalk, hesitating before I pulled my phone from my back pocket. The wind blew my hair across my face as I stood there, staring at it. I wanted the truth. I wanted to know what happened to Johnny, but I hadn't considered what else I would learn about my brother in the process. It took several seconds to convince myself to dial Autumn's number again, and I cleared my throat while it rang, heart racing until the voicemail picked up.

"Hi, it's Autumn! Leave a message!"

When it beeped, I tried to sound as sane and calm as possible.

"Hi, my name is James Golden, and you knew my brother, Johnny?" I grimaced at the awkward tone in my voice. "I, uh, I wanted to see if you could give me a call back." Another pause. "I'd really appreciate it. It's important."

I ended the call and let out the enormous breath trapped in my lungs, trying to replace it with the cold sea air. When I glanced at the phone again, it was only two minutes until the time I was supposed to meet Josie.

I pulled open the door and stepped inside, scanning the faces until I saw one that might be her. She had a laptop open and a stack of notebooks at her side, an abandoned pot of tea on the table. Her curly auburn hair was cut short, springing up in windblown ringlets along her chin. She had a weathered look that reminded me of Amelia Travis, but she had to be around Johnny's and my age.

I'd almost made it to the table before she noticed me, and she clumsily stood, hand extending warmly. "James?"

"Hi, yes." I shook her hand, bristling a little at the firmness of her grip. "Nice to meet you."

Josie waved at the man behind the register. "Brett? Can we get another?"

He answered with a nod, reaching for two fresh mugs. Josie motioned for me to sit before she closed her laptop and attempted to tidy the table. Bunched-up napkins and torn sugar packets were raked into a pile, and once she had them cradled in her palm, she stuffed them into one of the dirty mugs.

"Sorry about this." She laughed. "I'm not used to working indoors." She brushed off her hands, propping them up on the table. There was a beat of silence before she spoke. "I would offer my condolences, but I imagine you're tired of those by now."

"Yeah." I smiled. "I am, actually."

"Well, then I will instead tell you how grateful we are that you were willing to come up here and get your hands dirty. I speak for the whole team, honestly. We're really down to the wire, and Johnny's sector is an important one."

"I'm just glad I could help. This project meant a lot to Johnny."

She nodded. "It did. We were lucky to find someone like him, and he was very . . ." She searched for the word. "Dedicated."

My eyes ran over her face, settling on her stiff smile. It felt like maybe there was a double meaning behind the word.

"Now." She cut to the chase, just as the barista set down a fresh pot of tea between us. He took the used dishes up, leaning over the table, but Josie didn't break eye contact with me. "How can I help? You've got the originals of Johnny's logs. Are you having any trouble with the transcriptions?"

"That's actually not why I asked to meet," I said.

Josie's brow wrinkled as she picked up the teapot and poured. The movement was a little stilted. "Oh, okay. What's this about, then?"

"I've been in Six Rivers dealing with Johnny's affairs—including the CAS project, of course. But I'm also just trying to get a sense of Johnny's life. I know that probably sounds strange, but we weren't really in touch as much as I wish we were, and I guess . . ." The words faltered.

"You're trying to get closure?" she offered, gently.

"Yeah. Something like that."

She slid the teacup toward me and the fragrant scent of bergamot curled into the air with the steam. "Okay, how can I help?"

My hands clamped together in my lap, my palms slick. "Were you and Johnny . . . friends?"

The shadow of something passed over her face and she picked up her steaming cup, taking a sip. "We were."

I waited.

"If you're asking whether we were more than friends, then I suppose I could tell you it's not really any of your business." She smirked. "But sure. Yeah—sometimes more."

"Sometimes?"

She shrugged. "This job doesn't really lend itself to steady relationships, and Johnny wasn't really a steady guy, anyway."

"When were you guys together, if you don't mind me asking?"

"I don't mind. There's not much to know. I wouldn't say it was ever really serious. When he came onto the project, we connected. He had a lot of talent and passion, and that's not always easy to find. He inspired me, I guess. Made me remember why I started doing this in the first place." Her gaze drifted past me, as if she was watching a particular memory play out. "He had a very unique point of view."

"How do you mean?"

"It was remarkable, really. He had a gift. He could get so *close* to them—the owls. And it felt like he viewed them, I don't know, like . . ."

"As human." I cut her off unintentionally. "Sorry."

She gave me a peculiar look. "You don't need to apologize. But I don't know if I'd put it that way, exactly."

It struck me suddenly that there was something about her that *reminded* me of Johnny. The way she held herself and carried the frame of her body was so like him. She took up the space around her and she didn't even look like she meant to.

"How would you put it, then?" I asked.

She thought about it, mouth screwing up on one side. "I was thinking the opposite, actually. That Johnny seemed to understand that we're not so different. That in the end, we—us, the owls, the fish down there"—she pointed at the window that looked out over the water—"we're all just . . . animals."

That, too, felt like it had more than one meaning.

"When's the last time you talked to Johnny before he died?" I asked.

Her lips pressed together in a hesitant way. "We hadn't really talked in a while."

"I'm asking because—" I set the cup down on the saucer, trying to decide exactly how I wanted to ask the question. "I know it's probably awkward to mention, but I was going through his things and saw an email from you."

Josie met my eyes, her expression unreadable. "Yes?"

"In it, you were threatening to report Johnny to the board at CAS. I was wondering if you could tell me what it was about."

Her gaze didn't break from mine. "It doesn't matter much now, does it?" she said, matter-of-fact.

"It does to me."

She considered for a long time, letting the silence drag out before she finally answered. "I found out that Johnny was poaching."

I couldn't hide my stunned reaction. That wasn't at all what I'd expected her to say. "*Poaching?*" I repeated, my tone unmistakably disbelieving.

She nodded. "In our line of work, there are controversial tactics that *some* employ to skew the results of a study or to impact a specific problem occurring in the ecosystem."

"What does that mean?"

She lifted her hands in front of her, like she was weighing her answer. "I don't know how much you know about the project, but the most direct threats to the northern spotted owl are deforestation and another species called the barred owl."

I remembered reading about them in Johnny's field notes. He'd written pretty extensively about them, and when I'd run across it, it had summoned a vague memory I had of him bringing it up in conversation early on in the project. According to his notebooks, their growing population had impacted the survival of the subjects he was studying.

"As an invasive species, they compete with our highly endangered subjects for food, shelter, and everything else," Josie continued. "And in situations like these, there are those in our community who think that extermination is an acceptable solution."

Immediately, my mind went to the gun I'd found in the closet.

"I got a couple of calls saying that one of my guys was poaching, and when I asked Johnny about it, he didn't deny it. I thought about firing him off the project, but his work in Six Rivers was vital to the goal of CAS, and I knew we would have trouble replacing him. Especially that late in the game."

"So, you didn't report him?" I asked.

"No. If it had gotten out what he was doing, it would have jeopardized our entire study. If he was an actual scientist, he would have understood that. But he was very stubborn. It was hard getting through to him." She shook her head. "Like I said, it doesn't matter much now, does it?"

But it did. It mattered more than she could know. I couldn't deny the fact that I was surprised by what she'd told me, but there was no reason I could think of for Josie to lie. Deep down, I could feel that it was true, and slowly a realization was snaking its way through me.

That maybe, despite everything I'd ever believed, I didn't *know* Johnny. Not like I thought I did.

Twenty Years Ago

It was a Friday night in April, only weeks before summer, but a late frost was coming to Six Rivers.

Micah, Johnny, and I had planned to drive out to the gorge that afternoon, and Griffin decided to join us at the last minute. I'd been irritated when Johnny told me, because Griffin had been doing that a lot lately—showing up unexpectedly.

Telling him about Byron had been a mistake, and I wasn't sure why I'd even done it. The secret formed a kind of bond between us, and it seemed nearly every time I was alone, he was suddenly there. Finding me in the studio after school or on the walk home. Catching my gaze from across the diner or inviting himself into our weekend plans. Every time his eyes lingered on me or his arm brushed mine, it felt intentional. Like we had a silent agreement about *after* Six Rivers.

I could feel him wedging his way into the cracks of my life, fitting himself between me and Micah. Me and Johnny. The unspoken thing that hung in the air every time he was near me was that he knew what I'd kept from them. And the longer I did, the bigger the lie became.

I didn't argue about Griffin coming along to the gorge because I was walking on eggshells with him. At least until I came clean with

Johnny and Micah. I didn't like that he had something to hold over me. It felt like leverage, an unbalanced set of scales.

Griffin drove his own truck out to the gorge because he couldn't stay the night. He had soccer practice early the next morning and would make the trip back alone while the rest of us camped. We did what we always did, peeling off our clothes when we got down to the ravine and jumping from the cliffs as the sun went down. The temperature started to drop before it was dark, and Griffin stayed close to me, not letting the distance between us stretch too far. I could feel Micah watching us. No one knew about the nights he spent in my bedroom. I hadn't even told Olivia because I didn't want the spell to be broken. I was terrified of when it would end, because I could feel in my bones that it would.

Once my fingers were numb with cold, I found a spot on the other side of the ravine to sit and watch the others jump from the cliffs, while I sipped from a bottle of whiskey that Johnny had brought. It didn't take long before Griffin trudged up out of the water to sit beside me, and his fingers brushed mine as he helped himself to the bottle, taking more than one long drink. I sat there stiffly, my eyes on the water, hoping that if I didn't look at him, he would keep his distance. But only seconds later, Griffin's cold hand found my knee, sliding up the curve of my inner thigh until it was between my legs.

I shoved him hard, looking up to the cliffs, where Micah and Johnny were about to jump again. Micah was talking, distracted, but Johnny's attention was pulling in my direction. Like some flicker in the back of his mind had caught the uptick in my pulse. When he looked at me, I snatched the bottle from Griffin's hands again, taking a drink. And then Johnny was stepping off the ledge and falling through the air.

Come on, James.

Griffin leaned toward me, his mouth close to my ear and his breath stained with whiskey.

What the fuck are you doing?

I could still feel those hoarse words on my lips and hear the shake in them. I could still see the blaze in Griffin's eyes.

Don't ever touch me again.

When I left Griffin on the bank, I didn't know he was going to finish the bottle of whiskey. I didn't know that he'd stumble back to the trailhead when we were done at the swimming hole, too drunk to drive home.

I kept my distance from him as Johnny got the fire going, but I could still feel my brother's attention on me, a question in his eyes every time they met mine. But I'd handled it, I thought. I'd dealt with Griffin Walker and I didn't need Johnny to save me. I also wouldn't risk my secret about Byron coming out until I was ready.

The night drew on with a growing pressure in the gorge, and the more Griffin drank, the more visibly agitated he became. More than once, I caught Micah and Johnny meeting eyes in a building tension that made me regret the sips of whiskey I'd taken. I was beginning to feel sick.

Griffin went to his truck to turn up the music, and while he was gone the atmosphere around the fire eased just a little. I could see that Johnny and Micah had had enough, but we were stuck with him for the night. The only thing we could do was to let him sleep it off.

The crunch of footsteps on ice-crusted earth sounded before the firelight fell on Griffin again. But when it gleamed on something clutched in his hand, I felt colder. It was the rifle that was always stowed behind the seats in the cab of his truck.

Immediately, an uneasy feeling bled through me, an electric buzz waking in the air. The firelight glinted on the barrel of the gun as he raised it, pointing it into the dark, and I didn't expect the sound that followed. He fired, making me jump, and a rustle of wings took off in the trees overhead. When Griffin raised it again, Micah stood from where he was sitting on the other side of the fire.

Cut it out, Griffin.

Micah was noticeably annoyed, but there was a serious undercurrent to his tone. An edge of nervousness. Griffin ignored him, the barrel of the gun arcing in the air like he was sighting an imaginary bird across the sky. When he pulled the trigger again, I flinched.

Griffin.

The warning came from Johnny this time, but Griffin was laughing now. Slowly, the gun tilted down and goosebumps raced up my arms when its aim drifted close to me.

Johnny was immediately on his feet, moving in the dark beside me, but Micah caught Johnny in the chest with his hand, stopping him. Like he was afraid that any sudden movement would result in Griffin pulling the trigger a third time.

The flood of adrenaline in Johnny's body poured into mine, making me feel like I was on fire. Then they were both shouting—Micah and Johnny. But their voices were a blur lost in the sound of my own racing heart. Griffin's eyes met mine, a furious gleam in them that I didn't recognize.

It's not fucking funny, Griffin. Put it down.

Micah took a step closer to him, hand still twisted in Johnny's shirt, but Griffin only laughed louder.

You're the only one who gets to fuck her, right?

Griffin's words were slurred and sloppy, his eyes still on me.

I could see the shift on Micah's face. The rigidity of his posture. He glanced from me to Johnny, but my brother's face was unreadable.

You think it's a secret? When are you going to tell them you're leaving, James? When are you going to tell them you're too fucking good for this place?

The gun wasn't just close to me now. He was pointing it at me. And I was frozen, beginning to tremble as the blood drained from my face.

I could see that Griffin liked it. That he was *enjoying* it.

You're so full of shit.

He muttered the words before finally lowering the gun, and instantly, Johnny was closing the distance between them. I could viscerally feel the flood of his emotions, racing by so quickly that I could hardly get hold of them. And before Griffin even knew what was coming, Johnny had his hands on him. He tore the gun from Griffin's grasp, driving him backward until Griffin lost his footing. And Johnny didn't stop. He shoved Griffin with so much force that he went flying back, disappearing from the glow of firelight until he was swallowed by the dark.

That sickening sound—Griffin's head hitting the stone—made me stop breathing. I think I knew right then. In that very second. Before I scrambled to my unsteady feet. Before I fell to my knees beside his still body. Griffin's wide eyes were open, staring into the sky, and he was just . . . gone.

It was an accident.

I honestly don't remember who was the first one to say it—me or Micah. I only know that it immediately became true. In a matter of seconds, there was a story.

He was drunk.

He tripped.

There was nothing we could do.

I could see that Micah believed it. And why wouldn't he? He hadn't felt what I did. He hadn't almost audibly heard that scream of fury resounding through my brother's head. I was the only one who knew, in that moment, how badly Johnny had wanted to *hurt* Griffin Walker.

And then I'd watched with my own eyes as he did.

EIGHTEEN

I sat on the beach, my fingers buried deep in the sand as I stared out at the opaque water. This sea reminded me of my brother. The weary, windblown cypress trees on the bluff, the brutal cliff face.

The harshness of the environment made things grow differently here, and maybe Six Rivers was like that, too. I wondered now if that's why Johnny had always said that we were made in the dark.

I wasn't thinking about Autumn anymore. My mind wasn't twisting around the photographs or the timeline or even the day Johnny died. There was only one moment that kept replaying in my mind—Griffin Walker.

The memory was like a brick in my stomach. One I'd gladly swallowed for my brother. But with every day that I was back here, it seemed that night was cast in a brighter and brighter light.

I had always wanted to believe that I understood Johnny in a way that no one else did. That I had a handle on what he was and wasn't capable of. But my mind wasn't just spinning now. It was unwinding. I had the distinct feeling that the world around me was coming undone. And there was nothing I could do to stop it.

What I had never allowed myself to consider was whether my

brother was really, truly broken. Whether he didn't fit in this world for a reason. And maybe between the two of us, I was the only one who hadn't actually known that.

Micah found me after the sun began to set, rippling on the water like liquid fire. The fog had cleared just enough for the sky to peek through, changing the color of the sea. I didn't pull my eyes from the waves as he sat beside me or turn to look at him when his arm touched mine. We sat there in silence for a long time before I finally said it.

"He was going to get kicked off the project."

Micah turned to look at me. "What?"

"Josie. She told me Johnny was poaching the invasive owls that were impacting the outcomes of the study. He was worried his sectors would be eliminated from the report because they weren't viable. If that happened, his owls wouldn't be included in the protections. So, he started controlling the numbers himself and Josie threatened to report him to the board."

Micah let out a taut breath. "What the hell was he thinking?"

"That's the question, right? That's always been the question."

Micah didn't speak, but I could see that he was struggling to come up with some kind of explanation. Some reasoning that would dispel the implication of what I was saying. Because I wasn't just talking about the owls. I was talking about Autumn, Griffin . . . everything. I was even talking about him.

"How did you know that Johnny knew about us?" I asked.

Micah stayed quiet, turning his face into the wind blowing up the beach. It pushed his hair across his forehead, making that flash of his younger self come back to life.

"Tell me."

He thought about it a moment, as if deciding how much he wanted me to know. "Because he told me he did."

"When?"

"I don't know. A while before the night Griffin died."

I folded my legs beneath me, shifting so that I could look at him. "Why didn't you tell me?"

"Delaying the inevitable, I guess? He told me to break things off with you, that I was going to hold you back."

A bitter laugh escaped my lips. "From what?"

"From everything. Life, leaving, whatever."

"And were you going to? Break things off, I mean?"

His eyes were still pinned on the horizon. "I didn't have to."

A sting lit behind my eyes as a familiar anger bubbled up inside of me. I never had to break the news about Byron to Johnny and Micah, because Griffin had done it for me. And when I told Johnny I wasn't sure about going, he'd been furious. It was the worst fight we'd ever had.

I could still see him pacing our living room, my acceptance letter clutched in his hand. His voice boomed in the claustrophobic space of the cabin as I leaned into the fireplace, watching him. He was coming undone in the days after Griffin died, and even I couldn't hold him together.

For the first time, Johnny looked different to me. I couldn't un-feel that rage that had coursed through his veins. I couldn't erase the sight of him going after Griffin, of them both disappearing into the dark.

I think Johnny felt it, too. I think he'd scared himself that night. And in the days that had followed, he'd barely even looked at me.

You're going.

He said it with a finality that loosed the knot inside of me. I'd dreaded making the decision, but now Johnny was making it for me. Like he didn't just believe that I needed to get away from him, but that he needed me gone, too.

If you don't . . . I mean, if you don't, James, then what the fuck are we even here for?

What I hadn't expected was that Micah hadn't once tried to stop me. He'd never even said that he didn't want me to go. After that night in the gorge, he stopped calling. Stopped coming by. He pulled away from me until I was so alone that I didn't feel like I *could* stay.

It wasn't until Griffin's funeral, as the three of us stood side by side staring at that casket, that I'd made up my mind. I wasn't just afraid of becoming my mother anymore, getting stuck in this town and letting it erase me. I was afraid of the person I'd already become.

The waves climbed higher up the beach as Micah and I sat there, the sound of the ocean roaring.

"What if he wasn't who we thought he was?" I whispered, my voice nearly lost to the wind.

Micah didn't answer.

"Well, I guess he got everything he wanted," I muttered, voice broken. I couldn't say the same for the rest of us.

"He wanted you away from here, James. Away from *him*."

I wiped the tears from my face, trying to breathe through the pain waking inside of me. I wondered now if I hadn't known that, even back then. Because I wasn't ever actually scared of Johnny. I knew he'd open his own veins before he ever let anything happen to me. But I *was* scared, I was terrified, of finding out who he really was.

Nineteen

Over the next two days, I called Autumn a total of six times and texted her twice.

I'd done my best to leave messages that wouldn't scare her off from calling me back. But still, I hadn't heard from her. Now, I was sitting in the 4Runner with the engine running and Smoke sleeping in the back, watching the diner like a psychopath.

All day, people had been trickling back into town with blue and white paint smeared on their car windows from the melting flurries in the air. The team had won the game and the banner erected in the post office window had been switched out with one that said, WELL DONE, COUGARS.

Teenage boys climbed out of the cars one by one as they arrived, but I was waiting for one in particular—Ben Cross.

I watched the glass windows of the diner over the steering wheel, a chaotic hoard of complete and utter insanity on a loop in my mind. The minutes ticked by as I compulsively tapped through the long list of voicemails on Johnny's phone, listening to each one.

There weren't any messages from Autumn's unsaved number, and a majority of the voicemails were automated recordings from telemarketers or scammers. I propped my elbow on the edge of the car door window so that I could rest my forehead against my hand as I listened to the next one. After a few seconds, I was already hitting delete.

I was so unbelievably tired. Of all of it. The grief, the questions, the unknown corners of Johnny's life. I absently tapped the next message in the queue, and when I heard a voice I recognized, I looked down, realizing it was Micah's number. His name was at the top of the screen.

Hey, Johnny. There was a long pause. *Look—I know we're not talking, but I need you to call me back. I'm worried.* Another long pause. *Text me, whatever. Just get in touch. Then you can go back to being pissed.*

My elbow slipped from the window and I leaned forward, opening the details of the message. It was from the day Johnny died.

My eyes lifted to the windshield and I watched the wipers catch the snow, pushing it across the glass. Then I played it again.

Hey, Johnny. Look—I know we're not talking . . .

I paused the message, brow furrowing. Olivia had said that Johnny and Micah were on the outs, but Micah had brushed it off when I asked.

I hit play.

. . . but I need you to call me back. I'm worried. Text me, whatever. Just get in touch. Then you can go back to being pissed.

The message ended, but Micah's voice was still echoing in my mind. By the time he had left that message he'd probably called Johnny several times. He sounded worried, but there was also a weight to the words, like whatever was going on between them wasn't just two friends who'd known each other all their lives blowing off some steam. This felt like something different.

Ben's gray truck finally pulled up along the curb, parking illegally, and I sat up, hands hooked to the wheel. After a few seconds, he got out.

His eyes were fixed on the illuminated screen of his phone as he crossed the street, earbuds in with an apron thrown over his shoulder. He was starting his shift.

I waited for almost ten minutes before I finally got out of the

4Runner, attempting and failing to talk myself out of what I was about to do. The door slammed behind me and I crossed the street, dodging icy puddles and pulling my thin jacket tighter around me. The diner was still bustling when I ducked out of the cold, tugging my scarf from around my neck. Behind the bar, a woman I'd seen once before was ringing up a couple at the register.

I took the stool at the end of the counter, opening the menu in front of me and pretending to look it over. The bell jingled as the two women left, and a few seconds later, Ben came through the swinging door to the kitchen. I watched as he started clearing the table, thinking that every time I saw him, I saw more of Johnny. Except for those eyes—a piercing blue that made him look so much like Sadie. Even in the shadow that seemed to always be beneath them.

I couldn't help but also measure him against the description Olivia had given me. She'd called him *fragile,* and looking at him now, there *was* something that felt true about that, though I didn't know exactly what it was.

He made his way down the counter, but he didn't look at me, refilling the bowl of lemons beside the iced tea dispenser with a pair of tongs.

"Hey, Ben?" I kept my voice down, trying to avoid the attention of the women seated down the bar.

He glanced over his shoulder, those brilliant, glassy eyes catching the light. When he realized I was the one who'd called his name, his gaze moved over the diner slowly. Like maybe it was a mistake.

"Yeah?" He had that sheepish look again, like he thought he was in trouble.

I set down the menu, trying to figure out what to do with my hands. "I had a question for you, if you have a sec?"

He seemed to consider me for a moment before he left the lemons and came to stand in front of me. He leaned into the counter with both hands, making me aware of just how tall he was. Nearly as tall as Micah. I hadn't really gotten a good look at him up close. He was handsome and even looked a bit older than he was. But it wasn't my brother's face that flashed through my mind when I looked up at him this time. It was Griffin's.

"Can I get something for you?" he said.

The kitchen door swung open and Sadie came out, bracing a tall stack of plates in her arms. Without even looking where she was going, she slid them onto the counter beside the register.

I turned my body slightly away from her. "You know Autumn Fischer, right?"

Ben appeared startled by the question, taking his hands from the counter and finding something to clean instead. He tugged a rag from the ties of his apron, wiping at the surface along the back wall. "Yeah. I know her."

"I'm trying to get in touch with her, and I was wondering if you've heard from her recently?"

His wiping slowed, but he didn't answer. Behind him, I could see that Sadie was watching us now, eyes moving between us.

I tried again. "My brother was—"

"I know." Ben cut me off abruptly, and his gaze fixed on mine, unblinking. His tone had taken on an unexpected edge that I couldn't pinpoint the origin of. Was it the mention of Johnny, Autumn, or both of them?

"I haven't heard from Autumn since she left Six Rivers," he said.

I studied his posture, his body language exuding that same rigidity I could hear in his voice. "Do you know how I can reach her?"

"No."

He swept the rag over the counter again, but I leaned in closer.

"Are there any other friends in town that I could—"

"I told Johnny before. I haven't spoken to her."

"Johnny? When did he ask you about Autumn?"

He lowered his voice. "Look, if my mom hears me talking about this, she's gonna freak out."

My brow furrowed, trying to interpret what exactly that could mean. But when I opened my mouth again, Sadie was suddenly behind him.

"Honey, can you get that trash out for me? The bins should still have room." She had one protective hand set on her son's shoulder.

He answered with a nod, moving past her toward the kitchen.

"Thanks." She watched him go before she turned back to me. "Sorry." She smiled apologetically. "I couldn't help but overhear you two talking about Autumn, and honestly, it's a very sore subject."

"Oh, I'm sorry." My eyes went to the swinging kitchen door, where Ben had disappeared from view. "I didn't know."

"Is there something I can help you with?" she asked, carefully drawing my attention back to her. There was a vigilance in her face now, too, carefully concealed beneath her sweet, maternal expression. All at once, I could see both versions of her—the girl I'd known twenty years ago and the one who existed now.

"I was just trying to get in touch with Autumn Fischer. I have a phone number but haven't been able to reach her, and I thought she and Ben might still talk."

"Oh, no. They haven't spoken since Autumn left." Sadie picked up the rag Ben left behind on the counter, folding it neatly. "What's this about?"

I tried to think, stringing together bits of information that wouldn't sound suspicious. "I just ran across some of her photographs in Johnny's things—from when they worked together. At the school?" Now I sounded like I was trying to convince her or make excuses for Johnny. I attempted to change my tone. "I wanted to get them back to her."

"Oh." She laughed. "That's sweet of you, but I wouldn't worry too much about it. Autumn's kind of all over the place. The girl's hard to pin down."

"What do you mean?"

She shrugged. "She and Ben dated, and you know how it works in small towns like this one. Sometimes young people get to thinking way too much about their future before they're ready."

I swallowed, knowing too well what that meant. That was me and

Micah. Honestly, it was her and Johnny, too, though it had been one-sided. Sadie had thought for years that she and Johnny were inevitable. That eventually, he'd fall in love with her and they'd end up together. But it had never happened.

"I tried to temper the seriousness of the relationship, of course," Sadie continued. "But Ben had it in his head that Autumn was *it*, and when she broke it off and left, things didn't . . . go well."

I waited.

"She kind of dropped everything on him all at once. Hadn't even told him she was leaving for school."

She met my eyes pointedly, making sure I was drawing the same parallel she was. That was exactly what I'd done to Micah, wasn't it?

"To put it frankly, Ben didn't take it well. He really . . . *struggled* after she left. Back in September he actually tried to hurt himself."

My eyes widened. "Oh my god."

"I wouldn't have mentioned it"—she looked a little embarrassed—"but it's not exactly a secret around here. Everyone in town's already had their turn talking about it." She rolled her eyes. "I'm just telling you now to convey the seriousness of the situation. I've been trying to help him move past it, and it's important that this stuff doesn't get dredged up again, if you know what I mean."

Olivia's mention of Ben being fragile suddenly made sense. She'd probably been referring to the rumors about what Sadie alluded to now.

I let out a breath. "I understand. I'm really sorry. I had no idea."

"How could you?" She gave me another smile, the accusation still hovering between us. I'd broken Micah's heart when I left. I'd turned my back on this town. And I didn't know this place or its people anymore.

She let her gaze linger on me a moment longer before she went back to the stack of plates. The fact that there were uncanny similarities between me and Autumn was unnerving, to say the least. But that's what this forest did, wasn't it? Tell the same stories over and over?

For the first time, I was asking myself what exactly about Autumn Fischer had managed to transfix this sleepy logging town. Even Olivia had what felt like a shrine dedicated to the girl in her classroom. What hold did she have over this place? These people?

My gaze traveled over the pictures on the wall, looking for one of Autumn, but I didn't find one. If Ben hadn't heard from her since she'd left, then maybe Olivia was the only person who'd been able to get ahold of her. I didn't love the idea of going back and asking her more questions about Autumn, and I was long past the point where I should talk to Amelia Travis about all of this. That was the next thing I needed to do.

I stepped out onto the sidewalk and started up the street, but when I felt the hair-raising tingle of someone's attention on me, my pace instinctively slowed. I turned my head, scanning the road until I found a pair of eyes on me. It was Ben.

He sat behind the wheel of the gray truck, and as soon as I spotted him, he looked away, turning the key in the ignition. The engine rattled to life and he fumbled with the gear, pulling out of the parking spot a little too fast. Exhaust billowed from the tailpipe as he made it up the road, but just before he turned out of sight, he looked at me in the rearview mirror. My feet stopped and I held his gaze, trying to read him. There was something harsh and heavy in his expression before he turned out of sight.

As soon as I got back in the 4Runner, I checked my phone again for a missed call or text from Autumn. But there was nothing, and I was finished waiting.

I pulled up her Instagram profile, scrolling through the posts to find the handles that appeared most frequently. @sooziekyoo was a mostly dead account, and @firstfrostchronicle looked like nothing more than a hobby photographer's page filled with abstract macro lens shots.

I clicked on Autumn's tagged photos next. There weren't many, but several posts by other accounts had tagged her going back as far as three years. She wasn't the main subject of most of the pictures, but there was one particular post by @marimarimayhem where Autumn's face took up half the image. I clicked on it.

It was a photo of Autumn and another girl, their faces cheek to cheek. The caption read, *Roomies! Five weeks and counting!*

I tapped the handle of the account that posted it and the second girl's face filled the feed. The profile listed the name as Maria Alvarez, and the description beneath it had a few song lyrics and an emoji of a graduation cap followed by *Freshman at Byron School of the Arts.* According to the captions, the posts before and after the one with Autumn appeared to be from freshman orientation. This girl was Autumn's roommate.

I sat up straighter, tapping the message button. I knew I'd already taken this too far, but if Autumn wasn't going to respond to me, I needed to try something else. Anything else.

I typed, holding my breath.

> Hi, sorry to reach out like this, but I'm trying to reach Autumn Fischer. Do you know how I can get ahold of her? It's urgent.

I tossed the phone onto the passenger seat and started the car, but before I even had the gear in reverse, the screen lit up again. I picked up the phone, reading the notification.

@marimarimayhem replied to you

I hit the banner and the app automatically reopened to where Maria's message was nested beneath mine.

> lol if you find out, let me know
> She owe you money too?

My brow creased as I typed a reply.

> Sorry?

I messaged back and a symbol appeared onscreen to indicate that Maria was typing. I waited. Her response popped up a second later.

autumn ghosted me

                                                            When?

before the semester started

Before the semester started would have been back in, what? August?

                              Oh, I'm sorry—I thought you were her roommate?

i was supposed to be she never showed

i met her at orientation

the school matched us for off campus housing and we were supposed to room together, but she never showed up

just stopped calling me back and never paid her half of the stuff i got for the room

figured she decided not to leave her psycho boyfriend

I let the phone drop into my lap, fingers pressing to my bottom lip as my mind raced. I tried to fit it into the timeline I'd put together. Autumn had left for Byron in August. Johnny had made a large tuition payment before that, and everyone I'd talked to said the same thing—that Autumn was away at art school in San Francisco.

But what if she wasn't?

TWENTY

I stood on the top step of the back porch, staring into the dark.

Smoke was already whining at the back door when I got home. He wasn't used to being confined or left behind, and he was restless from being stuck inside all day. As soon as I'd opened it, he bolted out into the dark, leaving only the sound of his paws on the frosty grass.

I wrapped the sweater tighter around me, watching my breath fog in the air before it disappeared. Behind me, the cabin was just beginning to warm with the fire, but the moon was full and bright, lighting the tree branches overhead in a shimmer that looked otherworldly. I felt smaller beneath them than I ever had before.

I'd always known that Johnny was a tangled knot, but I'd believed I was the only one who could unravel him. I thought I knew all his secrets, but in the years since I'd left, he'd painted me a picture of his life that wasn't real, coloring in the details just enough so that I wouldn't worry or ask questions. I'd played along, because if I didn't, I'd have to admit to myself that Johnny wasn't okay. And now, I had to reckon with it.

The fact that Autumn never showed up at Byron felt like confirmation that whatever happened that day at the gorge, it wasn't as simple as Johnny being in the wrong place at the wrong time. There were too many questions now. Too many things that didn't make sense. I didn't know how they all fit together, but I wasn't going to stop until I found out.

I didn't know enough about Autumn to guess why she'd bailed on her opportunity at Byron, but I knew what it was like to not want to be found. To need to forget everything that happened before. I also knew that sometimes, you questioned everything, even the things you thought you always wanted.

The day after Griffin Walker's funeral, I packed a bag. I didn't know if I could do it. Leave Johnny, Micah, Six Rivers. I didn't know if I wanted to. But after what we did, everything I wanted to stay for was tainted with that decay. I didn't like who we were anymore, and I thought that if I left, I could erase it. I could somehow recast who I was in a different life.

There were plenty of people who wouldn't understand what had made Autumn throw away an opportunity like the one she had. It sounded like half the town had pulled together to ensure she could go to Byron, and then, what? She'd just taken off? There had to be a reason.

Then there was Ben. Maria's mention of Autumn's boyfriend didn't exactly match with the quiet, nervous teenager I'd met. Olivia's description of *fragile* felt somewhat accurate, but Maria had called him a *psycho*. Now, I wondered if the boyfriend Maria was talking about wasn't Ben at all. Maybe she'd been talking about Johnny.

Micah was the other problem. He hadn't been honest when I asked him if he and Johnny had been fighting, and I'd suspected that he wasn't telling me everything. The voicemail I'd heard on Johnny's phone proved that he was lying. I just didn't know about what.

I scanned the forest for any sign of Smoke's silver-gray fur, but there wasn't a single light visible through the trees and the road was empty, making it feel as if I was floating in a pool of black. I whistled, attempting to call him back, but it was still silent. A cold, tingling feeling crept over my skin as my eyes tried to focus. I came down the back steps slowly.

"Smoke!"

The frozen ground crunched beneath my feet as I walked toward the forest. The silence grew into a muted sound that swelled and stretched before an earsplitting *boom* exploded in the trees, making me jump. The sound echoed out around me, ringing in my ears.

I gasped, turning in a circle, and searched the darkness in the direction of Rhett's cabin, looking for any sign of light. It sounded like a gun.

I cupped my hands around my mouth, shouting, "Smoke!"

My heart was beating hard now, my breaths getting faster and shorter. My footsteps broke into a run and I caught myself on the trunk of a tree when I heard a rustling sound. I froze, turning my ear to the dark and listening. There was scratching. The rasp of breath.

When it didn't stop, I took a step forward, trying to focus my eyes on anything the moonlight touched. But it only came through the canopy in thin, broken beams that touched the forest floor in tiny circles of white. I took my phone out and turned on the flashlight, pointing it in the direction of the trees. But it was too weak, casting a dim glow around me.

"Smoke!" I called out again, following the sound.

I flinched when his eyes flashed, reflecting in the darkness, and I almost stumbled backward, catching myself on a tree. He was moving, his head dipped low, and when I got closer, I realized where we were. The fire pit.

"*Shit.*"

Smoke's fur was dusted white with ash, and I grabbed hold of his collar, dragging him back. Behind me, the cabin was lit up by the kitchen light, the back door cracked open. I yanked him toward it, trying to lead him in the opposite direction. But when the phone light landed on a flash of white in the fire pit, I stopped.

I kicked aside the fallen copper pine needles until I found it. Something pale that looked like a stone. I sank down, using the tip of my finger to unearth it, but when it lifted from the ashes, I could finally make out the smooth arc of its surface. It wasn't a rock.

I turned it over in my fingers, but the moment I realized what it was, I dropped it. It was a bone.

Smoke pulled free of my grasp, bounding back toward the cabin, and I sank down to my knees, eyes squinting. There was another one, half uncovered in the ash from Smoke's digging, but the shape of it was almost spherical, with angles and points. I picked up one of the wide flat stones that circled the fire pit and scraped the dirt until it was freed. I stared at it, blood running cold.

It was a small skull.

I turned it in the beam of my phone's flashlight. Two large, empty eye sockets peered at me above the curve and point of a beak. My eyes focused past it, to the drifts of pine needles that filled the fire pit. I dropped the skull and it hit the rocks with a crack. Before I even realized what I was doing, I was raking through the ashes with my hands. And I couldn't stop. I dug, ignoring the feeling of grit beneath my nails as my panting breaths fogged in the air around me. I could taste the ash on my tongue. Feel the bile climbing up my throat.

My fingers caught form after form, and I pulled them up, holding them in the light. Bones. There were dozens of them. More than that, even.

A small scream escaped my throat and I clambered back to my feet, staring down at them wordlessly. Josie had been right. Johnny was poaching. He had shot them in the forest, brought them back here, and burned them. Every single one.

I took a step backward, then another, that sick feeling uncurling inside me. Clumsily, my feet raced back toward the cabin, where the door had been pushed wide open by Smoke. He was standing in the kitchen when I made it inside, and I pressed my weight into the door, closing it. My dirty hand smeared on the glass as I pushed off of it, headed straight for the sink.

I scrubbed my hands beneath the scalding water, staring at my reflection in the window and trying to control my breathing. I could feel it all coming together, making a picture I couldn't quite see. Like the first lines of a drawing, the abstract forms that were only minutes from taking shape.

I turned off the faucet, hands still dripping as I slowly turned to face the hallway. Johnny's bedroom door stood closed at the other end. I hadn't dared cross the threshold since I'd gotten here. And why? Was it because I was afraid of facing the truth that he was really gone? Or was it because I was terrified of seeing Johnny—*really* seeing him?

I stared unblinking at the door. Usually, I tried to push Johnny's presence away, gathering it up and shoving it deep down into the place it was coming from. But I could feel him seeping through the cracks in that door, spilling out into the hallway and filling the space. Like he was waiting for me.

When I couldn't take it anymore, I opened it, walking straight toward the dresser and turning on the lamp. I pulled open the drawers and took out their contents, shaking the T-shirts loose for anything that might be hiding in their folds.

Johnny's presence intensified around me, making the ache bloom in my chest. He was everywhere, like smoke sucking the air out of the room. But I didn't stop. I opened the next drawer, and the next, until the dresser was empty. Then I was tugging back the sheets on his bed, feeling beneath the pillows. Then the mattress. I pulled out the storage boxes that were pushed beneath the frame and tore off their lids, not even knowing what I was looking for. I just needed something that felt like answers.

Smoke's barking echoed out in the hall, a sharp, reverberating sound that made me wince. I ignored it, opening the chest at the foot of the bed and rifling through stacks of negatives and old camera gear. There were lenses carefully secured in their cases and boxes of bulbs. The mess littered the floor around me as I turned, looking for any sign of another hiding place.

I went to the desk next, rooting through the papers and letting the stacks topple to the floor before I was raking through the items on the corkboard. But when I tore the loose papers from their pins, searching for the note I'd seen, it was gone.

You changed my life.

It was missing. The note from Autumn was missing.

When Smoke began to howl, I turned to him, anger changing the shape of my voice. "Smoke! Cut it out!"

I came around the corner of the wall to find him in front of the closet again, eyes boring into the door.

"What?" I was shouting now, on the verge of tears. "What do you want?"

I flung the door open and it slammed on its hinges before I turned on the light, shoving the jackets aside. Then I was tugging them from their hangers, furiously checking the pockets before I let them drop to the floor. But when I took Johnny's blue plaid coat into my hands, another sob broke in my chest. I stared at it, fingers clutching it tight, and when I pressed it to my face, I had to lean into the doorjamb to keep myself on my feet.

I knew my brother. I *thought* I knew him. But everything that had happened since I got to Six Rivers told me I didn't. I didn't know why I was surprised. Johnny had always had secrets; I just didn't want to see them. And now, standing in the aftermath of his life, all I could do was wait for the smoke to clear.

Maybe the truth was, Johnny had been showing me who he was for our entire lives. Maybe I'd just created a version of him in my mind that I could live with. But if he'd been lying and hiding from me before, he wasn't now. Since the moment I came back, I'd been able to feel him reaching out to me. Trying to tell me something. Now, it was time to listen.

The idea swirled in my mind, making the nauseous feeling in my stomach swell. Slowly, I opened the coat, slipping an arm inside. When I pulled it on, a rush of cold bled through me.

The sound of rain falling outside filled the house, but when I looked to the window, there was only snow drifting in the air. A flash of bright light filled the dark cabin, followed by the crack of lightning, and I tried to root myself down into it, forgetting the world around me.

There was a click—the sound of the bulb overhead being turned on. But it was still dark in the closet. I reached up, pulling the string, and the yellow light flooded the small space. Instinctively, I moved forward, hand braced on the open door. I leaned into the feeling of Johnny's movements, his position in the space around me. I stepped out of the mess that filled the hallway and fit myself inside the closet. The gleam of light on the barrel of the gun pulled my attention to the dark corner, but then I looked up, studying the ceiling. The bulb swung over my head, making the light bend and shift on the walls around me. I caught it with my fingers, and that's when I saw it.

The wall above the door was missing its panels, creating a cubby between the exposed studs. It was the singularity of the color that gave it away. Immediately, I recognized what lay inside.

I reached up, fingers grasping at the edge, but the opening of the hollow was just out of reach. I pushed out into the hall and went to the kitchen, taking one of the wooden chairs from the table. When I got back to the closet, I kicked the pile of boots and jackets out of the way, making room to set it down. I was shaking all over when I pulled myself up to stand on it. Both hands lifted into the opening, taking hold of what was stowed there.

The backpack. Autumn's backpack.

Instantly, Smoke stopped barking, turning in a nervous circle as he whined. I came down onto the floor beside him, tucking my legs beneath me.

The pastel pink canvas was stained with mud, the fabric stiff with it, but the black Sharpie designs were still visible, a tangle of swirling patterns that connected and flowed.

I pulled the bag into my lap and slowly unzipped it. Inside, there were a couple of water-stained notebooks with rippled pages and a smaller, toiletry-sized bag. I opened it, fingers sifting through its contents. It was makeup—a blush compact, mascara, lip gloss, and a pair of tweezers. I set it on the floor and dug to the bottom of the bag, where a couple of ruined pieces of paper and a smashed granola bar were buried.

With the large compartment emptied, the small front pocket sagged with the weight of what was inside. The zipper was caked in mud, and I had to fight with it to get it loose. As soon as I did, I opened it wider, letting the light fall on its contents.

There was a phone. And a wallet.

The gut-deep sense that something was very wrong here was coursing through me now. That ache in my chest had turned into a boulder of stone. I could hardly inflate my lungs around it.

I fished out the phone, impulsively tapping the screen and pressing the button on the side to be sure it was dead. When I tilted it in the light, I could see that it was cracked in several places. I unclasped the wallet. The leather was rigid from water damage, but Autumn's face was peeking out from behind the thin plastic sleeve. Her license.

There was a debit card, a Visa gift card, her student ID from the high school. There were even a couple of mildewed twenty-dollar bills inside.

I dropped it on the empty backpack, pressing my hands together in front of my mouth. Autumn's phone, wallet, keys—everything—were strewn on the floor around me. But where the hell was Autumn?

The idea was like a gathering smoke in my mind, choking out every thought, every feeling. The wide-open chasm that Johnny had left behind was now howling with a single possibility. A bone-chilling idea—that maybe Johnny *wasn't* just trying to tell me something.

Maybe he was trying to *confess*.

TWENTY-ONE

I pounded on Micah's door with a closed fist, pain exploding in my hand.

The cabin was awash in the 4Runner's headlights, and I watched my shadow shift on the windows, Autumn's backpack clutched to my chest with one arm beneath the opening of Johnny's coat. I was still trembling. Still trying to catch my breath.

I didn't remember standing up off the floor in the hallway or finding the car keys. I didn't remember thinking about where I was going or why. It was as if time had stopped completely the moment I unzipped that bag. Like I'd blinked and suddenly appeared here, standing on Micah's porch in the falling snow. I couldn't even feel the cold anymore.

Footsteps sounded on the other side of the door before it opened, and when he saw me, the lines in Micah's forehead carved deep with confusion. He eyed the blue checkered coat I was wearing—Johnny's coat.

"James?" When he spoke my name, it took on a shape I didn't recognize.

I just stared at him, willing my lips to move, but they wouldn't. The connection between my brain and the rest of my body had been severed. I had no clue how I was even standing upright.

When I said nothing, Micah pulled me inside. "What's going on?" He sounded scared. He *looked* scared.

Clumsily, numbly, I untangled myself from him, walking to the kitchen table, where I set down the backpack. I was still trying to convince myself that it was real. That I hadn't imagined it into existence. When I looked at Micah, he, too, seemed to not understand what he was seeing.

I paced back and forth along the length of the table, hands going into my hair. "It was in his house." I could barely hear myself. My voice was so thin.

"What?"

I gestured toward the backpack, the words unintentionally incomplete. "It was just . . . in his house."

"James, what the hell is going on?" He grabbed my wrist and held it between us, forcing me to stop. His touch was hot and burning on my frozen skin.

I pulled from his grasp, putting a few inches between us.

"Where did you get that?"

"I told you." I tried to slow my words down. "I found it at Johnny's."

Micah stared at it another few seconds before he stepped forward and opened the bag. He didn't react at first, moving around the contents until he saw the phone. When he did, he didn't touch it. "Is that . . . ?"

"Her wallet. Keys. Everything." I finished his thought.

Micah ran a hand over his face, palm pressing to his mouth.

"When's the last time you saw Autumn Fischer?" I asked, hollow.

His answer was distracted, his own mind racing. "I don't know. This summer? Before she went to school."

"Except she didn't. She never went."

"What?"

"Autumn never made it to Byron. Never showed up."

"What are you saying?"

"I'm saying that Autumn is gone! Missing! And her backpack was in my dead brother's house!" Saying it out loud made it, impossibly, more horrifying. "So you're going to tell me the truth. *All* of it. Right now."

Micah pinned his pensive gaze to the floor between us. He was biting back his words. Growing more rigid as he swallowed them down.

"*Now.*" My voice rose.

"I don't know anything about this."

"Stop lying to me!"

"I'm not!"

I was ready to push him all the way off the cliff. I pulled my brother's phone from my pocket, finding the voicemail and playing it on speaker.

Hey, Johnny.

I set it down on the table, crossing my arms.

Look—I know we're not talking, but I need you to call me back. I'm worried. Text me, whatever. Just get in touch. Then you can go back to being pissed.

The message ended, and slowly, Micah's eyes lifted to meet mine.

"What were you and Johnny fighting about?" My voice was barely audible. "What did he do, Micah?"

Slowly, Micah's expression shifted. He was meeting my eyes now, hands heavy at his sides. "I don't know. I mean, I'm not sure."

"Not sure about what?"

He paced toward the fireplace, and when he turned back in my direction, he wasn't looking at me anymore. "There were rumors going around that Johnny and Autumn were . . . getting involved. At first, I didn't think there was any way it was true, but they were spending a lot of time together and—and I don't know—I was just concerned."

I stared at him.

"I confronted him about it and he totally lost it. He wouldn't answer any of my questions, wouldn't even have the conversation. I told him that if something was going on, he had to end it. And that if he didn't, I wasn't going to cover for him. Not this time."

A shaking breath escaped my lips. "When was that?"

"Last summer. In June. He stopped talking to me. Wouldn't return my calls—nothing."

I tried to place it on the timeline in my head. That was before Johnny made the tuition payment to Byron. Before Autumn was supposed to leave for school.

"So, you hadn't talked to him for months before he died."

Micah's jaw clenched, making the muscles in his throat strain. "No. He'd still show up and borrow the camper sometimes, but he just completely shut down. Didn't want anything to do with me."

"I *asked* you." I took a step toward him. "I asked you if something was going on."

"I know."

"And now you're telling me that he was fucking a teenager? Is that what you're saying?"

"She was eighteen," he muttered, pinching the bridge of his nose.

"Are you serious?" I gaped at him.

"I know! Okay?" he shouted back. "It's fucked! But I never saw any actual proof that anything was going on, and he never admitted it to me."

"I can't believe this." I glared at him. "I can't believe *you*."

He stifled a laugh. "Me?"

"Yes, you! How could you not tell me about this? How could you let this happen?"

Micah sank into the chair beside the fireplace, a look of utter disbelief coming over him. We stared at each other, my blood boiling hot.

"That's what we do, right?" His voice lowered.

"What?" I enunciated the word.

He flung a hand toward me. "This! This is what we do."

"I don't know what you're talking about," I snapped.

"We cover for him. That's what we've always done, you and me. We take care of Johnny. We fix his mistakes. And deep down, *you* didn't want me to tell you," he said, dealing from the bottom of the deck.

My insides were writhing now. And not just because of what Micah was saying. It was how those words made me feel. He saw right through me, like always. There was no hiding with him. Everything always felt so naked. So exposed.

"That's why you always took the fall for him, right? Because you couldn't deal with who he was." He kept going, pushing farther into the territory we'd managed to avoid.

"That's not true." I swallowed, feeling sick.

"It's why you left."

"No."

"It is. And you know it. I mean, you blew up your whole life because of him."

"You think that's what I did when I went to San Francisco? Blew up my life?"

Micah's hand went to his brow, rubbing between his eyes like he had a headache. "That's not what I meant."

"Then what did you mean?"

"You just left, James. You couldn't cope with what happened, so you just cut it all from your life and pretended like it never existed. Like *we* never existed."

I closed my eyes, trying to find a way to erase myself from that moment. And not just because of what Johnny did. I didn't want to talk about the role I'd played in what happened.

"You have to stop taking responsibility for everything. What happened to Griffin was an accident. Did we do the right thing by lying? Probably not. But we can't change it."

I stared at him, that word—*accident*—twisting in my mind.

Micah looked so tired that the weight of it almost visibly dragged him down. "We're not kids anymore, James. I loved Johnny, but he was who he was. He was erratic and impulsive. Sometimes, he was fucking selfish. You can't just put all of that on me. Or yourself."

I stood there, unmoving, stunned by the truth of the words. I hated them. I hated him for saying them out loud. Because we both knew they were true. I couldn't feel the heat brimming beneath my skin or the stinging cold in my fingertips anymore. I couldn't feel any single thing because if I did, I'd feel it all—an entire ocean of pain and regret and fear that I'd held on to like a life raft for my entire life.

"And Autumn?" I rasped. "What if he did something to her, Micah? What if he . . ."

His eyes focused, more alert now. "You . . . what? You think he *killed* her?"

"I don't know what I think."

"He wasn't perfect, James. But Johnny wasn't a murderer."

I searched his eyes, looking for any sign that he was just trying to protect me from it. But Micah looked convinced. And why wouldn't he be? He didn't know what I did.

"It wasn't an accident," I whispered.

"What?"

"Griffin Walker. It wasn't an accident. Not really."

"What are you talking about?"

I was shaking all over now. "I could feel it, Micah. When Johnny went for that gun, when he went after Griffin, he wanted to hurt him."

An unreadable expression flooded Micah's face. He was still now. He didn't even look like he was breathing.

"He *wanted* to hurt him. And he did."

There was no way for Micah to know it. And I wasn't even sure what he would have done if he had. We'd all agreed to lie. I remember the three of us standing out there in the dark with the dying fire, watching one another to see who would say it first. And we'd all kept our promise.

His chest rose as he took in a long, measured breath. Like he was trying to line up this new information with everything else. Like he was trying to reason out what he knew about Johnny. About all of us.

That was a weight I'd carried for too many years, and now, it was on him.

"You think he meant to kill Griffin?"

"I don't know. But I know he wanted to hurt him. And even if he didn't, it doesn't excuse what we did. It doesn't make it right. We *lied*, Micah."

"I know."

"We were there. We saw what happened."

"I *know*."

"I don't want to believe it. But all of this doesn't add up. Something . . ." My voice constricted. I couldn't finish.

He leaned forward. "What?"

I let my head fall back, watching the firelight dance on the ceiling. "Something happened to that girl. I can feel it. And I'm terrified that it was him. That, in a way, it was all of us. What if Johnny was dangerous and we just couldn't see it? Didn't want to see it?"

"No."

I studied him, the tone of his voice—that desperate sense of denial. The urge to grasp at any shred of evidence. It was like trying to convince myself. Micah was maybe the only other person in the world who would extend Johnny the same benefit of the doubt that I had for so many years.

"You're right that I left because of what happened that night. And it wasn't just because I was terrified by the idea of what Johnny had done." I swallowed. "I was terrified of myself. Like I could suddenly see all those years, when I'd made choice after choice to take responsibility for everything he did. I loved my brother"—a sob broke the words—"but I knew I had to get away from him. And I knew that if I left him with you, he'd be safe."

Micah ran both hands over his face again, eyes cast across the room. He let the silence draw out between us before he walked into the kitchen, picking up his phone.

"What are you doing?" I sniffed.

"The thing you won't be able to."

I went for the phone, but he moved it out of my reach. "Wait. We need to talk about this."

"About what?"

My heart was racing, panic seizing every muscle in my body. "About what will happen if people find out about this."

"It doesn't matter, James. He's gone."

He didn't blink, meeting my eyes in a way that told me he meant what he'd said. And he knew that he was right about all of it. Johnny had protected me, but I'd spent *my* whole life protecting him, too. I didn't know how to not do that. I didn't know how to not be that person anymore.

Micah stood there, phone still in hand. He waited patiently for me to nod, and then he dialed. We stood there as it rang, and when he spoke again, the baritone of his voice bellowed in the room.

"Hey, Amelia, it's Micah." He paused. "Sorry for the late call, but I need to talk to you."

TWENTY-TWO

I t was the middle of the night and all was dark downtown except for the glowing window of Amelia's office. She sat behind the desk, looking between me and Micah. We were standing only inches apart, but I could feel the canyon that stretched between us. We'd ripped open the seams of a years-old wound, and it didn't matter how much time had passed, it would never heal. I was beginning to understand that now.

The idea that Johnny might be involved in something that happened to Autumn was the most sickening, terrifying feeling I'd ever felt. I didn't want to believe that he was capable of getting involved with her. But if there were rumors going around and he knew that Micah wasn't going to have his back, what would he have done? What lengths would he have gone to if he was backed into a corner?

"I need you to start from the beginning, James." Amelia's tone was even and measured.

The laid-back soccer mom I'd spoken to on the street a few days ago was gone now, replaced by a cool, collected law enforcement officer who was ready to start combing through a story. The last hour had triggered her instincts, and she was no longer hiding the fact that she was suspicious. Of all of us.

I strung together the events in my mind before I spoke, trying to arrange them in sequential order. I didn't know how to explain it all, especially when I didn't have all the pieces. And I didn't want to say anything about Johnny that I wasn't absolutely sure about.

"When you gave me Johnny's things the day I got here, there was a roll of film in his pocket." I decided to start there.

She nodded. "Yes, I remember it."

"The date he'd written on the canister was November tenth. A couple of days before he died. When I developed the film, this photo was on it."

I set the photograph of the backpack down on her desk. That moment in the darkroom immediately came back to me. The sense that Johnny was there in the shadows. The sound of my name being whispered in his voice. Is this what he'd been trying to tell me?

"It's Autumn Fischer's backpack," I said.

"This is why you were asking if I thought anyone was out there with him? Because you think Autumn was?"

"That's what I thought at first, so I tried to track her down to find out. I wanted to ask if she saw anything or knew anything about what happened that day. But Autumn isn't in San Francisco. She never was. I got in contact with her roommate at school, and she said Autumn never arrived for fall semester. Her tuition was paid, her housing set up. She just never showed."

Amelia's countenance shifted, her shoulders tensing. "But that was in August. This photo is from November?"

I nodded. "I think Johnny must have found it out there when he was working. I talked to Ben, and he says he hasn't heard from Autumn since she left, either. When Johnny got back from the gorge, he was trying to reach her."

Amelia's eyes dropped to the open backpack. The waterlogged wallet and cracked phone were placed in front of her, Autumn's license taken from the sleeve. It was obvious by looking at her things that they'd been out in the forest for a long time. Autumn had been missing for months, and no one had known. Not even Johnny.

"There was also a call to you," I added. "Do you remember talking to him?"

Amelia sucked in her bottom lip, as if trying to decide what she was willing to tell me. "I had a message from Johnny when I got back from Parker's soccer tournament in Redding."

"Do you remember what the message said?"

"Nothing particularly alarming. He just asked me to call him as soon as I got back, and I did. But Johnny was already back out at the gorge." Amelia turned her attention on Micah. "He didn't say anything to you about it?"

"We weren't really on speaking terms, which had to do with Autumn. I don't think he would have come to me about it."

"What do you mean it had to do with Autumn?"

Micah glanced at me, as if asking for permission before he really came clean. This time, I didn't try to stop him.

"I had some concerns. People in town were talking, and when I tried to ask to him about it, it didn't go well. I warned him that he should stay away from her."

"Why would you feel the need to tell him to stay away from her?" She was testing him now, poking at the unspoken implication.

"I thought they were getting too close," he said, simply. "I was worried that people were misinterpreting their relationship. Jumping to conclusions."

That was as close as he was going to come to accusing Johnny, especially when he had no proof.

"And what kind of relationship was that?" Amelia asked.

"Nothing you don't already know. He was helping her out with school application stuff, teaching her about photography. That kind of thing. Olivia is the one who set it up. But they were spending a lot of time together, and I just wanted him to be careful."

Amelia's face betrayed the fact that she'd had her suspicions about Johnny and Autumn. Maybe the whole town did. "You're not the only one who was concerned."

I could feel the defenses rising up in me. I couldn't help it. "What does that mean?"

"It means"—she gave me a pointed look—"the same concern was brought to my attention by another individual."

Micah looked surprised by that.

"And?" I pressed.

"And I looked into it. I spoke to Autumn and she insisted that there was nothing sexual or romantic going on between her and Johnny."

My first thought was that Autumn could have been protecting him. If she was, there was little Amelia could have done about it without any evidence.

"Either way, this changes things," I said. "What are the odds that Autumn going missing and Johnny getting shot are just a coincidence?" That was the question hanging over me. It just felt like too much of a stretch.

I could tell by the look on Amelia's face that she was wondering the same. There'd been nothing circumstantial to frame what happened at the gorge that day, and accidental firearm deaths were nothing new to a forest ranger. But this was more complicated than a wilderness photographer out at a remote location, caught in the path of a stray bullet.

"The first step here is confirming that Autumn is, in fact, missing." She scooted the chair back, reaching into the cabinet behind the desk. Then she took out a box of blue latex gloves, fitting them on her hands. "But it's important to keep in mind that anything's possible."

Micah and I watched as she slipped the backpack into a plastic bag. It was exactly like the one she'd given me when I got to Six Rivers. The one with Johnny's things. Now, Autumn's backpack and everything inside was evidence.

"Do you have any reason to believe that someone would want to hurt Autumn?" she asked.

Micah shook his head, but I hesitated, and Amelia caught it.

She fixed her eyes on me. "What is it?"

I swallowed. "Maybe nothing. But Sadie told me that Ben was devastated when Autumn broke up with him, and that he'd tried to hurt himself after she left."

The thought had crossed my mind more than once. Maybe Ben had done more than get upset when Autumn told him she was leaving. Maybe he'd done something he hadn't meant to. Lashed out in a way he couldn't take back. I'd seen the exact same thing happen that night in the gorge when Griffin Walker died. If Ben had done something he regretted, it was plausible that he might try to take his own life.

There was a shift in Amelia's expression now. "You think Ben Cross—"

"I don't *think* anything. I'm just telling you what Sadie said. If Autumn went missing when she left for school, that lines up with Ben . . . I don't know what he did. A suicide attempt? She didn't give me specifics."

But if the incident had made its way through the town rumor mill, then Amelia already knew what those details were.

"All right. And who exactly touched all of this?" She looked between us, setting a hand on Autumn's things.

"Both of us." I cleared my throat. "And Johnny, I guess."

I tried not to think about how his prints being on the backpack could be used. What kind of picture it could paint.

"And where exactly did you find it?" she asked.

"It was in a closet. Up on a kind of shelf."

"Any idea why he would have put it there?"

I shook my head. "I don't know."

"Would you say from where you found it that you think Johnny was"—she paused—"hiding it?"

The question was constructed carefully, spoken in a tone that I couldn't decipher. My eyes narrowed on her, the meaning of the question clicking into place. "What are you implying?"

Amelia stood, one hand resting on her belt. "I'm just asking for more information so that we can start to figure out what the hell is going on here."

If I was honest, I would tell her that it did seem as if Johnny had tried to conceal the backpack. If he hadn't, why not leave it out somewhere in the cabin? It hadn't just been tossed into the closet; it had been placed up in the cubby. But that didn't mean he was hiding it. It could just mean that he was keeping it safe.

"It was in the closet, like I said. I was looking for something and ran across it."

"What were you looking for?"

"A warmer coat. I didn't bring much with me," I explained, not missing a beat. Amelia already didn't believe me. I wasn't going to give her more ammunition by trying to explain that I thought my brother's spirit was communicating with me from beyond the grave.

"Do you think it's possible that Johnny hurt Autumn?" She asked the question point-blank.

"No." The answer was a knee-jerk reaction.

I waited for the complete and utter certainty to hit me with the words. The overwhelming conviction that it was true. But it didn't come.

She locked the evidence in one of the cabinets behind her. "I'll try to get in touch with Autumn's mom. See when the last time she heard from her was."

"All right." Micah nodded.

"And if you could both stay available and in town, that would be very helpful. I'm going to have more questions. And I'll request access to anything else you've found, James. Johnny's records, accounts, everything."

"Of course," I agreed.

Micah's hand found my back and he guided me to the door. But before we even made it outside, Amelia stopped us.

"I want you both to know," she said, looking between us, "I've spent a lot of time on this town's history since Johnny's death. I've spent a lot of time on *his* history. It goes without saying that the last time Johnny was implicated in the events surrounding someone's death, that due diligence wasn't done by the person who held this office."

Micah's hand tensed on my back.

"But I have every intention of getting to the bottom of what happened here."

The insinuation was clear. Amelia had done her homework not just on Johnny but on all of us. And she wasn't going to leave any stone unturned. Not like Timothy Branson had done.

The sky was still pitch-black when we made it outside, and there were still at least a couple of hours until dawn. But there was no way I was going to sleep tonight.

We walked to Micah's truck in silence and got in. The engine rumbled, warming up as we sat there, staring out the windshield without saying a word. What had just happened? What was *about* to happen?

"We'll grab Smoke and your stuff and you can stay at my place tonight," he said, not really asking.

He pulled onto the road, turning the truck around, and the headlights washed over the icy street. For once, I didn't argue with him. The idea of sleeping in the cabin with all of Johnny's buried secrets made me tremble. I didn't want to know what else I'd find there, and honestly, I was done looking.

TWENTY-THREE

I stood in the middle of the living room, watching the officers go through Johnny's desk.

It had taken two days for Autumn Fischer to be officially declared a missing person, and her face was already hanging in the windows of the shops that lined Main Street.

Interviews with town residents had determined that the last time she was seen was at an end-of-summer party with friends on August 18, the night before she was scheduled to take the bus to San Francisco.

It didn't take long for Amelia to obtain a warrant for the search of Johnny's home after the state police arrived in Six Rivers. Now, they moved through the small cabin wordlessly, stepping over the mess I'd left behind when I tore the place apart. The idea of people poking into Johnny's life made me nervous. It went against every instinct I'd ever had when it came to my brother.

The news about Autumn had engulfed the entire town, and I could only imagine the rumors that had started, especially if there'd been talk about Johnny and Autumn before. I imagined people recounting their suspicions, dredging up what they'd been happy to overlook before all this started.

Amelia's number one priority was to establish a timeline for everyone the night Autumn was last seen. Including Johnny. But it became clear very quickly that he had no alibi. Not one he could give, anyway, because he wasn't here to offer any kind of explanation for how all this looked. And there was no denying that it looked bad.

Micah stood at my side as we watched the officers move through the cabin. We had barely spoken since leaving Amelia's office, the accusations we'd both made like a ricocheting bullet. I'd blamed him. For all of this. And Micah had finally put words to what I'd never been able to admit—that when I left, I'd been running. And I hadn't just left Johnny, I'd abandoned *him*, too.

Standing in the middle of the house I grew up in, it all felt irrevocably true. I could sense Johnny everywhere, as if he was being stirred up like dust as the officers rooted around the place, and it put me on edge. It was as if I was just waiting to see him appear in that hallway or beyond the kitchen window. Like he was seconds from coming back to life.

There wasn't a single corner of Johnny's life that wasn't being overturned. The cabin, the school, there was even a team going through the 4Runner with a fine-tooth comb. And what would they find? Would there be strands of Autumn's hair in Johnny's bedroom? Her fingerprints in his car? Traces of DNA on his boots?

A man in a uniform took the gun from the closet, slipping it into a plastic bag before he carefully labeled it. The laptop was next, followed by the contents of the filing cabinet. A woman went through the papers on the desk, and I watched as she studied the items on the corkboard.

The words scratched on the missing note were still burned into my mind. Autumn's words.

You changed my life.

And what did they mean, exactly? Were they the sentiments of a grateful student who'd found her inspiration, or the romantic adoration of a girl who'd been taken advantage of? I couldn't help but wonder if they were some of her last written words. But it was one piece of evidence the police wouldn't have. I'd scoured the place and still hadn't found it.

The woman bagged a few items before she moved on, and I took a step forward, staring at the bare place it had hung on the bottom right corner of the board. My eyes narrowed on that small, exposed space of cork, a thought surfacing in my mind. I'd wondered if I'd imagined it, and my blood had run cold at the thought that maybe it was Johnny who'd somehow taken it. But what I hadn't considered was that there was one other person who'd been in the cabin—Ben.

It hit me suddenly, and I tried to re-create that moment in my mind. He'd stopped by, letting himself in when I didn't answer the door. But I'd had the innate feeling that something was off when I came inside and saw him coming from the hallway. Had he . . . taken it? If he had, then why?

"James." Amelia was suddenly beside me. "We need you to come down to the office so we can go over a few things." She was speaking gently, the way I imagined a doctor would when it was time to give you terrible news.

Behind her, another officer was taking Johnny's camera from his bag. "Tell them to be careful with that," I said, stepping forward, but Micah stopped me.

"Why don't you go with Amelia and I'll stay here while they finish."

He and Amelia shared a look, like they both thought it was a good idea.

"It won't take long." Amelia reached up to touch my elbow.

I reluctantly started for the door and Amelia followed on my heels. The men outside had the contents of the 4Runner laid out in the driveway, one of them making notes on a clipboard while the other took photos of each item.

"Will everything be returned?" I asked, climbing into her truck.

She clipped her seatbelt. "Everything that isn't retained as evidence."

Amelia pulled out of the drive, and I looked back over my shoulder before the cabin was swallowed by the trees. It didn't look the same to me anymore. Nothing did. I was questioning every memory now, every truth. Taking apart and reshaping all the details of the lives we'd lived here and what they meant. But maybe that was just it. Maybe there was no meaning anymore.

Town came into view ahead, and Main Street was packed with cars again. With people, too, but this time there were no banners or streamers or blue and white paint. This time, there was only shouting.

"What on earth?" Amelia murmured, leaning over her steering wheel.

Several people were clustered in the middle of the street, surrounding a state police cruiser. Beyond it, the door to the diner was propped open and a sea of faces inside peered out through the windows, watching the commotion.

Amelia pulled the truck over, shifting the gear into park. Then she was getting out, and the shouting only grew louder before the door closed behind her.

I opened my own door, stepping onto the street and trying to see over the heads in front of me. A woman's voice cut through the clamor, and a tall police officer had a hand up, as if trying to calm someone down.

". . . you even think about it!"

I thought I could place the voice even before I saw her. Sadie Cross was red-faced, one hand hooked anxiously on the arm of her son, who stood at least six inches taller than her. The police officer had his other arm, trying to guide him toward the car.

"This is ridiculous!" Sadie sounded almost hysterical. "You can't question him without me there."

"Ma'am, he's eighteen years old," the officer replied.

Amelia made it through the packed bodies, getting Sadie's attention.

"Oh, thank god." She was almost in tears now.

Amelia set a hand on Sadie's shoulder, eyes scanning the scene around her. "What's going on?"

"They're trying to arrest my son! That's what's going on!" Sadie cried.

The crowd watched with varying degrees of concern, a few voices murmuring too low to hear. One woman shook her head disapprovingly, and I could tell that at any moment, the lot of them would be ready to tear Ben from the officer's grasp. If the wind blew just right, this whole thing could catch fire.

"Sadie, they're just having him make a statement, just like all the other kids who were at the party that night. They'll ask him some questions and release him. That's it." Amelia's smooth voice turned coaxing and her eyes locked with Sadie's in what appeared to be an attempt to de-escalate the situation.

Ben said something to Sadie, his back to the officer, and she finally let her son go. Her hands clenched into fists at her sides as Ben was put into the car. Once it was moving, the group of onlookers began to disperse, getting out of the road. That's when Sadie's gaze found me.

"*You.*" Her voice cracked as it deepened and her crazed blue eyes flashed before she started in my direction. "This was you, wasn't it?"

I looked around me, confused. Amelia tried to catch hold of Sadie, but she was already out of reach, closing the distance between us fast.

"Are you happy?" she shrieked, making me flinch.

When she finally made it across the street, everyone was watching again.

"Are you happy now?" The words repeated, and before I realized what was happening, her hand lifted into the air and came back down with a snap, striking me across the face.

"Sadie!" Amelia shouted behind her.

A collective gasp loosed from the crowd and I sucked in a breath, stumbling to the side and catching myself on the bumper of a car. When I righted, Sadie was already coming at me again.

Amelia caught up with her and wrenched her backward. She put herself between the two of us and shoved Sadie toward the opposite sidewalk.

My mouth hung open, the pain in my face radiating. I didn't even recognize Sadie. She looked like a wild, crazed animal, her eyes wide and teeth bared as she screamed.

"Get back! Now!" Amelia looked disturbed, taking hold of Sadie's jacket and shoving her backward again.

Furious tears glinted in Sadie's eyes. "What are you thinking, letting these people come in here and haul my son out like a criminal? Hasn't he been through enough because of that girl?"

"This is all procedure, Sadie. This is exactly what we would be doing if it were your child missing."

Sadie was still heaving. "He's a good kid, Amelia. We're a *good* family."

"I know." Amelia was trying to soothe her, a genuine worry in her voice.

"She's the one you should be talking to," Sadie spat, pointing a finger in my direction.

The circle of people was widening around us now and more were spilling from the diner. They were all looking at me.

"Why aren't you asking *her* about Johnny? About him and Autumn?"

Amelia put a hand on Sadie's back, strategically leading her in the opposite direction. Her voice was too low to hear, but Sadie shot a glance backward, that same piercing gaze fixed on me.

I was still frozen, hand pressed to my cheek, when they disappeared into the diner. The faces around me reflected the same expression I was sure was on mine. The whole thing was so bizarre, so unexpected, that I wasn't completely convinced that it had just happened.

Someone handed me a handkerchief just as the spectators began to thin, and I took it, staring at the soft checkered fabric folded into a square. When my eyes lifted to the figure beside me, they went wide.

It was Rhett Walker.

His stoic face peered out from beneath his hat, his wild dark beard hiding the set of his mouth. He stared at me, his squinted eyes painted that same muted gray as his son, Griffin. He was the last person I expected to be standing there. The last person I expected to show me any amount of kindness.

I swallowed. "Thanks."

I dabbed at my face, where a stinging stripe was now throbbing on my cheek. The handkerchief came away with a few blots of blood.

He gave me a nod. "I'm sure you've figured out by now people aren't at their best when they're afraid for their kids." His gravelly voice was like faraway thunder. "I've been there myself."

When I looked at him, I wondered if the strangeness of his expression was guilt. An acknowledgment of what he'd done that day when he came to our house and tried to . . . what? I don't know what he'd intended. But I'd seen that same wild look in his eyes. I'd heard the anguish in his voice. He'd been desperate for the truth. One I had never given him.

"She was at Johnny's the night they're saying she disappeared, you know," Rhett said, gaze fixed on the missing person poster that hung in the window behind us. "That girl."

"What?" I lowered my voice.

He pushed his hands into his pockets. "Heard arguin' and that goddamn wolf making a racket, so I went outside and she was there."

"Doing what?"

"She was leavin' with her boyfriend."

Through the window across the street, I could see Sadie with her face in her hands. Amelia was still beside her, the walkie-talkie raised to her mouth.

"Who was arguing?"

Rhett shrugged. "Don't know. By the time I got there she was climbin' in Ben's truck."

My eyes drifted back to the street.

So, Johnny had been with Autumn that night, but if she'd left with Ben, then Johnny wasn't the last one to see her.

"Did you tell Amelia this?" I asked.

"I learned a long time ago that the last people you can trust to find the truth are the people who get paid to do it." He glanced at the diner window. "Sometimes you have to take matters into your own hands."

Is that what I'd been doing? Taking matters into my own hands? Is that what Rhett Walker had been doing the day that he knocked on the door and took a handful of my hair, screaming?

I held out the handkerchief. "Thanks."

"Keep it." Rhett looked at me for another moment before he started up the sidewalk, adjusting the hat on his head. He didn't look back before he ducked into the market.

I waited in Amelia's truck, watching in the side mirror as the red mark on my face grew darker. When she finally got back, she sat in the driver's seat, staring at her steering wheel.

"I'm sorry about that," she said, voice tight. "It was completely un-called for."

"He was at home that night," I said.

Amelia turned to me. "What?"

"Johnny. He has an alibi." I wiped at my cheek again, folding the handkerchief. "Rhett just told me that he saw Autumn leaving Johnny's late that night with Ben Cross. He picked her up outside."

I watched as Amelia stacked the new information against what she already knew.

"They were arguing."

"About what?"

"He doesn't know. But my brother wasn't the last one to see Autumn Fischer alive."

Beside me, Amelia paled. I could see her thinking the same thing I was. No one had been looking for Autumn because no one knew she was missing. But if Johnny found that backpack out in the gorge, he would have known who she was with that night.

If there was anyone who'd want to be sure that Johnny didn't make it back to tell anyone, it was Ben.

TWENTY-FOUR

❧————•————❧

It took four hours to recount the odyssey I'd been on for the police, and I still wasn't sure I understood everything that had happened.

After going through the two weeks I'd spent in Six Rivers, struggling to exhume every detail of every day, I laid out the clues I'd uncovered about Johnny's connection to Autumn Fischer and the timeline before his death.

To call them clues felt like a betrayal. Like I was admitting that Johnny had something to hide. But that's what they were—breadcrumbs I'd followed to the fraction of truth I'd managed to mine from the quiet existence my brother led in this town.

The investigative team had come from Eureka, setting up a search that should have happened months ago. No one had said it yet, but the odds that Autumn Fischer was alive were almost zero. Some would even say the odds didn't exist.

I went through Johnny's phone with the police, waiting as they logged each phone call, text, and Instagram direct message. I pried apart my brother's life like an apple cut in two.

The door to the makeshift interview room opened and Amelia

stepped inside. She looked like she hadn't slept since the night Micah and I showed up here with the backpack.

"I think we have what we need." She glanced at me, as if searching for any last hints as to what I may be hiding. "For now, at least."

She tilted her head toward the hallway and I stood.

"I need to let you know," she started, "you're well within your rights to press charges against Sadie."

She spoke the words dutifully, but her meaning was clear. She was hoping, for all our sakes, that I wouldn't. That I'd chalk it up to the hysteria of a terrified, protective mother and move on. Honestly, that worked for me.

"And Ben?" I asked.

She glanced at the other closed door down the hall. "Still being questioned."

I had to shoulder my way through the packed office, where officers were huddled at cobbled-together workstations over piles of papers. I recognized some of them from Johnny's house. They were the same pages I'd tried to make sense of for the last two weeks, lining up details so that things would click. But I was finally accepting that there was no riddling out the puzzle that was my brother. There never had been.

By the time I got out to the street, my lungs felt like they might explode. It was snowing, soft flakes floating to the ground in a sweep that made me actually feel how tired I was. Like I could sleep for years. For millennia. That if I laid my head down, I'd wake to another time entirely.

I reached up, gently touching the cut on my swollen cheek. Sadie's blow had also managed to cut the inside of my mouth against my teeth, and it tasted like blood. I still had the urge to flinch, just thinking about the way she had suddenly snapped. I could still see her hand flying through the air. The sound when it struck me.

I took out my phone, finding my texts with Micah and formulating the only message I could muster.

Done.

Within seconds, he was typing a reply.

I'll be there in a few minutes.

I liked the message and stuck the phone in my pocket, marveling at the fact that I believed him. We still hadn't talked or made things right. But right now, wherever he was, Micah was grabbing his keys and his jacket, on his way to the car. He was coming to get me.

The door opened behind me and Sadie Cross stepped out, the red-faced woman from the street now gone. Only a few hours ago, that look in her eyes had been almost feral. Unhinged. Like she was ready to burn down this entire town for her son.

Johnny had done much worse for me.

She leaned against the window on the opposite side of the door, arms crossed over her chest. There were several seconds of silence before she finally spoke.

"I'm sorry about earlier," she ground out. "Really sorry."

I shook my head, meaning to dismiss the encounter entirely, but I was still reeling from it and I wondered if she could tell.

"It's just"—she sniffed in the cold—"all this Autumn stuff. I wish it would end."

That made two of us.

"That girl caused such a mess. Everywhere she went. And the way she broke Ben's heart . . ." She wiped her nose with her gloved hand. "It was like she didn't even care."

I said nothing because there was nothing *to* say. I didn't know what happened between Ben and Autumn, but I knew it couldn't possibly justify anyone causing her harm. I didn't think that was what Sadie was saying, but I also got the sense that she needed me to know that Ben had been a kind of victim. I couldn't help but think that the same had been true about her. Johnny had never loved her back.

The door opened again, and Ben came out with Amelia at his side. The pale, dead look in Sadie's eyes almost immediately vanished. She looked between them, expectantly.

Ben gave his mother a reassuring look that Amelia cemented with a smile.

"All done." She was looking at Sadie, not Ben. "Autumn's mother confirmed that Ben brought her home that night. According to the other kids at the party, he came back and kept drinking. Passed out until morning."

My lips parted, ready to argue, but a loud gasp broke in Sadie's chest beneath the hand she had pressed there. She looked as if the panic she'd swallowed down was finally detonating behind her ribs. She was genuinely frightened. No—it was more than that. She looked like she was in shock.

"Ben's story lines up," Amelia said.

Sadie was completely drained of color. She looked like she was going to be sick. "That's good," she said, her pleading eyes going to Amelia. It was meant as a question.

Amelia smiled. "Yes, very good. Like I said, you have nothing to worry about."

Sadie was crying now, her nose turning bright red. Her teary gaze jumped back to Ben.

It occurred to me in that moment that maybe the reason Sadie had been so desperate when the police came for her son was because she hadn't *known* where Ben was that night. It would certainly explain the unbridled look of surprise and relief on her face now. Maybe she'd been afraid that he *was* involved somehow, the way I was about Johnny.

Ben's eyes were on his mother, and he looked almost puzzled, as if he, too, thought her reaction was strange. The boy-turned-almost-man looked frail and sick, his freckles darker on his skin than I remembered. Again, I had to ask myself what exactly Autumn had seen in him. But then I remembered what Sadie said about small towns and limited options. This kid would probably be running that diner in twenty years with his own kid on the high school soccer team. Autumn was the one who'd gotten out. Almost, anyway.

Ben glanced back at me before he walked Sadie to her car, and Amelia stood at my side, watching them.

"He was out of town the weekend Johnny died," she said. "If you were wondering."

I turned to look at her, my hands so tightly clenched in the pockets of my jacket that my knuckles ached.

"He was gone for four days," she added.

The soccer tournament in Redding, I realized. Amelia had mentioned it when she explained why she hadn't been in town when Johnny tried to call her. If the team had been gone for a game, Ben would have been with them. My mind tried to find a way around it, unable to let go of the last thread I had hold of. If Ben was gone, he couldn't have killed Johnny.

"Sometimes the hardest kind of deaths to accept are ones like this, James," Amelia said. "Accidents are the worst kinds of losses."

She set a hand on my arm, gently squeezing before she went back inside, and I swallowed down the lump in my throat. I didn't know if there was a world where I could believe that, after everything, it was an *accident* that killed my brother. A stupid fucking accident.

There was a kind of cruel irony in that.

Ben opened the door to his truck down the street, and before I'd even decided to, I was walking toward him. When he saw me, he drew back like he was afraid of me.

"Can I talk to you for a minute?"

He hesitated, wetting his lips. "Okay."

"What happened at Johnny's that night?"

Ben searched my eyes, his dark brows coming together. "What?"

"The night you were there with Autumn. Rhett said he heard someone arguing."

He looked up and down the street nervously.

"I need to know, Ben."

"I . . ." He twisted the ring of keys in his hand, mouth opening and closing. "Johnny thought . . ."

"What?" My voice rose.

"He thought he was my dad." Ben spit it out all at once, immediately going flush.

I stared at him.

"He told me a few months before that."

So, Micah was right. Johnny believed that Ben was his son. And when Sadie had refused to give him evidence, he'd most likely gone to Ben.

"And was he?" I asked.

Ben exhaled. "I don't know for sure. I mean, I always kind of wondered, but my mom always said it was a fling with a logger. When I started really pressing her about it, she kind of stopped telling that story. When I asked her about Johnny, she just said . . ."

"What?" I whispered.

"She would just answer with, *You don't want him to be your dad, Ben. Believe me.*"

A white-hot anger rose up in me and immediately, my instinct to defend my brother was there again. But as I stood there, tracing the echoes of Johnny in Ben's face, I struggled to find fault with Sadie. She had her reasons for not wanting Johnny to be Ben's father, and I couldn't deny that at least some of them might have been valid.

"So, why were you arguing that night?" I asked.

Ben hesitated. "Johnny wanted to talk. Autumn and I had already broken up, but she was the only one I'd told about it, so she came with me. But Johnny just kept saying that he wanted to get a test, and I don't know. I just got freaked out. Told him to leave me alone. To stop calling me."

So, that's why Autumn had been at Johnny's that night and also why Ben had been acting so strange toward me since I got to Six Rivers. I couldn't imagine what all of this had been like for him. Finally getting answers only for Johnny to be ripped from his life before he could even wrap his head around it.

"Doesn't matter now, I guess," he said, reading my mind. "It's too late."

His eyes flicked up and there was that flash in them again. An almost imperceptible glint that I could swear I'd seen a million times. It was like seeing my brother from a far distance.

"That day you came by Johnny's, did you take something from his desk?"

Slowly, Ben's eyes widened.

I lifted up an open hand. "You're not in trouble. But I think I know what you took."

He stared at me, jaw clenching.

"I just want to know why."

He searched my face, as if looking for reassurance.

"It'll stay between us. I promise."

He sighed, shifting on his feet. "I kind of . . . broke into Johnny's cabin last summer."

"What?"

Again, his eyes dropped to the pavement. "I don't really know what I was looking for. I guess some kind of proof that he was my dad. But I saw that note from Autumn and I just . . . Things with her had been different. *She* was different, hanging out with Johnny a lot, and I was . . . I don't know. I was jealous."

I waited.

"I started to think that maybe something was going on between them, and when I asked her about it, she was pissed. But I didn't believe her."

Slowly, I was putting it together. This is where the rumors had started, I thought. Not with Sadie. It was Ben.

"I saw the note on the board by his desk and I knew Autumn had written it." Now he looked embarrassed. "I told my mom that I thought Autumn was hooking up with Johnny. I knew she was going to break up with me and, I don't know, I guess I just wanted to get back at them both."

"Why would you need to get back at Johnny?"

"Because he *did* change everything for Autumn. He's the reason she wanted to leave. The reason she applied to Byron." He swallowed. "I didn't want anything to change."

I couldn't help but wonder if that's how Micah had felt. When I left Six Rivers, he hadn't said a word. He hadn't argued or tried to stop me. He'd barely even said goodbye.

"So, why'd you come back and take the note?"

"Ever since what happened to Johnny, I've felt bad about starting the rumors about him. It never really died out. I just didn't want anyone to find that note and think it was, like, confirmation or whatever."

My mouth twisted. Olivia was right about this kid. He was fragile. But in the end, he'd been trying to protect Johnny like the rest of us.

Micah's truck pulled up in front of Amelia's office, the engine roaring and tailpipe pumping a steady stream of exhaust.

"Ben, I want you to tell me honestly. Do you believe Autumn was having a romantic relationship with Johnny?" I tried to keep my tone even, my stare fixed on his face.

"No." He paused. "At least, I don't think so."

I let out a long, heavy breath, my hands finally unclenching. Ben got into the truck, pulling out onto the street, and I watched him drive away before I made my way to Micah's truck. Smoke was in the cab, and I opened the door and climbed inside. Micah had already clocked the cut on my face before I had my seatbelt on.

"What the—?"

"It's nothing."

I batted his hand away when he reached for me, but Micah cupped my chin, forcing me to look at him. He inspected the cut on my lip, tension hardening the look in his eyes.

"What's going on?" His hand slid from my cheek.

I stared out the windshield, a cold, empty feeling flooding my veins. "He didn't do it." I whispered. "Johnny didn't do it."

TWENTY-FIVE

I came down the stairs in one of Micah's old sweatshirts, pulling my hands into the sleeves. Smoke was curled up on the rug, sleepily watching Micah stoke the fire, the dance of the flames reflecting in his eyes.

I sank down onto the sofa, tucking my legs up beneath me and reaching for the half-empty glass of whiskey on the coffee table. I finished it in one swallow, eyes watering as it burned down my throat. As soon as I set it down, Micah refilled it.

He sat down beside me, close enough that his hip touched my leg, and I tried not to let it summon to life the memory of him touching me. For days, he'd been putting distance between us, but here, between the walls of the home he'd made without me, I felt like maybe there was part of him that was within reach.

"I think we should talk," I said, taking another sip from the glass and handing it to him.

"Yeah, I think so."

He shifted so that he could turn toward me, hooking one hand inside my leg, and the feeling of it anchored me. Made me feel steady.

"I don't blame you for what happened. I only said that because I blame myself."

Micah stared into the glass before he leaned forward, setting it on the coffee table. "You blame yourself for what?"

"All of it. All of Johnny's problems. Not protecting him enough. Leaving him." My voice was already on the verge of breaking. "What happened with Griffin."

"How was that your fault?"

I drew in a long breath, trying to gather the courage to say it. "For weeks before what happened, he was trying to . . . I don't know, start something with me. I'd told him about Byron and I think he had it in his head that we were both leaving and that once we did, there would be something between us. That day in the gorge, he tried to"— I paused—"touch me."

Micah's hand slid from my leg and I caught it with mine, holding it there. My fingers wound into his.

"I shoved him off and he was pissed. That's why he got wasted. Why he pointed the gun at me."

"James, there's no way you could have known he was going to do that."

I shook my head. "I didn't."

"Then how can you be responsible?"

"I just feel like everything Johnny did was my fault. I felt like it was my job to keep him safe. Contained. Every minute of every day, I could just feel this anxiety about what he might do or say. How other people perceived him. And eventually, it just all got to be too much."

"You loved him."

I nodded, my mouth twisting. "And he was all I had."

"You had me," he said.

I should have been used to the way Micah just came out and said things, but still, it seemed to always catch me by surprise. The truth was, I'd known that. I'd known that Micah was in it with me. That he got Johnny like no one else did. That's the only reason I'd been able to leave.

I smiled, but it hurt. "You were right, you know."

"About what?"

"That we could fill an ocean with the things we never said."

Micah picked up the glass again, finishing it. It was a long moment before he asked the question. "If there was one thing you could say right now, what would it be?"

I didn't even have to think about it. "That I know what I did. I know that when I left, I put Johnny on you."

His eyes searched mine. "You didn't put anything on me. He was like a brother to me, James."

"You know what I mean. You were the only one I trusted to look out for him. And I knew that when I was leaving, I was putting it all on you."

When Micah didn't say anything else, I pulled his hand closer to me, clutching it to my chest. I could feel my heart beating wildly beneath it.

He looked down at our fingers tangled together, jaw clenching. "That's not what hurt me, James."

There was a visible pain in his eyes that appeared to travel through his body, finding the tension in every angle of him. "You cut me off. You just . . . erased me. Like I never existed." The tone in his voice shifted. "I mean, I get it. You had to make a choice. And even if I wanted you, James, I was never going to be a guy in a tuxedo at an art show, living in San Francisco with you."

My heart sank as he said it.

"I just wanted to find a way to pretend like I was someone else."

"And did you?"

"Yeah," I said. "I did."

What no one knew was that I'd questioned that decision a thousand times since I made it. Looking back now, I didn't think I would change it. I wouldn't give up Byron or my work or the life I'd made in the city. But I also didn't know if it was what I wanted anymore.

"You don't hate me?" I took a chance in asking the one question that I was most afraid to have answered.

Micah's mouth tilted in a half grin. "I wish I could hate you. It would have made things a lot easier."

We both laughed, and it felt good. Like we were speaking a language we'd forgotten.

"What about you? What's one thing you would say right now?" I said.

He thought about it. "If there were no consequences? No cost?"

"Yeah."

"Are you sure you want me to say it?"

I nodded.

He unwound his fingers from mine and his hands came up between us, taking my face between his palms. The warmth that swelled there made me want to melt into it. I held on to his wrists, holding him in place, and my heart raced, waiting for it.

His thumb moved over my cheekbone, finding my temple. "All right. Then here it goes."

I braced myself, my eyes running over his face. He drifted closer until his mouth touched mine, and he kissed me softly. The words were a whisper, spoken against my lips.

"Don't go back to San Francisco."

TWENTY-SIX

⟫————⟪

I stood in front of the post office, watching the end of Main Street with the package cradled in my arms. Any minute, the courier would arrive.

Quinn didn't know anything about what was happening in Six Rivers, and I wanted to keep it that way. I'd managed to get everything I needed back from Amelia just in time for the CAS deadline, but with everything going on, I wouldn't be able to deliver it in person as planned.

I hugged the parcel to my chest, fingers fidgeting with the twine I'd knotted around it to keep it safe. Quinn had arranged for someone to pick up the physical copies in addition to the scans, and as soon as I handed them over, all of Johnny's work would be the property of CAS. Every notebook, spreadsheet, and photo.

The negatives in particular, I had a hard time letting go of. Because of Johnny's aversion to digital photography, they were the only finite, ephemeral elements of his unique fingerprint on the study. The only thing that couldn't be replaced or replicated.

A man and woman huddled in thick coats passed me on the sidewalk, shooting me a side glance but not deigning to smile. Johnny's name hadn't officially been cleared in Autumn's disappearance, and the town had fully descended into the rumors about their relationship. The majority rule in Six Rivers were those who "always had a *feeling* about those two." No one had seen fit to acknowledge that if they had, in fact, thought something was going on, they'd failed to address it when it actually could have mattered.

There was still no evidence to confirm that Johnny and Autumn had had an inappropriate relationship, and until there was, I was inclined to believe Ben Cross. Both he and Rhett could attest to the fact that Autumn had left Johnny's place that night, but the more the thread of the story was pulled, the more it unraveled. People compared notes to try and add to the narrative—that maybe Johnny had gone and found Autumn after Ben left her that night. Or that the day he'd gone to the gorge was the act of a murderer revisiting the scene of his own crime. There were some who even believed the backpack had been a kind of trophy. The thought made my stomach turn.

An enormous part of me wished I could go back in time to that darkroom when I first arrived in Six Rivers and forget the little pink blot on the negative. If I'd never enlarged the photo, no one would be looking so closely at Johnny's life. But that would also mean that Autumn's disappearance would remain erased from time. She didn't deserve that.

I glanced up the street again, hoping to see a car on the road. The drive from San Francisco was more than six hours, and the courier was supposed to arrive more than twenty minutes ago. I pulled out my phone, compulsively finding Autumn's Instagram profile while I waited, which I did several times a day now. Scrolling through her dormant feed had become a kind of self-soothing habit, one I wasn't ready to look at too closely.

The picture in the grid from the day before she was supposed to leave Six Rivers was still at the top, and it had been taken on this very street. It was posted the day she'd gone to the end-of-summer party, the day she'd gone to Johnny's house with Ben. It was the last day she was seen by another soul.

I read the caption for the hundredth time.

Last party in Six Rivers. At dawn, we ride.

That was how it should have been. She should have had her entire life ahead of her, a sea of possibilities with no end. From what I could tell, that's what Johnny had wanted for her, too.

The comments on the post had multiplied many times over since I'd first seen it. In the days since they'd announced Autumn was missing and the posters went up around town, it seemed everyone had come out of the woodwork to leave messages for Autumn. The few that had been there from the beginning were still at the top.

My phone buzzed and a message from Olivia came up on the screen, covering the photo.

Saw that Johnny's things are still in the darkroom. They're in his cubby if you want to come by.

I'd totally forgotten about the folder she'd left for me. The sentence was punctuated with a glasses-wearing emoji, and I smiled. Olivia had been one of the few people in Six Rivers who didn't seem hell-bent on casting Johnny as a villain, and I felt more guilty than ever for ghosting her after I left. It turns out, she was one of the only real friends we had in this town.

The soft squeal of brakes made me look up just as a shining black sedan made it to Main Street. It couldn't be more out of place, with its glossy paint, tinted windows, and jaguar mount on the hood. It slowed, coming to a stop along the curb, but when the door opened, it wasn't a courier. It was Quinn.

"James!" My name bent with the British accent.

I looked from him to the driver, unable to hide the confusion on my face. Quinn was the last person I expected to get out of the car, and maybe the last person I wanted to see right now. Six Rivers was crawling with gossip that might not bode well for the pile of research cradled in my arms, not to mention my brother's reputation. In a place like San Francisco, that kind of association mattered.

"What are you doing here?" I gave Quinn a tight smile, my voice giving way to nerves, but he didn't seem to notice.

"Decided I'd feel best collecting Johnny's work myself."

He leaned forward, kissing my cheek, and I immediately glanced up the sidewalk for anyone who might be watching. I was stiff as he hugged me, my arms still wrapped tightly around the parcel.

"Or maybe I just wanted an excuse to see you. Check in and make sure you're doing okay?" he said, more tenderly.

His brown eyes moved over my face, like he was taking stock. Trying to ascertain whether I was really all right. Quinn had a seriousness to him, but that gentle look made him even more handsome.

"That's really sweet. Thanks, Quinn."

"I know I've just pushed in a bit, but have you got time for a coffee?" he asked, hopeful.

"Sure."

His smile widened before he exhaled, clearly relieved. "Great. Where to?"

I licked my lips, eyes going to the diner's painted windows across the street. In the city, there was a coffee shop, tea shop, café, or bistro on every corner. "It's kind of a small town. Not really a lot of options."

"I'm not picky." He closed the car door, signaling to the driver. "Lead the way."

I forced myself to mirror his smile, and again, I scanned the cars parked along the street. The sidewalk. It wasn't until that moment that I realized who I was looking for—Micah. There wasn't any sign of his truck, but he was in town today.

I hadn't answered him when he asked me not to go back to San Francisco, and when I'd woken in his bed this morning, he was already gone. The words had caught me so off guard that my head was still spinning with the idea. And now my life outside of Six Rivers had suddenly shown up, chasing after me.

We started walking and Quinn took in the view of Main Street, eyes full of wonder. "Gorgeous country, isn't it?" he mused. "Can't believe you grew up here."

"Yeah, it is."

I studied the forest in the distance, trying to see it from his perspective. The picturesque town was like a painting against the unruly beauty of the forest. On the surface, it seemed like such a perfect place. A refuge from the chaos of the world. And maybe it was once, before the trees were scooped out to build a town for people to live. Before this place had been touched by humanity. Now, where there were people, there was pain. Even in a place like this.

When I opened the door to the diner, the conversation inside quieted, and this time, the people seated along the counter and at the tables weren't just looking at me. Quinn's cashmere sweater, suit jacket, and tortoise-rimmed glasses made him stand out against the sea of flannel and denim.

He scanned the room with another polite smile, but it fell a little when no one seemed to smile back. I could see the questions spinning behind their eyes, the curiosity bordering on suspicion. In the last week, Six Rivers had been filled with the kind of strangers these people weren't used to. Police, investigators, social workers. A man in dress shoes with a city haircut was another to add to the list.

"Not very friendly, are they?" he murmured.

But when I looked up at Quinn, his humor was still intact, which was a credit to him. "Not really, no." I stifled a laugh.

Sadie came out from the back, her steps faltering a little when she spotted me. It took a few seconds, but she attempted a warm smile, her posture a little sheepish. I hadn't seen her since Ben was questioned, but now that her son was out from under the spotlight, she was trying to smooth things over. That part of her personality was familiar to me, even after all these years. She burned hot, but eventually she came around. She always did.

"Hey, James." Her hands twisted around the rag in her hands. "What can I get you all?"

"Just a couple of coffees," I answered, only meeting her eyes for a second.

She nodded, reaching for the mugs, and I swallowed hard when I realized the only open table in the diner was Johnny's booth. I led Quinn toward it, trying to relax the tension in my shoulders.

"I ran into Rhia the other day." He slid into the booth. "She says the show is shaping up nicely."

I took a seat, trying my best to ignore the rush of cold that filled my body. Outside the window, the view flickered in and out, the clock rewinding to a scene in autumn. The snow-crusted sidewalk was suddenly replaced by cracked cement littered with pine needles, and the sky was gray. The sounds of the diner changed, too, going quiet as if the place was mostly empty.

I pushed the vision away, trying to center myself in the present moment by focusing my eyes on Quinn's hands folded on the tabletop.

"I was thinking of going," he said, ducking his head a little to try and meet my gaze. "To the show."

I blinked, the realization hitting me. That's what this was—Quinn hadn't just come all this way to pick up Johnny's research. He'd come to make a gesture. For the last year, he'd been trying his hand at the unhurried, subtle type. And after Johnny died, he'd mostly backed off. Now, he was testing the waters, and by the look of it, he was nervous.

I hadn't meant to string Quinn along, but he wasn't the type of man you just hooked up with or invited over when you were lonely. He was warm and cultured. Successful. He had passion and focus. But someone like Quinn just felt so . . . permanent.

Sadie appeared at the edge of the table, setting down the mugs and a small pitcher of creamer, eyeing me. "Just let me know if you need anything else."

"Thanks," I choked, reaching up to loosen the collar of my shirt.

Slowly, the sounds of the diner resurfaced, the view out the window becoming static. The moment—the memory—was gone, making me feel like I could finally breathe.

I slid the parcel across the table, fingers slipping from the brown paper wrapping, and Quinn looked at it for a moment before he set a hand on top. I hadn't answered his question about the show, and it wasn't a completely smooth change in subject, but he let me off the hook.

"You've no idea what his contribution means to this project, James. What it will mean for the generations to come," he said.

But I did have some idea. For the last few weeks, Johnny's words had been on a loop in my mind.

What the fuck are we even here for?

He'd been asking that question for a long time, and I felt now like he'd just been trying to do something good.

"It's in good hands. Don't worry," Quinn said, reading my face.

I cupped my hands around the mug to keep them from feeling empty without the parcel. "You didn't really know Johnny." I paused. "But this project was important to him. Gave him a purpose. It means a lot that you gave him this chance."

Quinn had given Johnny an opportunity that had changed Johnny's life. For better and for worse. I could see now that everything that led to the moment he died had more to do with the randomness of things, the unpredictability of the universe, than it had to do with me. I'd tried to control it all for so long only to find that in a way, none of it mattered. And yet, all of it did.

"Why don't you let me take you out to dinner when you get back?" Quinn asked, a slight apprehension in his eyes. "Maybe we can try this thing for real this time?"

In that single look, I could see an entire future. A sequence of events that aligned with the life I'd built for the last twenty years. Prix fixe tasting menus, an apartment in the Marina District, a seat on the San Francisco Arts Council. It was all a far cry from the life that I could live here.

Don't go back to San Francisco.

Micah's deep, breathy voice was still alive against my lips, but it was just the remnants of a long-lost dream. Coming back here was like falling back into the dark. I didn't want to live a haunted life. But across the table sat a whole reality at the tip of my fingers, with a good man in a place that had been my refuge when I left Six Rivers. All I had to do was reach out and take it.

TWENTY-SEVEN

⟡————•————⟡

My footsteps echoed up the empty hall of the high school's east wing, my reflection a shifting shape on the floor. The entire building changed on the weekends, with light casting unbroken beams at an angle through the windows and the open emptiness of the rooms almost resonant.

The darkroom had been left ajar, allowing the scent of the developer and the trickling sound of the water bath to drift out into the hallway. I didn't even blink when I caught the shape of Johnny as I passed the open door, and I wondered if that was how it would always be now—splices of him folded into the periphery of my life.

Olivia's classroom was empty when I stepped inside, and I glanced at my phone, checking the time. I was a few minutes late. Beams of sunlight pierced through the air, striping the linoleum floor as I walked along the wall, letting my fingers trace over the paintings. Every time I came here, the smell of ink and clay and a hundred other familiar things transported me back to Byron.

I stopped when I reached Autumn's photography series mounted and framed on the wall. The little star in the corner of the images had been written in pencil, the same one I'd seen on that message at

Johnny's. But those trees looked different to me now. They meant something different. What I wished I could know was what they'd meant to Autumn.

"James!" Olivia appeared at the classroom's entrance, one hand hooked to the edge of the doorframe.

"Hey."

"Thought I heard you. You barely caught me." She walked straight toward a row of large binders on a shelf behind her desk, pulling two of them down.

"Sorry, I got caught up with something," I said, surprising myself that I was actually tempted to tell her about Quinn. Like the teenage girl in me still wanted to pull it all apart with a friend, analyzing the details of everything. I'd missed that, I realized.

"The folder's still in the darkroom." Olivia found the binder she was looking for and pulled it down with a grunt. She opened it on top of the messy desk calendar and flipped through the plastic sleeves. "But I also ran across a few prints and I wanted to be sure you got them."

I leaned a hip into the desk. "I appreciate that."

"I know I put them in here," she murmured, eyes skipping from one photo to the next. She kept flipping until she found it. "There they are!"

A photograph of Smoke and a few others were clipped together and slipped into the same sleeve. She pulled them out, handing them to me.

The corners of my mouth tugged into a smile. The shot of Smoke was of him sitting on the porch of the cabin, his ageless tawny eyes on the road and tongue lolling out one side of his open mouth.

"How are you holding up?" Olivia asked.

I could feel the smile falling from my lips now. "I'm okay. You?"

She closed the binder, crossing her arms over her chest. "It's been a weird few days."

"Did you talk to Byron?"

She nodded. "They'd been trying to reach Autumn because a portion of her first semester of tuition had been paid for and then she never showed."

A sinking feeling traveled down to the pit of my stomach, remembering the payment on Johnny's bank account. I'd have to contact them about that.

"Everyone here has been just devastated. The students, teachers, it's all so hard to believe."

I'd come close a few times to outright asking Olivia what she knew about Johnny and Autumn's relationship, because she hadn't brought it up once. That tracked with the Olivia I had known before. Sadie had always been a straight shooter, someone who didn't shy away from things, but Olivia always seemed to exist in the background. Always on the edge of what was happening.

"Olivia," I began, trying to choose my words carefully.

But when she looked up at me with those wide, innocent eyes behind her thick-framed glasses, I thought twice. There had been so much stirred up, so many questions raised, that I could feel the weight of it all crushing this town. And that made me feel like the fewer people who were dragged into Johnny's mess, the better.

"Just"—I sighed—"thanks. For being a friend to Johnny."

"You're welcome." A sweet smile stretched on her lips, her head tilting to the side.

"When do you head back to the city?"

"In a few days. Waiting to see how things . . ." I didn't finish. I didn't have to.

She gave me a sympathetic look. "Can we grab a drink at The Penny before you go?"

"I'd like that."

She turned back to the shelf, stacking the binders in place, and I let my gaze drag over the classroom one last time. Olivia and I had spent half of high school conjuring up the same dream, but only one of us had lived it. And now I found myself wondering who'd been better off. She seemed happy here. Content. It made me ask myself if I could be, too.

I followed the hall back the way I came, finding the darkroom and flipping on the light. Johnny was gone. The chemical trays were empty and turned upside down, the water bath turned off, but the prints hanging on the line were still glistening. I smiled, realizing that they must be Olivia's.

I took a step inside, scanning the series of photographs. At first, I couldn't quite tell what they were. But slowly, my eyes began to make sense of the intricate shapes. They were shots of ice taken with a macro lens, so close that the patterns looked like something else entirely. Or maybe it was snow, I thought.

I was happy that Olivia was still shooting. There was something that was almost romantic about the idea—producing work just for the sake of creating it. Not for show or display or even the world's consideration. Away from opinions or opportunities. It was just . . . free.

The smile melted from my lips as I thought it. When was the last time I made art like that?

Olivia's footsteps echoed down the hall, followed by the screech of the double doors that led to the parking lot. I found the piece of tape with Johnny's initials on the row of built-in cubbies that covered the opposite wall. The manila folder was still there.

I let it fall open, sifting through what was inside. There were some pieces of scrap photo paper, a tattered notebook that had exposure and developing times jotted down, and a few homemade dodge and burn tools.

I closed the folder and tucked it under my arm, then I reached up, flipping the switch just for old times' sake. The stale white fluorescents flicked off and the safelight clicked on, painting the room in a saturated red. I turned in a circle, taking it in. My hand skipped along the edge of the cold counter as I walked to the enlarger and turned it on, just to hear its hum.

I stood there for another few seconds before I turned the light back on. The colors of the space instantly flattened, and I let myself look around the darkroom one more time, then opened the door. But just before I stepped into the hall, something made me pause.

I let go of the knob, eyes pulled back to the photographs drying on the line. I reached out, fingertips brushing the intricate constellation of lines. Not quite ice or even snow . . . it was frost.

A sense of familiarity was itching at the back of my mind, like I'd seen them before. I took out my phone, opening Instagram, and immediately pulled up Autumn's account. I tapped the comments on the last post. When I spotted the one I was looking for, the thought was already forming.

@firstfrostchronicle Bright and early!

I clicked the handle and the profile's grid populated, filling my phone screen with pictures that mirrored the ones hanging before me. They were Olivia's. They had to be.

She'd told me she was working on her own photography series, and this was it. Olivia Shaw was @firstfrostchronicle.

The profile had no identifying information, but the handle interacted with Autumn's account constantly. She liked all of Autumn's pictures and they followed each other. But it was that comment that chimed like a bell in my head.

Bright and early!

The realization settled slowly, like stones in my gut. Autumn was posting about leaving for school the next day. When she said *At dawn, we ride,* maybe it hadn't been a figure of speech about the future that awaited in San Francisco. Maybe Autumn was talking about actual plans early the next morning. Plans with Olivia.

I snatched one of the photos from the clips on the line and opened the door, my steps quickening as they took me back to the empty classroom. I walked straight toward Olivia's desk, letting the folder slide from my hands before I cleared the clutter from the calendar. Olivia's looping handwriting was everywhere, spilling outside the lines of the boxes, notes jotted down in every color with every type of writing utensil there was. I flipped back through the months, finding

August, and my finger stopped on the eighteenth, the day of Autumn's last post. Beside it, there was a scribbled note written in the corner of August 19. The day Autumn left for school.

Shoot with ✦ *—5:30 am*

The night Autumn went to Johnny's house wasn't the last time she was seen. That was the next morning, with Olivia.

The jingle of keys in the hallway made me flinch and I dropped the calendar, heart lurching in my chest when I saw Olivia in the doorway again. She looked surprised to see me still there.

"Oh!" She laughed. "Sorry, didn't mean to scare you. Just forgot my . . ."

Her words slowed with her steps as she looked down at her desk. "What are you doing?" Her tone was still light, but her gaze turned probing.

"You're first frost." I could hardly hear my own voice, still working it all out in my head.

Olivia laughed again. "What?"

"On Instagram. Are you @firstfrostchronicle?"

She relaxed a little, but now she was blushing. "Oh, yeah, I am."

Bright and early!

The words echoed in my mind again.

"How'd you know that?" She was smiling now, almost proudly.

I lifted the print I'd taken from the darkroom between us.

She frowned. "Oh, those really shouldn't be touched until they're dry." She reached for it, carefully taking it by the edges.

"It's the series you're working on," I said.

"It is. A never-ending work in progress, I'm afraid."

I stared at the photo in her hands, but the shapes were distorting now, my vision beginning to warp and fragment. Slowly, my eyes traveled across the room to Autumn's series that hung on the wall. Olivia followed my gaze, falling quiet, and before I could manage to keep the thread on the spool, the air around us shifted. It was almost as if she could see me thinking it. Like she could see it playing out behind my eyes.

I couldn't keep the words from finding my lips. "You were with her that morning, weren't you?"

Olivia didn't move. She didn't speak.

I picked up the calendar, holding it out to her, and she took it, eyes running over the notes.

"You were with her the morning she was leaving for Byron."

Olivia sucked in her bottom lip and her bright, round eyes instantly turned glassy. Her entire appearance, even the way she was standing, withered, almost like a frightened child's. She pushed the glasses up her nose, mouth twisting to the side. It looked like she was about to cry.

"I admit, I didn't think about that," she said. "The calendar."

Instinctively, I reached to my back pocket for my phone.

"I hadn't thought about the Instagram account, either."

She'd already tracked my thoughts to the conclusion I'd made. She set the calendar down slowly as one tear striped her cheek. "What I need you to understand is that I really cared about Autumn."

My pulse quickened, making me feel light-headed. I glanced down at my phone, unlocking it.

"She was just so . . ." Olivia bit her lip again. "*Special.*"

She walked past me, crossing the room to the mounted photographs of Autumn's series, and I stared at her, unable to speak.

"And lucky. That was the thing." She sniffed. "Some people are just *lucky*, you know? People notice them. Open doors and create opportunities. Autumn was just one of those people, like everyone just wanted to help her get where she was going."

She wasn't just talking about Autumn anymore. She was talking about herself. About the young budding artist in a rural town who no one had noticed. Who no one had thought to open the door for.

"I know it's because of her talent. I mean, you'd have to be blind not to see it, right? And she just had this confidence about her that made it seem like everywhere she went, there was a spotlight moving to follow." Tandem tears fell down her cheeks as she spoke, her eyes full of awe. "She was like you, James. Johnny thought so, too."

"What happened, Olivia?" I whispered.

Her mouth twitched as she looked up. She searched my face, as if trying to decide whether she could trust me with it.

"I know it wasn't exactly aboveboard to spend time with a student outside of school, but we were both working on our series. And Autumn, she really loved the work I was doing. Once, she even told me it was *distinguished.*" She sniffed. "We started going out on shoots together her senior year, and we'd planned to go one last time that morning. Then I was going to drop her off at the bus stop." She pulled at her lip with her fingers over and over, like a tick. "It was an accident," she stammered, turning to face me again.

My lips parted, but my lungs wouldn't inflate. It suddenly felt like there was no air in the room.

"There was a tree up on the cliffs she wanted to photograph again. It had been struck by lightning."

I blinked, remembering it. I'd seen it when I went there with Micah.

"We had to hike down from the ridge above to get the right angle, and she was just standing there with the camera up." Olivia pantomimed it, her face blank as she acted it out, her voice hollow. "And then she was just *falling.* Screaming. And when she hit the bottom . . ."

My stomach lurched. I took a slow step backward, toward the door.

"It *was* an accident," Olivia repeated.

Her hands lifted before her and she shook them manically. She was breathing hard now, like she might hyperventilate. Her eyes moved all over the room, as if she couldn't see me anymore.

Immediately, my mind plucked that sentence from the air, summoning the memory. *It was an accident.* How many times had we said those very words that night, standing over Griffin Walker's body? How many times had its echo chased us, reframed us, into something else?

I took another step toward the door. Then another. Until I was standing in the hallway and watching her through the large glass windows. She paced the floor back and forth, muttering to herself.

"It was an accident." Her voice cracked. "It was. I'm almost sure it was."

I found Amelia's number and dialed, holding the phone to my ear. It rang only twice before she answered.

"This is Amelia."

"It's James." I swallowed. "You need to come to the high school. Right now."

Twenty-Eight

A week after Olivia Shaw was arrested for Autumn's murder, there was still a wrinkled missing poster plastered to the glass door of The Penny.

Autumn's eyes stared at me as I sat at the bar with the band playing at my back and a second glass of whiskey in my hand. I had the innate sense that I knew her now. That I understood her. The reflection of my own life that had played out in Autumn's had bound us together in some cosmic way that I would never fully comprehend.

Micah and I had volunteered in the search for Autumn's body that went on in the gorge for five days before they called it off. Still, no one was completely sure exactly what happened. Olivia had recounted the story in so many different versions to police that, in the end, the only common thread that wove the versions together was the fact that Autumn fell.

History repeated itself in this forest, and in the years that Olivia was Autumn's teacher, Olivia had relived her own experience as the less talented art student who never made it out of Six Rivers. The girl who'd never really been noticed, never been given a way out. But none of that was true about Autumn.

Autumn Fischer had been standing up on those cliffs the day she was leaving for Byron, only hours away from playing out the ending to Olivia's story. Left behind. Forgotten. A faint imprint on someone else's life. Autumn was poised to take a photo as Olivia watched, simultaneously consumed with adoration and envy. Did Olivia actually touch her before she fell? If she did, had she meant to push Autumn, or had she slipped? No one, not even Olivia it seemed, would ever know the answer to that question.

Micah had been out on the Klamath River again for two and a half days while Smoke and I went through Johnny's things at the cabin. I'd made three trips to the thrift shop to drop off donations, but I'd kept a few things for myself. His blue plaid jacket was one of them.

There'd been no more evidence—physical or circumstantial—that indicated that Johnny's death was suspicious. It was generally agreed upon now that he was, in fact, out in Trentham Gorge looking for Autumn, and the town's narrative had shifted once again, recasting into a version they could live with. Now, Johnny was being regarded as a kind of hero.

Down the bar, I could see a smudged version of him sitting with a drink. He'd been there for the last hour, his elbows up on the counter, fingers tangled together with a glass before him. As always, I waited for him to look at me, but he didn't.

Maybe I was imagining it, but he felt just a little farther away now. Just a little more out of focus. Like he was slowly disappearing, and honestly, that scared me. Since I'd first gotten the call from Amelia, I'd never been able to digest the idea that my brother, with all his storm clouds and kinetic energy and the sheer force he used to move through the world, could ever truly be dead. And I guess that was what was so horrible about accidental deaths, like Amelia said. In a moment, with no meaning whatsoever, someone could just be . . . gone.

Micah came in through the door of The Penny, letting the light of the streetlamp flood into the dark bar, and I lifted a hand into the air.

He made his way toward me, taking the stool next to mine, and I slid my glass of whiskey toward him.

"How was the trip?" I asked.

"Cold."

Neither of us had brought up the fact that I was leaving in a few days for the opening of the show at Red Giant Collective. Most likely because if we did, we'd have to talk about whether I was ever coming back. Instead, we'd spent each night finding our way into each other's arms, trying to drown out the aftermath of everything. Autumn's death. Olivia's arrest. The loose ends of Johnny's life. The bottom line was, I didn't know if I could leave my life in San Francisco unless I knew what I was leaving it for. And maybe that *was* my answer.

"You ready to do this?" Micah asked softly.

We'd decided to spread Johnny's ashes, just the two of us, but back in town, we'd be joined by whoever wanted to honor Johnny's memory at the diner. My guess was that Sadie had planned the memorial as a kind of peace offering for what happened when Ben was questioned, but things hadn't quite thawed between us. Maybe they never would.

Micah and I drove the twisting roads deep into the canyon at the heart of Six Rivers, with Johnny's ashes on the seat between us. I'd wanted to go at night when the darkness felt like liquid black, and with the whiskey warming my belly, I could feel that it was the right decision.

Micah eased off the road onto a crude gravel track and the headlights washed over the broken asphalt. When he turned off the engine, they cut out, and that strange, muted silence enveloped the truck. We sat there for a few seconds until I looked at him. This was the last time it would be just the three of us.

We got out and walked, the urn cradled in the crook of Micah's arm. The sound of night in the forest was like a hive of bees, and with every step, it seemed to grow louder. I didn't stop until it felt like we were swimming in it. Until it felt like we had disappeared.

Micah waited for me to nod before he opened the urn, and we didn't speak any special words or try to mark the moment with wisdom or nostalgia. What could we possibly say? I couldn't even pretend to know how you could take a whole life, a whole person, and put it into words. Goodbye is a lost language. A silent one.

Micah turned over the urn, gently shaking out the ashes over the roots of a giant tree, and a hush fell over the forest that dove deep into my chest. It had taken losing Johnny to fully know him, but there was more to it than that. I had to lose him in order to even know myself.

When the urn was empty, we stood there, watching the thin veil of moonlight fall through the trees. Then we turned and left him where he could hide. Where he would find the quiet. Where he'd never be found.

We left him in the dark.

TWENTY-NINE

I t seemed the whole town had shown up at the diner to say goodbye to Johnny.

When we made it to Main Street, there wasn't a single open spot to park, and Micah had to double up next to Sadie's truck. The drive back to Six Rivers had been a quiet one, but I thought that maybe I could already feel it lifting—that heaviness that had plagued me since I'd gotten the call in San Francisco. That weight of Johnny in the air.

I got out of the truck, heart coming up into my throat as I stared at the colorful scene behind the large, foggy windows. The yellow painted script of SIX RIVERS DINER stretched across the smudged view of dozens of people standing and sitting inside.

Micah's hand slipped into mine. This time, he didn't ask if I was ready. We followed the sidewalk up to the door and he pulled it open, sucking a draft of cold air into the place. It was loud and hectic, with laughter and the sound of forks hitting plates. It was alive. No one seemed to notice us as Micah pulled me through the crowd, and that felt both good and worrisome. What did it mean if I wasn't an outsider here anymore, folded into the landscape of Six Rivers like I'd never left?

Micah greeted those we passed with a nod, and when their eyes landed on me, they were warm, almost reverent. I tried not to think about the fact that so many of the people in this room had turned on Johnny, and in my heart, I knew I'd been close to doing the same. The brother I'd laid to rest deep in the heart of the forest only minutes before had been unraveled and inspected. Picked apart. And for the first time ever in my life, I felt like I really understood him. He *was* this forest. Vastly unknowable and enduringly steady. A persistent force at the center of my world. And maybe in that way, he would never really be gone.

When Sadie spotted us across the diner, she cut her conversation short, leaving the group of women gathered at the back. She wasn't wearing her usual jeans and button-up with an apron. She'd put on a dress and her hair was even curled, showing that she'd made an effort for the occasion. Looking around the room, I realized a lot of people had. It was as if the forest had been dusted off of them, and even the diner looked dressed up, with bouquets of flowers scattered about and a framed picture of Johnny on the counter beside the register. I wondered if it would be crowned with dying flowers and hung as a tribute, like the one of Griffin Walker.

Sadie gave me a timid smile as she walked toward us. When she moved to give me a hug, I let her wrap her arms around me, but it took a few seconds for me to do the same. I set my chin on her shoulder as her hand moved in a small circle at my back. The feeling made me swallow hard.

"Thank you for letting me do this," she said, pulling back to meet my eyes.

Beside me, Micah gave her a halfhearted smile. He hadn't gotten over the fact that Sadie had hit me, and knowing him, it wasn't likely he ever would.

A woman with a tray of wineglasses stopped at our side and Sadie picked two up, handing them to us before she grabbed one for herself. Then she turned toward the room, clinking the rim with a spoon she'd plucked from the counter. Slowly, the commotion died down, and one by one, every set of eyes drifted toward us.

Sadie hooked her arm in mine. "Hey, everyone!" She lifted her voice, waiting for the last of the room to quiet. Somewhere, someone turned off the music. "Hey, thanks for being here."

The hush fell like a heavy blanket, and I instinctively reached behind me for Micah's hand. He squeezed it.

"We're here tonight to say goodbye to Johnny Golden," Sadie began. "A soft soul with a wild heart."

Already, I was swallowing down tears, and just when I thought it couldn't get any quieter, it did. Again, Sadie met my gaze, a silent exchange passing between us. She'd cared about Johnny. Of course she had. For years, she'd loved him.

Those words—*a soft soul with a wild heart*—were the only kind of eulogy that made sense for my brother. It also made me hope that despite everything, maybe he wasn't so misunderstood after all.

"I won't say a bunch of mushy stuff that would have embarrassed him," she continued, making a few laughs bubble up in the back. "Many of us knew Johnny his entire life, and I think we all know he wouldn't have liked that much."

I glanced back at Micah. He was smiling now, too.

"So, I'll keep it simple." Sadie lifted her glass and every person in the diner followed.

The silence deepened, as if the muted quiet of the forest had somehow gotten in. I could almost feel it climbing its way inside of me, making my bones feel heavy.

"To Johnny." Sadie's voice filled the air.

"To Johnny!"

The chorus of voices saying my brother's name was more than I could bear. I watched as people took a drink in his honor and hugged one another. The sight was followed by voices striking back up and the music restarting.

"You okay?" Micah's voice was low beside me.

I nodded.

The crowd parted as people made their way to the spread of food at the back, and I spotted Ben by the kitchen, standing with Amelia's son. His gaze traveled over the room apprehensively, those dark circles under his eyes more pronounced than they'd been when I first met him. He still just looked like a kid, but I could see more clearly than ever that he had a lingering air of something shadowed about him. Just like his dad.

I let go of Micah's hand. "I'll be right back."

I made my way across the room, and when Ben saw me coming, he stiffened a little.

"Hey, can we talk for a minute?" I said, eyes jumping to Amelia's son.

He dismissed himself, giving me a polite nod, and Ben leaned against the wall, keeping his distance. "Is something wrong? I can get my mom if—"

"No," I stopped him. "I just wanted to tell you . . ."

Ben stared at me, eyes intent as my words died out. That look— that glow beneath his expression—was like looking right into my brother's face.

"I wanted to let you know that if you ever want that test," I paused, "we can do it. You and me. It's not too late."

Ben's eyes went past me, and I followed his gaze to where Sadie stood on the other side of the diner.

"If you decide you want to, Micah knows how to reach me," I said.

He nodded, a shy smile lighting up his face just a little, and I thought, not for the first time, that I didn't need a test to know. I wasn't sure Ben did, either.

Micah was only a few steps away when I turned back into the crowd. "What was that about?"

"I'll tell you later."

I eyed the long counter stacked with food. There were already people making their plates, and for the first time in days, I was actually hungry.

We got in line behind Harold, and Micah stuck close to me as I said hello to familiar faces and accepted a string of condolences. When he set a plate into my hands and nudged me forward, I was grateful. I cradled the plate in one arm, leaning over the table so I could reach the bowls of salad and trays of lasagna. Everyone had brought something, and I couldn't help but compare the entire scene to the ones I was used to now. Champagne fountains and cocktail dresses and twinkling votive candles. Six Rivers was a far cry from all of it. I wasn't sure anymore which one felt like home.

Ahead of me, Harold took up a spoonful of mashed potatoes, roughly plopping them onto my plate.

"James," he greeted me.

I grinned. "I'm starting to think you live here, Harold."

"I don't trust anyone to cook for me but Sadie."

I glanced across the room again, to where she was tucked into a corner talking with two other women. The champagne glass was still dangling from her hand.

"'Bout rioted when she closed up that one day a while back. Nearly starved to death." He handed me a dinner roll.

"Thanks."

Once Harold moved along, I cut into one of the lasagnas and served myself, then Micah. But when I looked up, Micah had a lost look on his face, eyes roaming over the table like he was thinking.

"What's wrong?" I tapped him with my elbow.

"Wait," Micah said, his attention jumping to Harold. "What day are you talking about, Harold?"

Harold scratched his beard, balancing his overfilled plate in one hand. "What now?"

"What day was that when the diner closed up?"

He frowned. "When the whole blame town was shut down for the tourney in Redding."

The question was just beginning to thread together in my mind, but I was several beats behind Micah. Beside me, I watched as the color drained from his face.

"What is it?" I whispered.

His piercing gaze met mine. "That was the weekend Johnny died."

Slowly, sickeningly, the circle of thought connected, like a snake eating its own tail. Sadie had told me that the reason she couldn't leave town on game weekends was because she had to keep the diner open. That it never closed.

The weekend Johnny died, Six Rivers was in the middle of hunting season. But the town had been virtually emptied of its residents thanks to the high school soccer tournament in Redding. Even Amelia Travis, the only law enforcement they had, was gone.

"James?" I heard Micah's voice beside me, but I couldn't move.

Johnny had gone out to the gorge to work on November 10. He'd found the backpack, but then he'd come back to a ghost town. When he couldn't get ahold of Amelia, what had he done? Exactly what I did. Johnny had come here, to the diner. He'd come to ask Ben if he'd heard from Autumn. Only, Ben wasn't here. But Sadie was.

My gaze trailed the room until I spotted her again. She was smiling. Laughing.

I could see it, suddenly. Johnny standing at the counter. Telling Sadie what he'd found in the forest. How long would it have taken her to think back to that night when her son disappeared only to show back up in the morning wasted? How many minutes would have passed before she connected the dots to Ben's depression that followed? To the moment he had tried to take his own life? She was a mother with a broken child. A mother who had been undeniably shocked when Amelia gave her the news that Ben had an alibi for that night.

I stared at Sadie, unblinking.

When she found out from Johnny that Autumn was missing, she'd believed the unthinkable. That her son was responsible. And if Sadie suspected that Ben had hurt Autumn, and that Johnny was about to unwittingly expose him, what would she have done? What lengths would she have gone to in order to protect her son?

"James." Micah said my name again, but now my eyes were fixed on the wall of framed photographs that hung behind the bar.

The glow of the pendant lights reflected off the glass, and I set down my plate, moving toward them. I wasn't sure I was walking, exactly. It felt like floating. Like drifting through space.

Dozens of smiling faces peered out from the photos. Children with balloons, an old woman with a walker, two men clinking together glasses of beer. It was a story, the tale of a town dropped in the middle of the wilderness, where things could easily disappear. *People* could disappear.

My eyes ran over the pictures, searching for one I'd seen before but hadn't cared enough about to remember it clearly. When I found it, I reached up, taking it off the wall. Sadie Cross stood beneath a wide canopy of trees in her hunting gear, kneeling beside the carcass of a buck. The gun propped up beside her wasn't totally clear, but I could guess that it was old. An heirloom, even. I could guess that it was the gun that shot the bullet that killed Johnny.

That's why the diner was closed that day. While the rest of the town was in Redding and Johnny was looking for Autumn, Sadie had followed him to the gorge.

I couldn't tear my gaze off that photo. Sadie's sparkling blue eyes were like little shining jewels, her wide, genuine smile infectious. There was a warmth that emulated from her, even through the picture. I could almost feel it.

Micah's hand finally came down on mine and I looked up to him, everything inside of me twisting.

"It was her," I rasped.

His eyes trailed from the photo to the place across the room where Sadie stood. As if she could feel us watching her, her face slowly turned in our direction. In only a few seconds, she knew. That bloodless color returned to her face as her eyes dropped down to the picture in my hand.

When Micah was suddenly moving toward her, her eyes widened.

"Micah?" The smile returned to her lips, but it was wooden now. "Something wrong?"

Slowly, every head in the room turned, and I watched as Micah took hold of the collar of her dress, wrenching her toward him.

"What did you do?" he shouted.

A strange sound came from Sadie, and immediately, Amelia was pushing through the crowd. But Micah didn't let go. There was more shouting. A tangle of voices that warped in my ears. But there was no denying that look of guilt in Sadie's eyes.

"What the hell is going on?" Amelia's voice rose above the others.

When Micah finally unclenched his fists from Sadie's dress, she nearly fell backward. Her hand caught the table behind her and the wineglass fell, shattering on the floor.

"Where were you, Sadie?" Micah spat. "Where were you when Johnny died?"

Every soul in the diner fell silent, making the sound of the music twist eerily around us. No one appeared to so much as breathe, every eye on Sadie Cross. But no one looked more stricken than Ben. He stood across the room, staring blankly at his mother. He was putting it together, too.

Sadie swallowed, her mouth opening and closing. "I—I didn't . . ." She gulped in a breath. "I don't know how—" She was looking at Ben now.

Amelia took a careful step toward her.

"I thought I was protecting him." Sadie faltered. "You can understand that, can't you?" Her gaze swept the room, but no one answered.

"Sadie, let's step outside," Amelia said, lowly.

Sadie didn't move. Her hands shook, dangling at her sides until Amelia took her arm, moving her toward the door. Then they were gone.

The photo was still clutched in my hands as everyone turned toward me. But my eyes were on the window, where a face I knew was visible behind the glass.

Johnny.

He stood in the falling snow, hands in his pockets. But this time, he was looking at me.

Everything blinked out, disappearing around me, and for those few seconds, it was just us. James and Johnny.

And then he turned and walked away.

THIRTY

The city had no soul.

I stood in the window of Red Giant Collective, watching the twinkling lights of San Francisco glitter in the hills. It was impossible not to compare it to the wild, hot-blooded forest. The city had its own skin and bones and there was something about it that felt alive, but the mystical hum that lived in Six Rivers was an animal that couldn't survive here. Not even the hungry waves of the Pacific could find a home in the bay.

My glass of champagne grew warm and flat as I watched the people stream in and out. The slip dress I'd ordered rippled in the breeze coming through the door, and I was cold beneath the blue silk. Like I was too far from the fire of home. I also felt like I was too far from Johnny.

I hadn't felt his presence since I'd gotten back, and I'd kept busy to distract myself from that sense of quiet. That stillness felt too much like loneliness, and the more days that went by, the farther from him I was.

I'd left Six Rivers only a few days ago, and I imagined myself as an astronaut, drifting through space with no tether. That's what it was like being up on the hill that looked out over the lights, far from the scent of evergreens and the taste of rain in the air.

The show would get a glowing review in the *San Francisco Chronicle*. The editor who'd come by invitation to the small soiree had told me as much, saying that the pieces were *reliable*. That word was still chiming in my head, like a sound I couldn't decipher the meaning of.

When a face I recognized finally walked through the door, I felt myself relax a little, walking toward him. Quinn hadn't waited for my invitation this time, and now I found that I was glad. He felt like a small connection to Johnny in this foreign place. A confirmation that my brother was real. That he was here. That he wasn't a figment of my imagination.

Quinn shrugged off his jacket and handed it to the host, beaming when he saw me. His black tux made him look taller and he'd gotten a haircut. When his gaze traveled down my body, his eyes grew hungry.

"James." He took my elbow, kissing me on the cheek. "You look quite beautiful."

"Thank you."

Quinn spotted my trio of paintings on the east wall. "These are yours," he said, not questioning.

"They are," I answered.

"You really are amazing, James."

"Sarah Manchester at the *Chronicle* says they're reliable," I said, eyes roaming over the largest painting in the middle. "Any idea what that means?"

Quinn frowned, eyes focusing on the details. "I think it means that people know what they are going to get from a James Golden piece. That you're consistent."

I considered that, measuring the painting against the other two I had in the show. The abstract textures and melting colors made more of a feeling than an image. It was meant to take its shape in the eye of the beholder. But looking at it now, it just appeared as a mess.

"What do you see?" I asked him, really wanting to know.

Quinn looked delighted by the question. He turned to the painting again, taking a long pause. "I see a sunset over the water?" He
arched an eyebrow at me, as if looking for confirmation.

I smiled weakly. "Yeah," I lied.

Quinn brightened. "Yeah?"

I nodded. I didn't have the heart to tell him that there was no right
answer. That there'd been little inspiration behind the piece at all. I
didn't *see* anything anymore when I painted. I didn't feel anything,
either. Even looking at it now, there was nothing in me that felt connected to the canvas. Had it been that way before I left for Six Rivers?
I couldn't remember now.

"Can I get you a fresh one?" He looked down at my glass.

"Sure. Thanks, Quinn."

He lifted it from my fingers, melting into the crowd, and I wrapped
my arms around myself, shivering. The sound of the cello somewhere
in the gallery was a vibration on my skin, making it hard to tell if the
goosebumps were from the music or from the cold.

Across the room, Quinn had already gotten caught in conversation
and a few attendees had begun to crowd around him. That's how it
was everywhere he went. He was respected and had influence. There
wasn't a foundation in the whole state that wasn't trying to give him
money for something. Most importantly, he was kind, and for the last
year and a half, he'd been patiently pursuing me. I couldn't think of a
single sensible reason for why I'd resisted.

I stared at the painting again, willing myself to feel *something*.
Anything. I held my breath, like I was listening for a heartbeat.

A horn honked outside as the cello finished its suite, interrupting
the last prolonged note, and again, I itched for the silence of the forest. For the claustrophobic cabin and the firelight at the gorge.

"Excuse me, ma'am. Sir."

A woman wedged past me and I stepped aside, thinking that when
I turned around, I would find Quinn waiting, champagne glass in
hand. But the eyes that met mine made me let go of that breath I was
holding, and all of a sudden, I could hear that heartbeat.

Micah.

He stood only inches away, his blond hair swept back and his sun-warmed skin more golden in the low light. His black jacket and tie were cut close to the line of him, and it was such a paradoxical scene that a smile broke on my lips. No haircut. No shiny watch.

"I thought you said you were never going to be that guy in a tux," I said, my voice as brittle as snow.

"Guess I figured out I can be anything if I'm with you."

He held out his hand, waiting for me to take it. When I slipped my fingers into his, they closed around mine. Instantly, that quiet was back, encircling us. Like we weren't in the gallery at all. Like there was a space that only the two of us created.

His eyes lifted over me and I turned to face the painting, my bare shoulder touching his.

He looked at it for a long moment, his voice deep and steady beside me. "What the hell is it?"

I stifled a laugh, pressing my fingers to my mouth, and when I turned to look at him again, there were tears in my eyes. Slowly, my hands found his face and I pulled him low to kiss me. The soft, gentle press of his lips was like fitting myself into a shape I was made for.

"What do you want, James?" he said, hands feeling the shape of me beneath the silk of my dress.

The question felt like finding land, and my answer was a boat running ashore.

"I want you to take me home."

THIRTY-ONE

❋

I'd believed my whole life that there was no me without Johnny. It turns out, I was wrong.

My fingers smudged the edges of the charcoal as I sat at the drafting table in the sunroom, racing against the dying light. Micah had converted it into a studio for me after I moved in, and I spent the hours he was gone working in it with Smoke curled at my feet.

Wherever there wasn't a window, the wood-paneled walls were covered in iterations of the pieces I'd been working on, and my fingers were perpetually stained with pigment and ink. I lifted my arms over my head, stretching through the tightness coiled around my spine, and my belly hit the table, jostling the pencils. I caught one before it rolled off the edge.

I'd recently graduated to wearing Micah's sweatpants because everything in the closet no longer fit, and it didn't matter if I was sitting, standing, or walking—I couldn't get comfortable no matter what I did. Hours at the drafting table were becoming less and less feasible, but I could feel the world shifting around me. Everything was about to change. Again.

Micah's shadow moved over the floor and he pressed a kiss on top of my head, a bowl coming down through the air in front of me.

"You need to eat."

"I'm almost finished." I reached for a new piece of charcoal and he caught my hand, turning me toward him.

"Eat," he said again.

I peered down into the bowl of stew, my mouth watering. "Fine."

He went and got his own bowl, sinking into the armchair beside me. I propped my feet up on his knee, taking a bite.

"Quinn's invited us down for the exhibition at CAS next week." I spoke around a mouth full of food.

His eyebrows lifted.

There was a gala planned to celebrate the conservation effort, where the work of Johnny and the other contributors would be displayed. Features were being written on each of them, and Johnny's photographs would have their own gallery at the event.

"It's black-tie," I added. "And you *are* a tux man now."

He laughed. "Johnny would have hated that."

"He really would have."

Johnny would have called the gala a hypocritical waste of money. In fact, he probably would have drunk too much and offended someone before being asked to leave. Just thinking about it made me smile.

"Do you want to go?" Micah asked.

I thought about it. Johnny wasn't the only one who'd be a fish out of water in a place like that. "As much as I want to try and fit this"— I pointed to my stomach—"into an evening gown, I think we should just let him have his moment."

Micah's face shifted into a sweeter, softer smile. He nodded. He set down his bowl and sat up, taking hold of my chair and rolling it toward him until I fit between his legs. "Six weeks until we're family."

I set my own bowl beside his, wrapping my arms around his neck. I looked down into his face. "We've always been family."

His hands moved over my stomach between us. "This is different."

It was. I could feel that in my bones.

It was one thing to share a life, to share memories and spaces. But this child growing inside of me that neither of us planned was made by the two of us. It was the place Micah and I—our bodies and blood and even our souls—came together. It was a whole new story waiting to be told.

I looked past him, to the drawings overlapping on the wall, meeting the eyes of Autumn Fischer. I woke up in the middle of the night sometimes and drew her. That was the only thing I drew in the dark. She'd find me in my dreams, and I would wake almost convinced that the moments were real. That I was somehow tapping into memories Johnny had of her.

Her body was never found, and we never revisited the site where we left Johnny's ashes. After everything, Johnny and Autumn had died in the same place, for different reasons. That was enough to make me wonder if in some twisted way, their fates *had* been tied together.

I rubbed at an ache below my ribs, thinking that this baby was going to be born into a world that Johnny wasn't in. It still felt so wrong. Like there would be no way for this child to know me, if she never knew Johnny.

Micah drew my face back in his direction, meeting my eyes. He'd read my mind. "We're here. Now."

He'd said that to me before, a reminder that what happened before didn't matter. Not anymore. We were starting our own lives, the two of us, for the first time.

I set my forehead against his. "You know how we agreed not to leave things unsaid?"

"Yes."

"I feel like I should finally tell you that I've always found it annoying when you know what I'm thinking."

"I know." He laughed. "But I should probably tell you something, too."

I waited, pulling away from him so that I could see his eyes.

His hands moved around the shape of me, pulling me closer. "I have loved you for a very long time, James."

"I know." I echoed his words.

He let me go, leaving me in the golden hour light, and I turned back to the drawing, hand itching for the charcoal. It was a portrait of Johnny standing on the cliffs at the gorge exactly how I remembered— a rendering that captured all the versions of him that lived behind those eyes. I finally understood that they all could be true, all at the very same time.

Maybe we were made in the dark, like Johnny said. But we'd found a way to create our own kind of light.

ACKNOWLEDGMENTS

No book that comes to shelves is a solo endeavor, and that is very true for *A Sea of Unspoken Things*.

This story is dedicated to my twin brother, Adam, to whom I'm sure I owe a lot of thanks for a lot of things over the span of our lives. For now, I will just thank him for playing a part in the inspiration for this book and for being a good human. It is a strange, mystical thing to have been there the moment someone first existed, and I'm grateful I get to share a part of my soul with you, Adam.

I wrote this book during a very difficult year of life, and it would not have made it to print without the diligent, faithful support of my agent, Barbara Poelle, and my editor, Shauna Summers. That very big thank-you of course extends to my entire team at Penguin Random House. Thank you also to Kristin Dwyer and Natalie Faria, whose feedback helped shape this story into what it was meant to be, and to Rachel Griffin and Adalyn Grace, who let me borrow their imaginations so that I could see the heart of this book.

All my gratitude to my family and loved ones for carrying me through the evolution of this story. I will be unpacking the things I learned from this experience for a long time, and I am very thankful to have such an incredible support system. I wish everyone in the world could be so lucky as to be loved the way I am.

ABOUT THE AUTHOR

ADRIENNE YOUNG is the *New York Times* and international bestselling author of *The Unmaking of June Farrow*, *Spells for Forgetting*, the Fable series, and the Sky and Sea duology. When she's not writing, you can find her on her yoga mat, on a walk in the woods, or planning her next travel adventure. She lives and writes in the Blue Ridge Mountains of North Carolina.

ABOUT THE TYPE

This book was set in Caslon, a typeface first designed in 1722 by William Caslon (1692–1766). Its widespread use by most English printers in the early eighteenth century soon supplanted the Dutch typefaces that had formerly prevailed. The roman is considered a "workhorse" typeface due to its pleasant, open appearance, while the italic is exceedingly decorative.